I'm F★cking
Amazing

I'm F★cking Amazing

Amazing

A Novel

Anoushka Warden

DOUBLEDAY

New York

For Moo (when you're old enough!!)
You're fucking amazing.

Copyright © 2024 by Anoushka Warden

All rights reserved. Published in the United States by Doubleday, a division of Penguin Random House LLC, New York. Simultaneously published in hardcover in Great Britain by Trapeze Books, an imprint of Orion Publishing Group, a division of Hachette UK, London.

www.doubleday.com

DOUBLEDAY and the portrayal of an anchor with a dolphin are registered trademarks of Penguin Random House LLC.

Front-of-jacket painting © Nancy McKie
Lettering by Lynn Buckley
Jacket design by Emily Mahon

Cataloging-in-Publication Data is on file with the Library of Congress
LCCN: 2023009597

ISBN: 9780385549820 (hardcover)
ISBN: 9780385549837 (ebook)

MANUFACTURED IN THE UNITED STATES OF AMERICA

1st Printing

Wet Fanny

By my mid-twenties I thought I had my fanny and its workings all figured out. I'd spent almost 10 years observing its ways. From the start I embraced its look and goings-on. I didn't feel ashamed when it bled in Year 7 maths. I didn't feel awkward when it got wet from Year 9 fingers. I didn't even mind its random discharges (hockey bus, school-canteen queue, end-of-year tutor-group song). I never worried what it smelled like (sometimes metal, sometimes onions, occasionally a bit fishy) or how hairy it was. Or the sometimes-mingers it picked. I just had this deep trust in it. That it was doing what it was supposed to be doing. Which, primarily, was finding orgasms from all the ways possible to it, i.e. fingerings, lickings and dry humping.

And for many years, with a couple of systems in place (to account for the mingers), I let it lead the way, which seemed to work out quite well. It found me orgasms and also love—a really big, terrific, kind love.

But then something changed. Things got crapper in the fanny department and the rest of me went along with this as if it was normal. Which maybe it was, as the problem with growing up and doing proper adult long-love stuff is you've not done it before, so how the hell are you supposed to know what the fuck is going on?

Maybe fannies and long-term love don't work well together.

Part One

The System

I had a scale that I used for marking all males I had ever been with or was about to get with. It involved considering how much my fanny fancied them out of 10 and how much my brain did out of 10 and then working out the average. If it was above eight, I was allowed to engage in long-term love with them. If it was below, then it could only be short-term pleasure. I created the scale when I was 15, as it turned out my fanny had much lower standards than my brain did. It desired things all the time and was always easily wet, even from mingers. Which I didn't mind for small encounters, and it often felt like a bit of a superpower as I could walk into any room and, chances are, I'd probably quite fancy someone in there as the joint desires of my brain and my fanny meant that I had no type. It was like my own version of beer goggles, minus the alcohol. If you stuck pictures on the wall of all the faces of the people who had made my fanny wet between the ages of 14 and 24, I don't think you'd be able to pull out a pattern, apart from them all being male, having hair and being either my age or a bit older. But this lack of a type wasn't a very helpful thing when I was trying to make choices about people I wanted to be with properly, since especially with the guys from the lower end of the scale, after the fanny-wanting had worn off (i.e., I'd come), they usually then utterly repulsed me.

Like Mayo Dan. I fancied the shit out of him for a couple of weeks when we were rehearsing *Grease* for the school play.

In real life he was boring and unfunny, so not a high scorer on my brain scale, but he was cast as Danny and so my fanny went wild for him. After snogging him during the interval at the dress rehearsal I was excited to see him after the show—until I ran into him in the changing room and he was eating a chicken sandwich, which had left loads of mayonnaise around the corners of his mouth. In that moment everything changed and my stomach did an actual gag thing, as looking at him with the chunks of white goo on his face was so gross.

This became quite an occurrence, hence the creation of the scorecard system.

TOP HUMPS

NAME: Rob S.

AKA: The Sneak

AGE: 14 (him), 14 (me)

BUILD: Quite skinny compared to the other boys in Year 9.

GENERAL VIBE: Bit of a wimp. Moderately popular at school.

ACTUALLY LIKE: Nice-ish.

SPECIAL SKILLS: Low-level lying, v. convincingly. Massage fingers.

FANNY SCALE: 8/10

BRAIN SCALE: 3/10

OVERALL RATING: 5.5/10 = Short-term Pleasure

PRE-GAME: During the queue for snacks from the tuck shop he squeezed my side with his hand and my fanny got wet.

THE DEED: I had to share a bed with him at a sleepover party. Fanny got really wet as he breathed into my neck, so I rubbed my bum against him until he finally got brave enough to put his fingers down my Superman pyjama bottoms. I came, then went to sleep without bothering about him.

PLEASURE (me): 1 × orgasm due to fingering.

PLEASURE (him): No climax as I went to sleep as soon as he made me come.

Summary: He was probably just happy to have touched a girl's fanny who was actually in the same year as him. We all normally only ever went older. People who went with guys in the same year or below had something wrong with them. The next morning I felt confused and grossed out a bit, but not for too long, as it's always nice when you come, isn't it?!

Three

I met my third proper boyfriend when I was 24. I had slept with 24 and a half people, which was a number I was proud of. A businessperson on the news once said that in terms of salaries you should try to earn the age you are and if the figure is higher than your age you are doing very well. I like to apply that rule to knobbing. I'd done very well on that front.

With Proper Boyfriend Number Three, during the first few moments of meeting I got totally the wrong impression of him and thought he was a bit of a player, which, for me, is the secret ingredient I need when falling in love with someone who is actually a very nice guy. This niceness cannot be demonstrated too soon in case of retreat and dulled desiring feelings, but it is, of course, eventually what I want the man I am in love with to be.

I was working my usual shift in the Red Dragon and a darts final was on. The pool table had its DIY wooden top fixed to it so all the men could rest their beers on it as the projector screen came down across the window next to it, so it worked as a good use of extra counter space on a match day. The pint glasses would stack up fast, and during sports shifts the main goal was to recover and wash. This meant having to climb and push through all that drunk maleness to bring back their empties. Karen and Mollie, who I often did shifts with and who were working that day, hated doing this as they couldn't handle the leering/bants they'd get on the round-up. So, it was always my job, not because I liked the leering—I did not—but I enjoyed telling the fuckers to do one, and also I did like the leering a little bit, from the right ones.

It was on one of the round-ups that I noticed Three. Some guy who had a belly that looked pregnant had thrown his dart and Three shouted "CUNT!" really loudly at the screen just as my head was passing by. It was very hot. He was wearing a white T-shirt (with no stains on it) and some loose navy Adidas sports shorts—the kind that cling to the right places. I couldn't see what shoes he had on as my view was obstructed by all the men. He was tall, looked a little bit older than me and had a nice amount of blond floppy hair. I fancied him a lot.

Later on, after most of the darts losers had left or been kicked out for being too aggro, I went to sit in the garden with Mollie to eat our dinner. For our breaks we were allowed to pick whatever we wanted off the menu, which was the best thing about working there. For this meal I had asked the chef to combine the cheesy mash from the fishcakes dish with the spicy sausages (which were usually served with rice), creating one of the best things I had ever tasted. I don't know why they didn't put it on the menu. Three was sat on the table opposite with his friends and as I listened in on their conversation, I noticed he didn't swear once, and I also noticed he was in quite a good mood even though the guy he wanted to win hadn't, which is something my brother can't achieve when his team lose at football. I thought all men had to be affected negatively by this kind of thing, so it was exciting to see one behaving in a different way. When he came over to me to pay his tab, he asked if I'd like to go out with him sometime and I said yes but on condition that we had one phone call first. So that's what happened. We swapped numbers and spoke for almost an hour the following Wednesday and then I agreed to meet him at the Cardinal on the river. I strongly hated the jeans he was wearing when he turned up; they had a rip designed into both knees and it made me feel a bit queasy. I considered leaving immediately, but once they were out of sight under the pub table it wasn't so bad and I spent the rest of the time thinking how amazingly hot his teeth were. They just had such a lovely way about how they were put together in his mouth—the formation in which they hung down and how the front two slightly rested against his bottom lip. I'd never thought about anyone's teeth before; it was clear this was going to be something.

Within the month I had got him to swap his ripped jeans for a pair of light-blue Diesel ones and we had agreed to be together.

Lying on my bed after a particularly exciting chair-sitting sex session where I had purposefully worn my favourite bikini top, not my bra, as all my bikinis were way sexier than my actual underwear, he asked me how many people I had been with.

I told him I'd slept with eight coz he had started the conversation by telling me that he had only slept with six, and looking in his lovely eyes I felt a bit overwhelmed and I really, really, *really* wanted him to fall in love with me soonish because he was definitely a 9/10 on both my fanny and brain scale.

Philadelphia

Three was a dreamy combo. He knew every capital city in the world, but also played football at the weekends. I loved that he was from London; he seemed more grown-up or clued in than the male friends I had from home. Like his brain thinking for himself was much bigger coz he'd grown up in a huge city as opposed to a tiny rural town. When he was 18, he went to the Philippines to help build things in villages there. When we were all 18 none of us would have even heard of it, let alone known where it was—I would have assumed it was some new kind of spreadable cheese.

By the time I met him, Three had a proper job that he had to wear suits for. His suit game was very strong, and it turned me on that he would spend large amounts of money getting them specially fitted and not buy those crappy Burton ones that all the boys from uni got when Mr. Williams, our lecturer in Films: Now, Then and Beyond, weirdly invited us to his wedding.

Three's job was the sort where he had to sound clever to do it and most of the people who worked in his office had all been to the same university, had very posh accents, were in cricket teams together and shortened their surnames to create nicknames like Diko (Dickens), Wilko (Wilkins), Hamo (Hammings)—which they always said like a football chant. Three was not like that. His voice sounded like a proper London person and he'd gone to a normal school in Ealing—i.e., a bit of a shit one. He showed me a newspaper article of a report on it that the *Daily Mail* did where some of the recent students had gone a bit mad one lunch break and locked four teachers up in the walk-in bin store. Three said that would have been a much nicer day for them than teaching that lot.

"Did your year do that kind of thing too?!"

"Not as bad—we ignored them, locked them out of the classrooms, never handed in any of our work. Oh, Kevin Jacobs once went round to our chemistry teacher's house during double science and kidnapped all her garden gnomes, and then over the rest of term they would turn up, one by one, in different areas of the school with little chunks missing from them, fingers cut off, nose smashed in."

"That's quite harsh!"

"Yeah, but by sixth form he had been sectioned, so probably the exception, not the rule. What about you?"

"We swapped the soap in Mr. Lennard's sink for a blue dye one. He was the art teacher so that was pretty funny. And at the end of term once we put itching powder in Mrs. Day's 'desk shoes'; not sure it was that strong, though. We would spray fart gas everywhere, and someone was always shoving a banana up one of their exhaust pipes."

"A-ha, so you went to school in Beanotown!"

In our early days of dating Three would often explain what he actually did at work, but it was so far from anything I'd ever thought or known about that my brain could never hold on to the exact info. But it involved contracts and accounting and you needed some letters after your name to do it—some kind of a qualification or accreditation. FSA or FAS? But basically, if he lost those letters, he could lose his job, which was why, after he passed the exams to get those letters, he stopped doing his regular drunk party trick of getting his balls out and pulling them into a funny position while making a silly voice, which all his friends would crack up over and one of them would always take pictures of.

I loved falling in love with him. He'd take me on driving dates around different parts of London where we would find obscure fudge and chocolate shops we'd never heard of. I was still very easily excited by males who owned and could drive cars and would sit in the passenger seat, giant slab of fudge on my lap, getting progressively wetter, waiting for the time we would be back in my room.

After my fanny had been satisfied, my brain would then go on little love explosions where it would need to create something physical for him. This is how I knew I was in love with him.

I once spent a whole evening picking out all the banana chips from six boxes of his favourite cereal as he didn't like them so would always spend ages moving them out before he'd pour the milk in at breakfast. I had to walk to the nicer side of Ealing to a Waitrose as the Sainsbury's and Tesco didn't stock it. I repackaged the now-banana-free cereal, making my own label with hearts decorating it, and gave it to Three as a gift. He was so surprised a few tears came to his eyes, although neither of us acknowledged that was what was happening. It was too early for that.

But I knew and it made my brain want to do more of those things. How amazing to have someone so in love with you they are brought to tears when you do nice stuff for them. Maybe I could give him enough love surprises that I could fill a whole glass with his tears and then freeze them or drink them. No, that is too much, but love makes you think odd things. The point is, it filled me with huge amounts of happiness. That was it. That's what I wanted to be. Someone who made someone else's life nicer through loving them. I was quite surprised by this revelation as I didn't think I was that kind of person. I'd not been brought up in that way.

Do you want to hear about that? I don't mind telling you; it's just quite long so feels like a bit of a tangent from all this love-story stuff. I can go into it more later, but basically I had two parents who weren't together but who loved me, just in ways that might not look like conventional parental loving styles. I officially lived with my dad and stepmum. My older brother Jay, from Dad's first marriage, had a room there too, but he lived at his mum's down the road. I would see my mum every other weekend, but it was always a bit annoying as she had moved quite far away, so I spent a lot of time on the motorway being driven to or from one of their houses. So much time that Dad and I had got up to date with the car registration game (it is such an awful and dull task I can't bring myself to write it out, but basically it involved not being able to move on to the next car registration letter till you'd spotted the one before. Marginally better than I Spy, but only in the moments you got one). Then, when I was 10, Mum fell in love with a man who ran an animal sanctuary in San Francisco, so she moved there. Making the car registration game redundant.

If I needed help and asked, one of my parents would always talk to me about it, but I didn't see or feel love from them in the ways a lot of my friends seemed to. Like having nice conversations around dinner tables or spontaneous moments of touching and hugs, or just being able to eat Jelly Babies while singing along to Radio 1 when on long car journeys. And, mainly, just having them around, as Dad was often away for work. Which ended up being one of the only things him and Mum had in common. Dad would always send me lots of postcards with funny pictures on the front and "miss you" and "love Dad" written on the back, and Mum would regularly send letters with funny stickers on them saying "miss you" and "love you" and I didn't doubt that they meant it, but that's all actually quite easy and not very time-consuming to do. If there had been a conveyor belt of parents to pick, they aren't the ones I'd have chosen. They were much more focused on living their adult lives, doing fun social things or cool work stuff, which now I am an adult I get; I can totally see how that is way more enjoyable than looking after children, which is why I wouldn't have any.

But also, if I did, I would make sure I showed love in much better ways than them.

TOP HUMPS

NAME: Richard P.
AKA: Dull Dick
AGE: 14 (him), 14 (me)
BUILD: Quite a good-sized body and height with lovely brown hair but wore thick-rimmed glasses so . . .
GENERAL VIBE: Maths geek. Not exactly popular but not despised either.
ACTUALLY LIKE: Very nice.
SPECIAL SKILLS: Could tell you how far away something was just by looking at it. (He'd have been very good at the car registration game.)
FANNY SCALE: 8/10
BRAIN SCALE: 5/10
OVERALL RATING: 6.5/10 = Short-term Pleasure
PRE-GAME: After months of sitting behind Dull Dick in physics the back of his neck suddenly became very hot to me when I overheard him telling James, who sat next to him, how far away the bin outside the window was from us. It made my fanny v. wet.
THE DEED: After a school BBQ I made him come to the hedge with me.
PLEASURE (me): 1 × orgasm due to fingering.
PLEASURE (him): 1 × orgasm due to hand job.

Summary: Being with Dull Dick was a similar experience to going in a shop and trying on the one thing you know you're not into and that really isn't your taste or style but then ending up wanting to buy it, so you do and you think you love it the first time you wear it to your pal's birthday but after you take it off later that night you never, ever consider wearing it again, which would be okay, only it had been a special birthday and there had been loads of photos taken and when you catch a glimpse of you in these pictures you feel shocked that you ever made such a choice (i.e., having to see him all the time in class).

Clingfilm Kisses

Three was the best male person I had ever come across. EVER. And all my bits worked with his bits very well in a very exciting manner. I wanted to kiss him all the time and I loved how he looked at me when we were getting it on. We did a lot of sexual firsts together, like sitting on his face instead of just lying on my back when being licked out, using fluffy handcuffs and letting his finger wander down to the bridge close to my bum-hole area when I was about to come.

Because my fanny has never been able to have an orgasm from a penis being inside its hole, that was never a part of sex that bothered me that much with whoever I was with, especially if I had already come. This no-orgasm-by-penis feeling didn't change with Three, but I liked it in a different way—like when you know you're going to the kind of restaurant where you're getting three courses. I really liked the pattern of how our early sex moved into an arrangement of kissing course followed by licking course followed by sex. He never not wanted to lick me and I felt very, very lucky.

We also did all of the serious non-sexual firsts together. First romantic holiday to faraway places (we went to the Land of Cheese Spread!!!), first big-money gifts to each other (my first and only designer boots!!!), first "our restaurant" (Las Tapas in Shepherd's Bush), first rented flat of our own (in Ealing), first joint travel-insurance policy (World Travel), first joint car (an Escort), first joint bank account (RBS), first life-and-death situation together (in Argentina), first wills (via WHSmith) and first life-insurance policy (too boring to remember). So all the big ones. Three took our future planning very seriously because this was a forever thing. And also because his parents hadn't been very good at all that, so I think he made sure he would be.

"I've put you on my work life insurance."

"Do I have to fill out any forms for that?"

"No. It means if I die, you'll be looked after."

"Oh. For how long?"

"It's a lump sum."

"Oh! How much?"

"£150,000."

"Oh, wow! Right, thank you, so exciting, so much money!!"

"You only get it if I die."

"Yeah, of course, and I'd prefer to have you than not, but if we ever get sick of each other and you look like you may be on your way out, it's not all bad for me!!"

We didn't have weird tip-toey conversations about marriage as I was and have always been very clear and open to everyone I've ever met that I am not interested in it, due to the fact that both my parents had been married a number of times and it seemed to be the thing that made things shit. This was my theory.

Three agreed. His parents had only been married once, to each other, and they did it when they were really young. He was pretty sure they didn't enjoy each other's company when he was growing up. They separated when he went to uni.

Plus, times had changed. Buying a home was just as big a commitment these days and I informed Three over email that I would be very happy to do that hopefully at some point if we ever had any money.

From: Me
To: Three
Subject: I would really, really, really like to . . .

Buy a home with you one day.
Just thought I'd let you know as I thought this thought and it excited me very much.
Shall we have lamb and my special pea thing for dins?!!
xxxxx

From: Three
To: Me
Subject: RE: I would really, really, really like to . . .

Sweet Bean.
Yes that sounds lovely. Should be 7:30 at latest hope that's ok?
x

We had started calling each other Beano in a soppy couple-nickname way but often the "o" dropped off, which I was trying to encourage, otherwise it felt like we were conforming to his annoying work-people rules.

My theory about marriage was actually more specific than what I had shared with Three. I think marriage makes men more likely to cheat. And marriage plus children definitely makes men cheat. My dad had cheated a lot on both my mum and Jay's mum, who he was with before he met Mum. But then, with his final partner, who he didn't marry and didn't have children with, he has been faithful and happy and they've been together for over 20 years! I don't see this as sad, bitter history—I see it as extremely helpful, almost scientific-like information to help guide me.

In basic formula form it would look like:

Lover Marries Lover = 25% chance of success
Lover Marries Lover Plus Children = 0% chance of success
Lover With Lover = 100% chance of success

I haven't done any official research into "Lover With Lover Plus Children," but my guesstimate would be around 25 per cent chance of success for this one too.

Either way I would never, ever, *ever* be in something where there was cheating. So I really wouldn't be marrying any men any time during my lifetime or having children with them.

I'd been honest with Three about that too and he had said he wasn't into having children either. We were on the same page.

Living with Three was lush. I'd always thought of the area I'd grown up in with my dad in Bridport as home. That feeling when I got older and Dad would pick me up from the train station after a weekend spent at Mum's and I'd see someone I knew drinking outside my favourite pub—that immediately made me feel happy things inside. And I didn't think there was more to a home feeling than that. But after living with Three and walking in the door to our flat, especially after a holiday (once I'd checked that my stash places of important earrings and clothes and my designer boots were still safely hidden), the feeling I felt was like home × 100. Being there, knowing it existed with all our stuff in it, permanently, not having to ferry my stuff between two houses, or not being allowed in certain rooms and knowing that all my belongings could stay in just the one place was a new feeling and I liked it very much.

I loved rushing home from work to make dinners that we'd eat together followed by decision-making about which choc-olate mousse we should eat on the sofa, and touching feet as we watched telly, and hugging and saying we loved each other every night in bed just after the light had been turned off, and how, when we rolled away from that hug to go to sleep, we'd always still have one little part of us touching, like maybe right hip to middle of bum, or left heel to bottom side of inside left knee. And Three letting me have two-thirds of all the wardrobe and drawer space in the bedroom plus the bottom cupboard in the kitchen for my extra shoes.

Our love became so strong that we couldn't handle talking seriously about death as it became paralysingly painful to think of one of us gone. We'd each worry about the other one cycling around London or flying on planes without the other in case it went down with no chance of survivors. When Three got ill once with a very bad cough/cold thing, by the evening of day four I felt so sad that we couldn't kiss that I created clingfilm kissing—I tore a bit of clingfilm off and put it between our lips so that they could be pressed together and feel almost-contact. This then became the norm whenever one of us was ill.

TOP HUMPS

NAME: Tom M.

AKA: Millsy (Serious Boyfriend Number One)

AGE: 17 (him), 15 (me)

BUILD: Overweight; blond, salty, long hair.

GENERAL VIBE: Surfer dude. Very popular in his year (which was two years above mine!!!!).

ACTUALLY LIKE: Bit of an arrogant dick. But would bring me cheese scones wrapped in clingfilm to school.

SPECIAL SKILLS: Surfing—he was really good. And his mum owned a bakery, which is why I guess he had a weight issue as he got to eat baked goods whenever he liked.

FANNY SCALE: 9/10

BRAIN SCALE: 7/10

OVERALL RATING: 8/10 = Long-term Love

PRE-GAME: I spent weeks sussing out his lesson timetable to walk past where he'd be at just the right time for him to start noticing me. My planning and patience paid off!

THE DEED: After Nell P. started going out with one of Millsy's mates, I made her have drinks at her dad's doctor surgery after school as she had keys and there was a garden and after a few ciders we got off with each other after I followed Millsy to the toilet.

PLEASURE (me): 20-plus orgasms, mainly through dry humping on his mum's sofa.

PLEASURE (him): About the same number of orgasms, mainly through dry humping on his mum's sofa!

Summary: We went out for just under a year. There was something so thrilling when we were dry humping on his sofa, him on top, the distant smell of a recently cooked cheese scone floating overhead, him crushing me, almost suffocating me with his fat belly and heavy weight, me not wanting to move him off and relieve my lungs coz . . . I-was-just-about-to-comeeeee. After, he'd always get me a still-warm cheese scone. They were the best savoury cheese snack I have ever tasted. At this age, having a hugely heavy boy lover was fab for your confidence as it meant you always looked tiny next to him and didn't need to worry about being fat, or saying no to another two cheese scones.

Asda

Three and I saw the world together. Apart from mum-visits to San Francisco, I had never travelled anywhere else other than Spain before meeting him, but by the end of our second year together we had been to Rome, the Philippines, Argentina and Sunderland. I'd never thought of going up to Sunderland as it seemed so boring and sounded like it was always cold, but we had such an amazing time, visiting beaches and seeing Newcastle and meeting his mental Granny Aggy who lived there and who pretty much hated everything possible about being alive. We also did big fun holidays with our friends, one with his uni mate James and his girlfriend Chloe, and another, a skiing one, with a random mix of people including Al and Fran, my best mates from school. I had always hoped I'd be in the kind of couple that did this sort of thing.

For the first few holidays Three would pay considerably more than me on them, as my pub job didn't allow for any savings. But after six months of us meeting I had got my first proper job at a science start-up company as I had lied and said one of the add-on modules I did on my media studies degree was in natural sciences when actually it had been in Spanish. I was their general office admin person, so I don't think it mattered about this lie as I didn't need to understand any of the weird and unexplainable stuff they chatted about above my head, which is actually what being in my Spanish class had felt like.

When Three and I would return home from any holidays I'd never get down or dread going into work the next day like most of our friends would, as the science job paid bonuses twice a year—an actual extra big amount of money for just doing the job I was already being paid to do. That just made it much easier to be cheery around the place, as there was never not another bonus about to be due. This was on top of every Friday's free Pret lunch. I was living the high life and my new salary meant that the girls on the tills in the Marble Arch Topshop knew me by my first name.

Around year two, among the weekly Asda shops and general life-together stuff, I had slowly started to forget the power of my wet fanny and how easily it used to be around, as now it was always, always dry. Growing up, no one gave me a detailed guide of what to expect from long-term love. I'd *never* have had that kind of conversation with Dad or my brother, and Mum wasn't around enough to develop those kind of comms. We didn't get newspapers in my house or play radio stations with talking conversations, and the only telly I watched regularly was *Red Dwarf* and *EastEnders*, so I'm not sure where one goes to find out this kind of intel. When things moved into a sexually duller place with Three it was just like, oh, *this* is what a relationship looks like a couple of years in. This is normal.

From: Three
To: Me
Subject: Shall I . . .

I'll try and get home on time so we can finish Interstellar, Shall I get treats?
x

Sex began to *really* hurt in about the middle of year two. Nothing had changed with the nice pattern of kissing, licking and then missionary, but I had obviously developed a majorly faulty fanny. It had completely stopped getting tingly and wet. I assumed losing this feeling was another normal part of getting older, like when you no longer create imaginary and magical cities when you're spending time swimming underwa- ter. Although, I do actually still do that when I'm swimming lengths as it makes the time pass more quickly.

I told Fran and Al about it at a bring-your-own curry place in Bournemouth, which is where they both lived now. Most people from school either stayed in boring dull-dull Bridport or went to live in Bournemouth. Fran and Al were my chief advisors. Al had brought the visible thong into fashion for us all in Year 12, wearing it very high with very low-waisted flared jeans. And Fran had once spent an entire day at uni continually making herself come with a vibrator to see what would happen. She said she achieved 22 orgasms before even- tually having some kind of zone-out fit, which resulted in an 18-hour straight-through sleep and a very throbbing and sore clit. She said she couldn't touch it for a week after. We were all massively inspired. Thank you, Fran, for bravely investigating and sharing your findings. She also said her hair had got 100 per cent straight since that day too, meaning she never needed to use hair straighteners again.

After Al popped Prosecco bottle number two, I explained to

them the circumstances, which were that I'd never now be wet before action started with Three, but that he was still always able to make me come through licking me, which was obviously ace, and that this would always happen before the sex bit, but as soon as I had come from the licking he would put his dick in me (normally in missionary position) and it was at this point that it would be very, very uncomfortable and stressful and painful.

Fran said she knew this, she had it nailed. She had studied biology at uni so her answers were often given quite a lot of weight. "The problem is, when the female vagina orgasms it contracts."

Yes, this made sense.

"And after it contracts it stays a bit tight."

Yes, yes, that also made sense.

"And what you are doing is putting something very hard into that very tightly contracting place."

Yes.

"So," Fran said, "you need to have the sex before the orgasm!"

"That all makes great sense, but the point of Three licking me before the sex is so it is a slippery area to enter, otherwise it is even more impossible and painful to get him in."

Al was thinking now. She often spoke quietly and with minimal words. She studied German and French at uni and she spoke in Arabic to her mum and Spanish to her dad, so I assume her brain was always frantically translating between all the languages in there. "Use lube."

Al had been with her current girlfriend for three years and her boyfriend before that for two years so obviously knew STUFF.

Great! I love a plan. I'd buy shitloads of lube.

TOP HUMPS

NAME: Alan
AKA: Spanish Alan
AGE: 19 (him), 16 (me)
BUILD: Very, very tall and strong and Spanish.
GENERAL VIBE: Laid-back cool guy. One of my brother's best mates. His dad lived in Spain. He rode a moped.
ACTUALLY LIKE: Clever, lazy, smoked too much weed, thought deep things about world affairs, drove drunk. Always carried lube in a mini bumbag (for his bike).
SPECIAL SKILLS: Speaking two languages and driving really fast around his town in Spain after a night of drinking and smoking blunts.
FANNY SCALE: 7/10
BRAIN SCALE: 7/10
OVERALL RATING: 7/10 = Short-term Pleasure
PRE-GAME: I spent years fancying him on and off when I'd see him occasionally at things for my brother.
THE DEED: After my GCSEs Fran's gran got ill and we had to cancel our celebration hols so my brother said I could join him and his pals visiting Alan in Spain. By night two we had kissed by the cigarette stand. By night four we'd had sex on the beach—the shagging, not the cocktail.
PLEASURE (me): Lots of orgasms mainly through being fingered on the beach late at night and one from the vibration sat on the back of his moped.
PLEASURE (him): Probably came about three times.

Summary: Alan and I kept our dalliances secret so as not to upset Jay, but as we were all pissed and high all the time our efforts weren't that slick and one night there was a big bust-up on the beach about it, which then made it all feel a bit crap and shit. Plus, months later when Alan visited England, without his summer tan or moped, he looked a bit average.

Lube

There aren't a lot of situations that can make my cheeks go red with embarrassment, but getting told off for trying out lube in Hammersmith Boots is officially one. A woman with a Boots badge approached me from behind the cotton pads while I had the lid off number two of four. They didn't have any testers and I wanted to make sure the one I was getting was really lubey—but I didn't really know what that meant, or even what lube looked like, so I'd had to pierce the cap on the selection they had in there in order to squeeze a small slime trail along the top of my left hand. Manager Lady said I had to buy them all. So I went home with four different brands. Shoved them in the back of my bedside cabinet drawer ready for testing at the weekend.

I instigated the lube test on a Saturday morning.

I'm really good at waking up just before my alarm if I say to myself the time I want to wake three times before I go to sleep, "Wake up at 9:15 a.m., wake up at 9:15 a.m., wake up at 9:15 a.m."

I woke at 9:11 a.m. and turned my back-up alarm off. Three never wakes before 10 a.m. at the weekends so that gave me time to wee, eat two digestive biscuits with Nutella spread on them (for stamina) and then lie back in bed, minus my pyjama bottoms and with a huge dollop of lube number two surrounding my fanny hole.

I reset my alarm for 9:55 a.m. and waited for him to be

woken up by it. As Three's eyes opened I kissed his lips while twisting my body to keep my hips and bum flat on the bed. He responded as I had predicted and moved on top of me, heading down to start the usual licking business. I stopped him, pulling him back up and round so I could get on top of him. He clocked that our usual getting-it-on pattern had changed.

"You all right?"

"Yes, just keep kissing me!"

"OK . . ."

And then, as my right leg sailed over his body, a huge dollop of the goo splattered onto his hip.

"What's that?"

I decided not to acknowledge this. "Relax . . ."

Right, this was going to be dreamy, easy, really great sex.

"I love you . . ."

"I love you too."

It was awful. Putting his penis in with all the lube hurt just as much as when he'd licked me first. I pretended it was nice and good, but being on top actually made the inside pain much worse.

This was depressing.

Immediately after, I rang Fran. "It didn't work. I tried everything we went through—it made no difference."

"Maybe you shouldn't have been on top . . ."

"I've got a proper problem with my fanny."

"Do you want me to send you some sexual crystals?"

Fran had recently completed a course in crystal healing. This side of her new studies I was less interested in.

"No, I'm OK, but thanks."

TOP HUMPS

NAME: Pete
AKA: Bummy Pete
AGE: 17 (him), 16 (me)
BUILD: Thin, short hair; all his trousers purposefully sat halfway down his bum displaying his boxer shorts.
GENERAL VIBE: Always wore T-shirts from the Krystal King, a local skate shop. Mega skater dude. But his sister was a proper nerd so this pulled his popularity down a bit.
ACTUALLY LIKE: A bit gross to girls.
SPECIAL SKILLS: Getting places super-quick on his skateboard and bumming girls.
FANNY SCALE: 8/10
BRAIN SCALE: 3/10
OVERALL RATING: 5.5/10 = Short-term Pleasure
PRE-GAME: Everyone knew that Bummy Pete would defo try to bum you, which did not excite me but everyone also knew he loved licking girls out too, so it was a bit of a weigh-up.
THE DEED: After a very drunk night at the only nightclub in town I agreed to let Pete have sex with me on our friend Grant's sofa if he licked me out first. He did and when he licked me he also licked my bum, which felt all right and gave a double meaning to his name.
PLEASURE (me): 2 orgasms.
PLEASURE (him): 2 orgasms.

Summary: After a second very drunk night at the only nightclub in town I agreed to let Pete try to bum me on Grant's sofa. His penis was like him, long and thin, and even though it wasn't huge my bum couldn't even handle the tip of it. So he gave up and licked me again instead. When I woke in the morning he had pissed on the sofa bed and wasn't planning to say anything. I didn't get it on with him again.

Ugly Bum Hole Theory

A lot of girls in my year were petrified of a boy they liked seeing their bum holes. Which is the main reason no one in our town dabbled in the area of bum licking. I was born lucky: a bit like not minding what my fanny could do and not being embarrassed by its wetness or look, I also accepted that the bum hole's purpose, whether on a girl or boy, is never to look good and therefore, if we all agree that as standard, it totally takes the pressure off. Bums should look gross. Enjoy them as they are. Thank you, Bummy Pete.

Acton

Three's mum got a bit ill in December just before we were supposed to go on a big trip to Australia. I had always hoped I would end up there someday—what with spending all of my growing-up years watching every single episode of *Home and Away* and *Neighbours*. I could not wait to visit this magical and obviously much-better-than-England land. I'd given Three an early Christmas present of a pair of Billabong navy board shorts, the kind that have a lace tie-up and don't have that lame elasticated waist that most swimming shorts have, meaning they sit just really sexily on the man's hips. I couldn't wait to see him coming in and out of the sea in them.

Three was adamant that we shouldn't change our trip, even though I said a number of times in a very genuine and properly supportive voice that I was happy for us to. It was an infection in her back and even though the doctors weren't treating it like it was life-threatening, it was taking ages to clear up and she had to stay in hospital for a few weeks so it felt a bit miserable leaving her to handle Christmas in there.

But Three kept saying not to worry about it, which made me wonder about how nice a person he actually was, as, compared to my parents, his were actually okay. His mum would always invite us round for Sunday lunch and get loads of special puddings in, and whenever we went to visit Three's dad he would always buy the takeaway and then offer to drive us all the way home, not just to the train station, which annoyingly

Three would never let him do. I pressed him again about being around for her during this time, but he shrugged it off, saying his mum wouldn't mind, that they weren't like that.

They were a bit different. When we first got together, we spent our first Christmas at my dad's house, and when we were doing all the present prep in the weeks before going Three didn't get anything for his family. He said they never swapped Christmas presents if they weren't spending the actual day together, which I think is absolutely mental and also quite depressing, but none of them ever seemed that bothered by it all. I got the impression they might not always do presents when actually spending the day together either, which would absolutely not be on if I was doing Christmas with them.

From that year on I got him to start doing presents for his mum and for his dad, his younger brother Mark, and his Aunty Hannah, as they all lived in London, and Granny Aggy would get a card. She was always miserable so no point in wasting money on her. Our first Christmas with his mum, everyone seemed well into the present giving/receiving, which was a relief.

"Are you sure we shouldn't be doing something before we go?"

"Mum will be fine with a visit and present drop."

"OK, I'll come too."

I suppose that was progress.

I had thought Three and I had been together for too a long time by now to discover anything new about the other, but it was only on the way back from the Wednesday-night hospital visit, as we drove past a giant building we had never passed before in Acton, he told me that when he was 12 he had to go and stay there for a few months on his own.

"What do you mean? That massive building there? What is it?"

"It was a warehouse, probably flats now."

"Why did you get sent there?"

"Mum was in a work accident and Dad couldn't manage caring for both me and Mark, so Aunty Hannah took Mark, and I got sent to that place to live with one of Mum's colleagues who was the guardian of it."

"Who was the work person?"

"Someone called Minna—I don't really remember her much; she kept to herself."

"Did you have a bed?"

"Yeah, it was pretty big, with beds in a few of the rooms. Was a bit spooky at night, though."

"Is that not really weird?"

"I don't think they had any choice."

"But that doesn't seem very fair. Why couldn't you both go to your Aunty Hannah's?"

"She only had her bedroom and Mark was the youngest, so they thought it was best. Plus, I was a proper handful, never shut up, so just easier all round."

"But you were only 12!"

Three ended up staying there for six months until his mum was fully recovered, and even though his dad would visit him regularly and take him to see his mum in the rehab centre, neither of them ever spoke to him about it then, or after, and so he was just very sad and worried throughout that time.

WHAT A FUCKING BUNCH OF CUNTS.

I didn't say this to Three, but I felt it angrily bubbling inside of me. Stupid fucking parents who don't know how to parent properly and never talking to him or making him feel okay. Little 12-year-old him. It made me so mad. And I get it, I totally get how hard that situation must have been for them, but why didn't anyone do any better by him?!

I didn't think I could love or care about him any more, but

34

when he told me all of this, I felt more feelings than I knew I had. And I wanted to look after and love him forever.

"I'll never do that to you. Even when you're old and annoying I'll look after you!"

He got the teary-eye thing he gets and squeezed my leg.

I decided to stop hassling him about why he sometimes seemed to be a bit of a dick to his parents. This explained it, and I could relate to that!

When we got home there was an answer-machine message from my mum. It was so annoying as we never actually used the home phone and only got it for the internet. We purposefully didn't give the number on it to anyone, but I had once rung Mum on it and she wouldn't wipe it from her records.

"You can use my mobile to call her back if you want."

Three had a work phone with loads of free minutes to international numbers.

"No. I want to do two episodes of *Spooks* before bed."

I know I am a bit of a dick to my parents. I don't try to be, or have it as my life mission, I just think it's incredibly hard not to be when they've been or done something majorly disappointing—something the adult you would never do. People say that when you become a parent yourself you then forgive your parents all their faults and mistakes: a) I think that is madness and b) how does that help someone like me who knows they never want to have children? Absolute useless bollocks!

Three would always encourage me to speak to Mum more than I did. Which, given this new information, was kind of surprising.

Dr. Butt

It turns out it's not so easy for Three to get to the point of being able to come in me when I'm wriggling around trying to pretend I'm not in pain. He didn't say this, and I didn't comment that that's what I thought was going on, as we didn't know how to have mature conversations about how to fix it. But it was clear that neither of us was having a good time during sex.

I was not equipped to tell the man I deeply loved how awful I found sex with him; however, I am a big believer in finding the answers to problems, so I went to the doctor. The trick for getting anything moving when it comes to the NHS is to have a "Condition Diary" where you input dates, given circumstances and the pain level of whatever the problem is. Then, when reporting to the doctor, you have a factual and credible account of how long it has all been going on for, and they can't say their immediate normal suggestion of, "You should start keeping a log and let us know how it is going in a few weeks." We're already there, buddy, get me the medicine and scans to fix this now, please.

Also, depending on how hesitant the doctor seemed, I would always increase the pain level recorded in the Condition Diary by 20 per cent. It makes things move along more quickly, plus I get the impression that a lot of male doctors cancel down the pain level a female patient reports, so it works out about right in the end.

For a few months I had been keeping a "Fanny Pain Diary."

The doctor who was seeing me was an old man called Dr. Butt. I had seen him a few times and he was kind, so I kept the pain levels as they were originally recorded. I had always wanted to ask him if that was the correct spelling of his surname and if he had felt pressure about the extra "t," as most humans are pretty immature, but I never had enough time because, although he was kind, he was a stickler for keeping to the allocated appointment minutes.

I presented him with my fanny diary and read him some recent entries.

Dear Diary, today my fanny turned to me and with a slightly sore and downhearted look begged me to help her.

Ha, I'm joking; not that kind of diary. I'm not into writing feelings or my adventures down in case they can be used as evidence against me.

Fanny Pain Diary

Friday 10pm—sex after normal on-back, lying-down licking. Very, very painful on entry (pain level 8/10). Pain continued in a different way once in (7/10). Relief when over. No more immediate pain. Slight sting when weeing from entry hole pain (1/10).

Sunday 11am—sex tried in sitting-on position with lube used. Went in slightly easier but very painful during all the up and down bit (9/10).

Saturday 10am—had to stop the missionary position sex coz it was making me feel sick. Pain level (6/10). I had eaten a whole packet of chocolate Hobnobs before though.

Dr. Butt immediately referred me to the gynaecological department at Chelsea and Westminster Hospital. Even without my exaggerated pain levels! This must be very serious. I was a bit worried and also relieved. He said the referral would take up to eight weeks. Now that it seemed I had some kind of actual problem I found it easier to inform Three.

From: Me
To: Three
Subject: Docs

Hello, great news Doctor Butt thinks there is something going on maybe in relation to pelvic stuff (haven't googled yet) so I'm being referred to see someone to look into it further. Might take a few weeks so he advised we don't put anything up there until then.
Love you,
SB xx

Quick nickname update: we still called each other Bean but now sometimes he called me Sweet Bean and shortened it to SB so sometimes I signed off as SB. Ideally we would *never*, EVER call ourselves these names around other humans, but one time it did slip out at a dinner party and Three's best uni mate James took the piss so much as he didn't believe the *Beano* story, said more like flicking the bean, so for Valentine's that year I asked Three to get me a gold necklace with Beano written on it, and I wore it solidly for the rest of that year, not for deep love reasons but for back-up proof.

From: Three
To: Me
Subject: RE: Docs

I didn't realise that was his name, I wonder why he never changed it!
Great news SB well done for going, would you like me to cook something special for dins?
x

I felt huge relief—I didn't have to worry or think about sex for ages! *And* it might all get solved.

> **From:** Me
> **To:** Three
> **Subject:** RE: Docs
>
> I know, the extra T makes it hard to separate from the body part.
> YES PLEASE, can you cook something amazing involving lamb or poached egg fishcakes, or puff pastry pizza??!!?!
> xx

Three cooked the most amazing celebratory meal of lamb two ways with potato dauphinoise, which took him two hours, and coz he knows I get very impatient when I can smell good things in the kitchen, he also bought a bumper-sized pack of the really expensive salt-and-vinegar stick crisps they sell in the M&S near his office. Sitting at the dinner table drinking Prosecco while Three yelled updates to me about his day as he put the food together, things felt very hopeful.

TOP HUMPS

NAME: Dave

AKA: Welsh Dave

AGE: 18 (him), 18 (me)

BUILD: Very short with long brown hair, always smelt of freshly dug potatoes.

GENERAL VIBE: Hippie music guy. Pretty sure he didn't ever wash his hair. He could play the guitar well.

ACTUALLY LIKE: Kind-ish.

SPECIAL SKILLS: Making things sound hotter than they were due to his accent.

FANNY SCALE: 7/10

BRAIN SCALE: 4/10

OVERALL RATING: 5.5/10 = Short-term Pleasure

PRE-GAME: Welsh Dave was at my uni and washed up in the Red Dragon kitchen, and when I'd come in he'd speak to me in Welsh and when I asked what he was saying he said "things that were too dirty to translate" and that really excited me even though the potato smell was a bit off-putting.

THE DEED: At a lock-in by the pool table he told me he could make me come with his cue. And then did.

PLEASURE (me): 10-plus orgasms.

PLEASURE (him): 10-plus orgasms.

Summary: After he came back from Christmas break his potato smell was so strong I was unable to get back to the hot and desiring place I had felt with him before the hols so I basically ignored all future moments alone with him.

Armpit Baby

From: Three
To: Me
Subject: Today

Good luck today, sorry I can't meet you after but I am thinking
of you brave Bean
x

On my first visit to the gynaecologist I had no clue of what to
expect. So I told work I needed the whole day off for a hospital
visit and figured if it was quicker I could have a bonus shopping
session in Westfield. On arrival at the right department the
nurse in the unit said I was to have a scan—an ultrasound.
I thought people only had them if they were pregnant, so I
checked. "Are you worried I'm pregnant?"

"No," she said, adjusting the bed, "this is just the clearest
way to get a look and see what's going on up there."

I lay down on top of a bed which had been covered with
one long strip of giant kitchen-roll and then she placed more
of it over my bottom half to cover me. I could have done with
finding out where they got this from as our Asda one was quite
weak and small. I got my belly out, ready for the gel and the
machine thing to be gently pushed over it. Weirdly I started
feeling like I was about to see a baby I didn't have, which made
me feel panicky. Good to see nothing had changed there—defo
no children for me thanks.

The nurse was taking ages to come back and I entered a weird daydream where a doctor came in to see what the problem was and they spotted a plum-sized lump in my armpit and everyone got really worried thinking it was cancer and kept me in for ages with doctor after doctor coming to have a look until eventually the head of the hospital came in and told me a miracle had happened, that I was the first woman ever to fall pregnant with a child in the armpit and that it would be a bumpy road ahead but with their team of experts they could help carry it to full term and it would be a miracle of modern science, and I informed them I didn't wish to have children and they said some big scientific funder would pay me £10 million to do it, so I said okay.

When the nurse comes back in, she's carrying a huge dildo thing, which she's putting a condom on.

"I thought the scanners were flat."

"No, they are like this. Take your trousers and knickers off, please."

"I'd prefer to keep them on."

She looked at me impatiently, 'Well then, how will I insert this inside you?"

"You don't press it on my belly?"

"No, we use these for internal ultrasounds."

I awkwardly took off my bottom half. This was not what I had expected. The whole problem was that my fanny hurt when large hard things went up it and now she was going to put a large hard thing up it.

She moved towards me. I decided not to open my legs.

"Are you OK?"

"I'm not very good at this. I don't think you'll get it up far enough to see stuff."

She became a bit nicer and gently moved my knees open.

"Don't worry. Just lie back and breathe through your nose. It'll be a bit cold, but just relax."

No one ever, ever, ever, *ever* relaxes during these things. These or smear tests or when doctors put fingers up your bum hole—it's bollocks. You can't relax; it's not normal or relaxing. Maybe it was fine for women who had super-big bucket fannies, but do they even exist? The only one I had heard of belonged to Lily Hughes, who in Year 9 was nicknamed Soggy Bucket by the popular boys because apparently Chris Cormack in Year 11 had put his whole fist up her.

Lying on the giant kitchen-roll sheets, I silently sang to myself most of "I'm Feeling Good," the shitter Muse version, not Nina Simone's, while the nurse prodded the dildo around inside me.

It actually *didn't* hurt as much as I had feared, and was a million times nicer than having a smear test.

After a good while of moving it all around inside me, the nurse informed me that, "This will determine if en-doe-mee-e-tree-us is to blame for your pain."

I mean, that was the word I had heard her saying; I had to google it later to properly know it.

Endometriosis = a problem women can get when the tissue that makes up the lining of the womb grows in other places in your body, e.g. in the lower abdomen or ovaries. Women with endometriosis often have pain with periods, lower abdominal pain, pain with sex and may have a hard time getting pregnant. Some women with endometriosis may not have any symptoms at all. Classic.

TOP HUMPS

NAME: Michael
AKA: Johnny
AGE: 29 (him), 19 (me)
BUILD: Quite tall, massive arms, builder's bum.
GENERAL VIBE: No-nonsense London builder. He was good at pool and always put Muse on the pub jukebox. For some reason all his mates called him Johnny.
ACTUALLY LIKE: Maybe a bit depressed.
SPECIAL SKILLS: He could fix anything.
FANNY SCALE: 9/10
BRAIN SCALE: 3/10
OVERALL RATING: 6/10 = Short-term Pleasure
PRE-GAME: Michael/Johnny could only come to the pub on Sundays, Tuesdays and Wednesdays so I swapped all my shifts to always work those nights.
THE DEED: We started playing pool with each other at the end of my shifts and one night Andy, the aggressive drunk greengrocer, wouldn't drink up and leave so I couldn't shut the bar down and Michael/Johnny stepped in, told him to do one and that was it for me. I needed to have sex with him.
PLEASURE (me): 5 orgasms from 69-ers.
PLEASURE (him): 5 orgasms.

Summary: After I came back from Easter break he was on one of his downer paranoid times, which made me stop fancying him. Plus, I had got it on with two boys from home and didn't fancy having that conversation, so I got the pub to change my shifts back.

Fist

On my second visit to the gynaecological department I still told work I needed the whole day off, even though last time had only taken two hours, as I thought it was nice to end it all with a "Well Done" trip to the shops.

I met with a consultant, and she had the write-up from my internal examination. "Good news: no endometriosis and no other suspect-looking lumps. So my recommendation would be some physiotherapy. Does that sound OK?"

The previous year I'd had a series of physio sessions for a bike accident and a painful shoulder thing. It was quite hands-on and I was shown lots of exercises to take away and continue doing to help the muscles around the injury in my shoulder heal. After three months I felt no more pain in my shoulder.

It was a no-brainer. "Yes, I'm very up for physio."

"Great, we can start now. Lie up on the bed . . . and take your knickers off."

I immediately felt stressed, but rather than voicing any of the very loud shouting happening in my head, I automatically went into don't-ask-any-questions-and-pretend-I-know-what's-

45

going-on mode—a very unhelpful and stupid mode that once I am in, I am unable to steer out of.

My consultant was called Donna. She had very short ginger hair with very strong large-earring game—classy, not Pat Butcher–esque—and she was lovely. Donna also had a private practice and often treated pregnant people who were scared of giving birth. As she fiddled around with getting supplies for our session, and as I lay naked from the waist down with their shitty paper-towel thing under me and more over my fanny area, I asked her how anyone who found a penis too painful could ever have a baby come out of them.

She laughed kindly and said, "That's a common worry but you'd be surprised how much you can actually fit through the hole."

"Maybe normal people's holes," I said, "but I think I might have an ultra-tight and tiny one."

"We'll see," she said, "we'll see."

We'll??!! What's she going to do, bring all her gyno pals in for the challenge? No thank you, Donna, not on my fanny hole, you're all right, you've got the wrong girl here.

"I think it might be an actual thing with me—all my holes appear to be very tight," I said. "Quite often when I'm pooing it can be the most intense squeeze of a thing, like, my bum hole isn't equipped to handle the size of the poos that come out. All my holes just feel a bit squeezy. Dr. Butt had to put his finger up there once to check a blood poo thing, and not even an eighth of the way in it got stuck and I was clenching so hard he could hardly get it back out, and he has quite small hands for a man."

"Right," she said, totally ignoring my hole talk, "legs open. I'm just going to have a feel of your pelvic muscle, OK?"

Of course I didn't know what that meant. But, as per the above mode, I smiled too enthusiastically.

It turns out that to feel the pelvic muscle you have to go

up and inside the fanny. This was the physio—to have Donna working on my pelvic muscle from inside my fanny. Like, RIGHT UP IN THERE!!! So for the 20-minute session we chatted and talked about how weird brain freeze was and the recent closures on the District Line while most of her hand was up and inside my fanny, pressing relatively strongly against different parts of my inside muscles. Always with a "How's that? Can I go a bit harder?"

No, Donna, please don't go any harder, I'm ripping this shitting kitchen-roll stuff to shreds and not sure how long I can pretend to be brave about all this pain and weirdness.

Donna informed me that my pelvic muscle was very, *very* tense and that with six sessions and some "homework" she thought we had a good chance of getting it into a more relaxed place.

Meaning sex should become easier again.

Neither of us talked about why it might have got so hard. Just that it was, and she felt hopeful.

She finished up the session at a part of my muscle that I think was near my bum hole. It all got a bit confusing for me to identify where exactly she was at any given point, as I had to keep my eyes closed to keep myself from freaking out. One look at her arm disappearing up me and I knew I'd try to leg it, which, with her attached, would no doubt be traumatic for my fanny.

"Can I press a bit harder?"

NO! "Yes, no probs!"

And then suddenly, from nowhere, I thought I was going to shit everywhere. While her hand was up me.

OH GOD, OH GOD.

"Please stop, something weird is happening around my bum area, I don't feel I have control."

"OK, I'll go slow."

47

"I think I'm going to poo on you . . ."

I started doing pregnant-lady breathing and my forehead went really hot.

"It's OK."

She gently pulled her whole fist out of my vagina and said, "That's very normal, that was a muscle spasm that I was working on, on your sphincter muscle. All better now?"

"Yes, back to normal." Thank fuck.

My breathing slowed down and I had a moment of clarity.

"Did you have your whole fist up me?"

"Yes."

"Oh . . . So I fitted a whole fist up there?"

"Yes."

"Ha, brilliant, woohooooo, I've never had a fist up there before, I didn't think I could, brilliant, amazing!"

I'd never actually believed the rumours that it could happen, that it was humanly possible, unless you were with someone tiny, with tiny fists, or an experienced and practised porn star. But it was!

Hold on, does that mean I have a bucket fanny . . . ?!

It was a bit weird—to be fisted for the first time in this manner. But so interesting. I didn't think my fanny had the ability to house such girth. I felt so powerful. I rang Three straight away. "I'm incredible, my fanny is incredible!"

"OK, so all good?"

Three had his annoying say-minimal-express-no-emotions work-phone mode on.

"No, but Donna fitted her whole fist up my fanny!!"

"What? Who's Donna?"

"She's my consultant."

"And was that the, er, plan? For her to, you know, up there?"

"Urgh, talk properly!"

"Hold on, let me go somewhere private."

I headed to Topshop for a treat spree, feeling confident and again hopeful that we were on the right track. Three came home on time and cooked pork knuckle in celebration. It was a great day.

Morse Code

I looked forward to my time with Donna. During week three's session she informed me that some of her physio with the scared pregnant women involved blowing up a balloon in their fanny and then getting them to squeeze it out, to show them they could pass large things. I asked her if any of the balloons had ever popped inside someone and she said no. They used strong rubber.

Donna seemed positive about my progress and checked in with me about my homework, which I was actually making an effort to do. Every night I had to lie on my back with my knees up and get my thumb right up my fanny hole and find areas of my pelvic muscle to apply pressure to for two minutes a go. I did it while watching *Hollyoaks*. I also had to, whenever possible, engage my pelvic floor. Donna had helpfully said to imagine being in a bath when the bath water was full of dirty swimming worms that you didn't want getting up inside you. What happens to your fanny after having that thought is engaging your pelvic floor. If you've got a fanny, imagine the worms now.

Hello!

I started to do it all the time—sitting on buses, in boring meetings at work. I'm doing it now.

Feeling my fanny respond felt like I had my old pal back with me, and we were starting our communications again, like an internal Morse code.

"Squeeze squeeze, squeeze, squeeze?"

"What's that? You want chicken Kiev tonight?"

"Squeeze!"

"You got it!"

This week's homework was in a brown paper bag. Donna handed it to me. Inside was a small-sized dildo, a medium-sized dildo and a fucking huge one. Like the start of porno Goldilocks. Goldi-knobs, ha!

There were also loads of individual sachets of lube included. I didn't need them as I still had 3.75 tubes left of my original stash but am always a sucker for something that comes in a smaller size than is usually intended; it pleases the part of me that used to lose my shit over Polly Pocket and her tiny world.

Donna said after doing the two-minute thumb exercise I was to start using the small dildo, pushing it in and out for five minutes. Once that became comfortable, I was to progress to the next size up. If I encountered any problems, I was to use the lube.

The NHS were basically giving me sex toys.

After I left her office, I took the dildos to the toilets and had a proper inspection of them. They were purely practical for just this task, as there was no battery-operated option to make them buzz. No women ever needed a dildo without a vibration option. They must have been designed by a male doctor.

I created a day-by-day paper chart that I stuck on the DVD cabinet and, as per my homework instructions, ticked off when each seven-minute session had been completed, noting which dildo size had been used. By week five of this I had graduated to the huge one!

In our final session Donna said she was very proud of my hard work and progress and after a final good digging around in my fanny, she informed me that my pelvic muscle was much more relaxed than it had been. She declared officially that I should have no more painful problems with my fanny!

So why was sex still hurting? I had made Three put it in me that morning so I could come armed with the info. It hurt, it hurt, it hurt, as bad as ever.

Donna handed me a final dildo, my graduation present, which was even bigger than the huge one, and told me to continue with my homework. She said that things would get better if I persevered but my treatment with her had to end—we'd used up all the allocated appointments. As I left her office, trying not to cry, she said I could always come and visit her in her private clinic, the one for the scared pregnant people that probably cost loads of money.

I did a fake smile and said thanks. I needed to get out of this stupid place before I cried.

She followed me out to tell me that if I was still experiencing pain in a few months' time, I could get my doctor to refer me again.

Oh just fuck off Donna.

I got in the empty lift and kicked the door, hard. It made a scary noise. I immediately regretted doing it.

What a pile of poo.

This morning, when sex with Three had hurt, I had felt disappointed but not mega worried, as I knew I still had Donna. But our time had ended with woolly, not-clear help, and now I felt stressed. Three would be waiting to hear and it was all shit, as not even the clever professionals could help me work out exactly why it was still not working properly down there. I didn't want to have only painful sex with the man I loved and I didn't know what would happen next if that never changed. It had already been nearly six months. Three might decide he didn't want to be with me. This thought made my head feel a bit hot, so I left the hospital at double speed.

Outside I saw the number 414 bus approaching, which takes

you to Topshop. I went to get on it but instead went into a phone box. Mum had sent me some phone cards that couldn't be used with a mobile, so I dialled the hundreds of numbers on it to try to get through. I don't know what I was expecting to say but it didn't matter as I got their answerphone, and no way was I listening to all of that. Mum and her husband, Bobby, had recorded the message together and it went on forever with loads of annoying info about the sanctuary, what to do if you found an injured animal, blah blah blah. I went into the nearest café, which was Starbucks, and sat down in the corner to think. I just needed to work out a plan. My fanny had to find a way to be able to handle Three's penis again because we were much too young to have a non-sexual relationship, plus I still wanted to be licked and to have orgasms, so it would be totally unequal if I got that and he didn't get to come too, and I know I could have achieved that through other methods but there was no way I was going to spend the rest of my life wanking him off or giving him blow jobs; they are far too physically tiring to do more than once every two months, tops.

I took out my notebook and pen.

Broken Fanny Plan
Option 1. Something alternative . . .

In moments like this, when the medical pathways have all been tried, sometimes people turn to alternative therapies. Fran had her crystals and I know she'd have come up for a visit to use them on me, but I wasn't into exploring those routes. I didn't want to give up either, though. I am a problem solver. I'd just have to create my own bespoke treatment plan. This is what the scientists at work would do. Last week I had to step in for Magda who usually interviewed the scientists we were working with to write up their inventions for the website blog. It was basically a marketing exercise for the company to demonstrate to the rest of the industry that they got the best intellectual property and how easy it was to take your ideas to them and have them be looked after and eventually created into a successful business, pushing forward important scientific development. I actually really enjoyed reading these pieces when I had my mid-morning poo in the big disabled loo, as it was the easiest way of understanding who we were working with and what our company actually did!

Magda had to stay home sick and I had to interview Professor Alessandro Ferrari who worked in Advanced Structural Design. Magda normally asked clever questions using her science understanding and words to match theirs, but as I had none of that I asked him questions that any person could understand the answers to, as I was the one who had to write this fucker up.

I pressed record on two Dictaphones (no chances taken) and asked:

What is your name?

What do you do?

What is your special area?

What are you trying to do?

Why is it important?

Professor Ferrari was super-kind and a bit of a joker, and he explained his research in a way that didn't make me feel lost or thick. He was working with a material that could move into different positions if voltage was applied or if there was a significant change in temperature. Basically, he could create machines that could morph. Apart from that sounding pretty cool and future sci-fi, I didn't get why that would be a super-helpful advancement for science, but it didn't matter as he gave me a really funny story (by scientist standards) to end the column on and I knew it would be a good piece.

Option 2. Morphing hole

I need the fanny-hole equivalent of a morphing machine. But how, really, could I change the actual shape of things down there?

That was enough thinking for now. I went to the counter to order something and as it was the end of November I considered buying my annual cup of coffee. I don't like drinking coffee but strangely at the beginning of the Christmas season, when all the coffee shops declare their new Christmas flavours, I get very excited and always like to christen the start of the festivities by having one. This year's options were: toasted white chocolate mocha, toffee nut latte, chestnut praline latte, caramel brûlée latte, eggnog latte or gingerbread latte.

I went for the gingerbread latte, then immediately regretted my choice and quickly got them to change it to a caramel brûlée latte, just in time.

As I went back to my seat someone caught my eye. It was a guy we used to call Creepy Nick at uni, except he wasn't looking so creepy now, he looked quite hot. Nick had been studying film making and I had helped out with his short film. I don't remember the narrative being that strong, but the film had ended with me being attacked behind an ice-cream truck while Rihanna's "SOS" blasted out. It really ruined that song for me as we had to do shitloads of takes, and it played over and over. It would always come on at the end of the night in Bluskey's, our shit nightclub, and in my drunken state, on hearing the song I'd always get momentarily confused and think for a minute that something bad had happened to me. Which it hadn't, obvs, but the tone of the night would then be changed for me. Stupid film. Creepy Nick always called that nightclub Slutskey's. Stupid creep.

We had our coffees together and then we stayed longer and

ate cake and after that he suggested another coffee and I broke my one-coffee-a-year rule and had the gingerbread latte. Morse code was going mad and I had a distantly familiar feeling: my fanny fancied him. I needed to investigate. I grabbed my parting gift from Donna and went to the loo. Inside the cubicle I whipped down my knickers and there it was—my knickers full of wet. It was all right, it was working as normal. I didn't have a totally broken fanny! Taking my suspicions a bit further, I grabbed the super-super-huge NHS dildo and whacked it up there without any problems. No NHS lube necessary. No scientific morphing hole needed. Ha! Welcome back old buddy!!

That night, because of the leftover Creepy Nick excitement feelings, I had really easy and wet sex with Three. He was so happy. And so was I. Sex didn't hurt!! He cooked me homemade baked beans with bubble and squeak for breakfast the next day, which he surprised me with in bed. Things felt great.

TOP HUMPS

NAME: Top Secret
AKA: The Actor
AGE: 35 (him), 20 (me)
BUILD: Old, in shape, short.
GENERAL VIBE: The kind of guy who dyed his eyelashes. His popularity was on the decline as it had been years since his big soap job so he had started a coffee-bean side business.
ACTUALLY LIKE: Quite boring.
SPECIAL SKILLS: Famous friends, a UK-wide-known catchphrase.
FANNY SCALE: 6/10
BRAIN SCALE: 3/10
OVERALL RATING: 4.5/10 = Short-term Pleasure
PRE-GAME: Minimal: he started dancing with me at a club and at first I was totally uninterested until Al said, "That's thingy from *Coronation Street*," and then I got turned on (a small bit).
THE DEED: Weirdly, he had driven his car to go nightclubbing, so I let him drive us all home. He wanted me to go to his with him but I said I couldn't as my school friends were only up for one night, which was true and also he did creep me out a bit. So I snogged him in his car and he gave me his number and as I left he told me to call, which I said I would but had no intention to. Fran and Al shouted his character's catchphrase at me as I approached the front door.
PLEASURE (me): None.
PLEASURE (him): ?? maybe a wank.

Summary: I had to call him the next day because I'd left my baccy pouch in his car and it was one Jay had brought back from India so I was quite attached to it. I arranged the handover in between classes on Monday so that I didn't have to talk to him for too long. Seeing him again made my stomach area feel queasy.

Option 3

I don't know what it's like for other people who are almost three years into a relationship but the doing of sex stuff for us popped up about once a month. This was now usually instigated by Three as I had definitely created a bit of a worry in my head about the pain, which blocked me from wanting it with him. If life could be just lickings and fingerings, I'm sure my desire would have felt stronger. But it wasn't.

After things finished with Donna I made sure not to talk to Three about the fanny pain stuff (which had returned post-Creepy Nick) as I didn't want him to have it in his head as a block too. But it was quite hard to control my reaction to the sex pain as my body would want to flinch when he went to go inside me. And once he was in I could feel my eyes changing and my face fighting not to look pained. Which meant I couldn't enjoy looking into his eyes during sex anymore. But as he neared coming I'd always perk up, sensing the end was in sight, and give him some encouraging noises and smiles and proper eye-to-eye looking.

Afterwards Three normally seemed happy and once the deed was over the pain didn't hang around so I was pretty cheery too and could get on with the important matter in hand: food.

"BLT with tomatoes and mayo, or BLT with butter and ketchup?"

I loved both equally and found it agonising to have to pick one, which is why I always had ingredients for both and would do a half-'n'-half one for me. Three could go either way depending on what mood he was in.

"Actually, can we have them later?"

I was about to kick off as I hated waiting to eat and it was the best thing to do after sex, but then I saw a worrying look on his face. "Yes, OK, what's going on?"

"Can we talk about sex stuff?"

NO! "Yes."

I had learnt from Three when we were buying our car never to offer too much info in the beginning of negotiations and let them do the talking. I liked to employ this strategy when on unfamiliar ground, so I let him go first.

"What are your thoughts about it?"

Cunning—he was using the same tactics.

"I think we have a good amount, don't you?"

"Yes."

"Good, me too!"

I kissed his ear.

A sad-looking expression crossed his face so I continued: "I did a quiz in *Glamour* magazine and the result said that we came in above average for British couples in long-term relationships!"

"That's good."

"It is, isn't it!"

He smiled, but then a different, more confused-looking expression came across his mouth and forehead.

"But I'd just like to feel it coming from you a bit more, too."

Ugh.

I can't handle how sad he seems and there's no way I can tell him that although I love him more than anything, I really, *really* dread having actual sex with him. I kissed his other ear. "OK!"

I needed to solve my broken fanny shit fast.

So alongside doing double the amount of homework with

Donna's final dildo, I would, where I could, also use the Creepy Nick Method.

Option 3. The Creepy Nick Method

I've had to have a lot of blood tests at the hospital, but I'm rubbish with needles, so one time a nurse helped me by telling me a trick of turning my head in the opposite direction, focusing on a point away from the needle and then recalling in my head the name of every human I knew and liked. This worked and I got good at blood tests.

The Creepy Nick Method was inspired by this. When the opportunity arose I gave myself permission to have exciting and flirty conversations with other men, in order to get my brain and fanny excited about those what-ifs in order to aid matters with Three.

It worked well! Using that wetness, I was able to initiate sex with him and also feel less pain doing the penis-in-and-out bit. This was the first really helpful tool in my new coping-with-sex toolkit.

In order to keep it all as intended I set some rules: the flirting couldn't be premeditated and nothing physical could actually happen. When I came across someone who excited me and who flirted with me I would flirt back; maybe graze my hand near them and then the tingles that the encounter would give me would build up the fuel I'd need for when I next got it on with Three. It wasn't the most reliable of tools, as it depended on me happening across someone beforehand. But as I still didn't seem to have a type, or very high fanny-fancying standards, I was normally able to get some kind of buzz off a new guy every three months or so. Since I've been sexually active, I've never been able to get overexcited about men in movies or in bands or on posters with their muscles and chests out—my fanny excitement always has to happen from an actual real interaction. The Creepy Nick Method was my mind's Viagra.

TOP HUMPS

NAME: Sam
AKA: Aussie Sam
AGE: 24 (him), 22 (me)
BUILD: Like a hot Aussie surfer.
GENERAL VIBE: Big party guy, was never not ordering shots. Everyone loved him. He loved coke.
ACTUALLY LIKE: Absolute player, obsessed with knowing if you preferred sambuca or tequila.
SPECIAL SKILLS: He could act really normal in front of workmates when minutes before he had followed you into the pub toilets and fingered you.
FANNY SCALE: 10/10
BRAIN SCALE: 4/10
OVERALL RATING: 7/10 = Short-term Pleasure
PRE-GAME: I hated sambuca and tequila but always let him buy me one.
THE DEED: He became a regular in the pub and would always be the one to round up everyone for after-closing lock-ins. He would flirt with me constantly when ordering drinks and was relentless in his quest to get me to kiss him. Which I eventually did.
PLEASURE (me): Lots of orgasms from toilet fingerings.
PLEASURE (him): He hardly ever came as he had always drunk too many shots and always wanted another line of coke.

Summary: His party-boy persona started to get boring and after a while I started dreading the thought of a sambuca on a Monday night. I began only staying on for lock-ins on Thursday nights, as Friday felt like an okay day to have a hangover, and then he suddenly moved back to Australia with the girlfriend none of us knew he had.

Proper Money

Three and Jamie from uni had been doing really well in their proper city jobs and so now they and their other workmates all earned really good money. Money that could be used for deposits on flats and flashier holidays and wasted on big nights out with bottles of spirits and drugs.

His work friends started bringing coke with them on nights out. It was so exciting, a group of us, having a shared secret, taking it in turns to hand it over/go to the loos together and then talk shite at each other excitedly and very fast. And brilliantly, when I took coke it was much easier to have sex with Three, which was a relief as alcohol had never been helpful for me with that, and there wasn't always someone I was having hot thoughts about to help in that way. I started siphoning off bits of coke from those nights out with his friends. I learnt how to make the little paper wrap it would come in and would have a pre-made empty one in my back pocket alongside a bank card so that when it was my turn I could super-quickly divide some off and pop it into my own stash. This was my emergency supply to be used during nights out when Three and I were on our own. Or if he was cooking me a romantic meal at home, which might end in sex. It made me feel relief knowing I had it if needed. He didn't know—I kept it secret and would only administer it in situations where I felt sex would be part of the night.

I've heard a lot of people say coke makes them horny and it definitely did for Three. It really doesn't for me, not at all, but it did desensitise my fanny area. Numbed something down there making it much easier to have sex. Tool number two in my coping-with-sex kit. I had decided that there needed to be rules for this tool as well, what with it being addictive and expensive. I was allowed two small lines to be sniffed on my and Three's date nights and up to six lines, still small, were allowed on big nights out with our friends.

It was such a wonderful drug. Not only did it improve things for that area, but being on coke made me feel much more generous to my mum's dull, not-my-world, full-of-injured-animals updates, emails. If I had trouble going to sleep, I would respond by writing paragraphs of news for her—something I found utterly boring to do at normal times.

A couple of months after being introduced to coke properly I had my own dealer, Ray. I was not an ideal customer; given the purposes I was using it for, I could make a gram last well over a month. On average, taken from a study of our friends, the normal (i.e., not addicted to drugs in a proper way) coke consumer seemed to do a gram in a night, sometimes two for special occasions. So my needs weren't really worth Ray's time. But we came to an agreement that every few months I would order two grams.

On getting my supply, I would cut the two grams up into a big pile and divide it into eight wraps, each one basically holding a quarter. Meaning I would never be tempted to take more than my rules had outlined. This system worked. And while a few of our friends were getting a bit out of control with their coke needs, doing it a number of times a week, always wanting more, I was very strict and never went into another wrap in the same night. When we'd have parties back at our place and they'd beg the room for any more, I'd never let on that I, in fact, had 1.5 grams, separated into six wraps, hidden in the bottom of the sewing box in my bedroom. Even the nights when I wanted more I wouldn't crack—I had created a system and needed that supply for when it really mattered—for sex with Three.

I'd always try to meet Ray around wrap six, to ensure a crossover so that the supply wouldn't run out. A dark moment happened when on a Friday night at home, after Three had cooked me beef wellington as a surprise, I popped to the bedroom to have a small line from wrap number five and it was almost all gone, even though I was only just starting that one and it should have been full. On opening it there was a very dried-up, tiny, hard-like-cement layer across the paper. I opened up wraps six, seven and eight and this was the case in those ones too. I was really confused and panicked. What the fuck had happened? I NEEDED it now! What was I supposed to do?

"Are you OK up there?"

"Uh-huh."

"Dinner in five!"

Somehow they must have got wet. It was winter and our flat was quite cold and we had issues with damp. I was really, *really* upset. Stressed. Had a pillow thump and cry. I didn't want to go back to the dinner table.

"Dinner!"

I tried to enjoy the lovely food but as Three went to nuzzle into my neck I couldn't help myself: "Why are you happy wasting hours cooking but you won't sort the window coverings?"

"I'll do them this weekend."

"You said that last weekend and it's getting damp and shit."

"Is it?"

"Well, it will."

After being mean, I told Three that my stomach was being dodgy and made fake sick noises in the bathroom. He brought up some water and told me to relax. I apologised and said that was probably why I was grumpy at dinner. He seemed happy with that. I'd have to text Ray tomorrow.

64

~

Al and Fran came to stay for a weekend when Three was away with the boys. It was day two and although we had downloaded and shared everything that had happened in the last few months since we'd seen each other, I still hadn't mentioned the Creepy Nick Method or coke coping sex plan, not so much because of the sex stuff but because someone who does drugs or drinks on their own is considered to have a problem, and although I did have a problem, it wasn't related to that.

That night I took them to a bring-your-own Moroccan place that had opened round the corner. As we finished the first bottle of cava, I told them about the Creepy Nick Method, and asked them what they thought.

Fran went first. "So you're worried because you've used another man to get you horny?"

"Not worried. I'm confused and relieved."

Fran opened the second bottle of cava—it is the best drink for bring-your-own as you don't need to wait for the waiter to bring a corkscrew.

Al added, "Do you feel guilty?"

"No, I don't feel guilt. I think the relief takes away from that. Just confused."

"*El plato adicional.*"

I had kept hold of some Spanish from uni, enough to understand that. "Spare plate?"

"Yes, a side dish. To accompany the main event."

Fran was sure too. "Exactly. You've got to use whatever you can to get you through. Remember Martin at uni? He could only fuck me if I wore my glasses." Fran took a massive swig of cava before continuing. "It's about finding whatever helps you, isn't it?"

"Yes, I guess so."

Shawarma

Over the next bit of time I used quite a few tools to help me. And so as not to get the tools confused, or overused, I formalised a clear set of rules for me to check in with and to help ensure a "happily ever after with Three."

The Tools Rules:

1. No premeditated meetings
2. Touching/grazing only
3. No suggestion of something more
4. No flirty texts/Facebook messages pre or post
5. No one Three knows
6. No coke without alcohol
7. No more than two lines of coke on a quiet Three night
8. No more than six lines of coke on a big night
9. No more than two big nights out a week

These rules kept me and Three on track, and four years after meeting we got married. I agreed to this as I had felt compromised when he asked since it was the second time, and I had declined the first one three years in . . .

I hated going for walks but if I knew food was at the end of it, or clothes shopping, I could be persuaded. Three *loved* walks so it was a constant battle. He had got me to agree to an hour-and-a-half walk from Hammersmith, through Holland Park and Hyde Park up to Edgware Road, where apparently there were the best shawarma places. When I moved to London for uni I used to knob on about this amazing shawarma that Jay and I accidentally found after a night out visiting him at his uni halls in Camden. It was the most magical-tasting one I had ever had—lamb not greasy, very fresh herb stuff and the best white sauce that exists. Jay and I ate two each and then shared a third, but I couldn't ever find it again and Jay couldn't remember where it was either. The shawarma itch became a lifetime search for another that could out-do those first ones. And it also informed a lot of Christmas and birthday presents Jay and I gave each other.

So I agreed to go on the walk with Three as maybe this was the day I would find it!

When we got to Edgware Road Three turned us down a street that only had antique shops on it, and then, looking in the window of one, Three asked me which ring would I like and would I like to marry him.

"WHAT THE FUCK WHERE'S THE FUCKING SHA-WARMA YOU LIAR??!!!"

A bit harsh but I was hungry and angry and had been tricked into taking a fucking massive walk. And I had always remained clear that I never wanted to get married. Very, *very* clear.

We had a huge argument and Three took back his proposal. And I felt immediate relief and very strong hunger aches. He stormed off, upset, and before heading after him I nipped into a Pret to quickly nail a hot meatball wrap.

A few months after that he came home very late from a work thing where he had only drunk whisky for about a million hours and he woke me up to have a little cry.

"I know you don't care about marriage and what it means and your mum and dad and all that, but I just want us to be a family—you and me and our little home. I want to have the family the right way for us to be it for each other and why should our parents fuck that up?"

I didn't yell at him for waking me up, or pick him up for half

67

of what he said not making clear sense. Instead, I gave him a hug while he did gross booze-breathing in my face as he fell asleep.

The next time we visited his mum's house she had an envelope of pictures for us to take home. Little him aged two to ten, being an absolute legend. She went through each one telling me of the troubles he had just gotten—or was about to get—into. "This one, right after Jack took that, he went and peed all over the hydrangeas. Oh gosh, this one, he looks like a little angel but he'd just buried all of Mark's Trolls in Grandad's allotment. And this one, he had screamed the whole car drive here!"

Three looked so happy in all of them.

And even though I still didn't want children, I wanted to look after little naughty him forever.

The second time Three asked me to marry him, I was deep into my tools and had worked out that long-term relationships were about *a lot* of compromises. Marriage was very important to him and I didn't think he fitted the usual marriage/cheating equation, as I had a theory that Three was below the average man in terms of his sexual wanting, since a) he always seemed content with the little amount of sex we had, b) I never caught him wanking or ever found any weird smell or shit loads of tissues in the bin if I was out or away, and c) he was resistant to watching porn with me. This all led me to believe that he had a very gentle sex drive and meant I didn't worry about him wanting more or going elsewhere. Plus, we had been accepted on to the Hammersmith and Fulham housing association help-to-buy scheme and just moved into our first owned flat, which is way more of a commitment and effort to manage than a marriage. So, I said yes.

We were at a beachside cocktail lounge in Mexico on those lying-down, smart-looking sofas for "cool" people. Three kept slipping as it is actually quite hard drinking a cocktail when you are in the lying-down position. We had a rug over our

68

legs and he suddenly slipped right down, falling off the side and spilling his drink, and I thought he was having a stroke or something as his favourite granddad had died from one. But it turns out he was just getting onto one knee and he pulled a ring out and asked me to marry him. The relief of him not dying added to the excitement of the moment, and knowing how sad I'd feel if he did die meant I knew I wanted to be with him, so my answer was "yes." It's very weird agreeing to marry someone when you're wearing a bikini in the middle of a strange country with no one you know around you and none of them available on the phone coz they are all asleep in their country. It meant the excitement and energy bounced back and forth between us, building like a hot happy ball, and gave us both the feeling we were on some kind of drug. Three said it felt like being on E, but I'd never tried pills so couldn't be sure. But it did make us cross insanely busy roads without thinking properly, which sounds like the kind of thing someone on E would do.

Three knew normal-looking engagement rings made me feel sick coz they are all so samey—shiny and boring-looking. So he got me a collection of thin, bumpy stacking bands in silver, gold and rose gold from last year's Xmas list and a note saying I could design whatever kind of ring I wanted. And I was *very* excited about that. He took me to a very expensive restaurant at the end of a very long, sandy path and we ate very expensive steak in four different ways. The food was AMAZING and I didn't even mind the walk there or back!!!!!

Aside from not worrying about the marriage/cheating theory, I still didn't believe in marriage as some kind of special thing, so to make myself feel okay about it all going ahead I told myself to think of it in a different way: the "wedding" could be just a brilliant party—a celebration of us. We didn't need to focus on the marriage side of it.

The rules to ensure this were:

1. The "W" word would not be used.
2. We would call it a celebration of our time together; not a wedding day, but our "Four-year Anniversary Party."
3. We would do it on our four-year anniversary date to help cement point two.
4. The service would not be in a church.
5. The readings would be made up.
6. The vows would be adapted to words like "try" instead of "promise/swear."
7. I wouldn't wear a wedding dress but a fabulous designer dress.
8. The dress would not be white.
9. I would have a wedding ring made based on my favourite ever Topshop ring.
10. I wouldn't take Three's surname.
11. We would never refer to each other as husband or wife, but each other's "partner."
12. There would be no soppy songs.
13. My dad wouldn't "give me away."

I *love* special occasions—for my birthdays I always plan months in advance. Sending reminders and nudges to friends and Jay to make sure they don't forget. Sending present wish lists to Dad, Jay and Three. Organising a whole week of birthday events and plans. Having a late-November birthday meant I did always lose some people to clashing early Christmas parties, and as the years went on I'd lose other people to geography, having children, etc. The Four-year Anniversary Party (aka absolutely not a wedding day) was the best day of my life because everyone that I loved had to be there. And they were all sent the date six months in advance, so no excuses!

I had saved up and bought Three a very expensive pair of yellow-gold cufflinks. He never spent money on himself, always frantically saving it for "our future" but also always spoiling me, so I wanted to get him something that he would love forever. Fucking hell, expensive cufflinks are fucking expensive. I didn't have even half the amount I needed to pay for them so I took out my first ever credit card, which was interest free for 18 months, and I created a repayment plan I knew I could achieve. I left the box with Jamie, who was best man, to give to Three before he went to bed the night before the big day. Inside I had written a note saying, "I've ripped up the receipt so they can't be returned!" because I knew that would make him laugh (and be one of the first things he would insist on, thinking they were too much).

Three and I had spoken a lot about the things I couldn't stand about weddings, and the number-one thing was wedding vows. I hated them; sitting at other people's weddings and hearing them say the traditional ones always made me feel queasy.

"Do you promise to love her, comfort her, honour and keep her for better or worse, for richer or poorer, in sickness and in health, and forsaking all others, be faithful only to her, for as long as you both shall live?"

In sickness and for poorer—it's all bollocks. What if he became a serial killer due to an undiagnosed mental health issue, or became riddled with debt and had a gambling problem due to an addiction that suddenly got triggered, or contracted a very contagious life-threatening disease? I would not be hanging around for any of that.

Promising promises in front of everyone is just not the most sensible way to try to be together for as long as you can. It's such pressure.

I said, "I will try to love and be there with you through all the times."

I think that was a pretty clear, honest and hopeful statement of intent. I did not make any promises.

Three's Aunty Hannah told me after the dinner that she felt what I said was a bit cold. But she was on her own and had very different ways of operating through a very different kind of life, so I smiled and kissed her on her cheek and passed her the plate of little cakes while my fanny had an angry Morse-code conversation with me via my pelvic floor. I shut them both up.

My dad and Three did amazing speeches, which were all about me and made me sound like a very excellent human, although Jay basically MC-ed alongside Dad's speech to add in some witty counter-remarks. The knobber.

My mum stood up after my dad's speech to "add something" but I gave her the stare of death and mouthed "not now" so she awkwardly sat back down. She cornered me later in the loo, trying to help tidy my falling bits of hair into my flower headpiece, which had purposefully been styled to be falling down. "I'm so proud of you darling."

I batted her away from my hair. "Mum, can you not?"

"Very, very proud of you!"

"OK . . . Thank you!"

"I just wanted you to hear that today from me as well as your father."

"Heard and received! Come on, I think you're pissed!"

"Darling, language!"

"I'm almost 30 and married and it's not even considered swearing over here now. You're so out of touch!!!"

"Well, I definitely think this champagne is stronger than what we get."

"It's Buck's Fizz."

The mashed potato song started to play and Mum got all excited and insisted we go and dance to it. She may be totally annoying and feel like a completely alien creature from me, but I also go super-mad for dancing to the mashed potato, so I went with her.

That night it felt like sex was *the* thing that should happen after such an event. Three had been referencing it in romantic ways throughout the day, plus I had managed to put it on hold a bit in the weeks beforehand due to reasons of wedmin prep and stress. Before the big day we had sent out a briefing to our friends who did coke to say, "Don't do coke at our wedding, motherfuckers." Too many family members and not enough loo areas meant it was a risk I wasn't willing to take. They all agreed. But I had an emergency pack hidden in our hotel room, so once it was all over I had something to help me with the sex bit. I had stashed it in the dressing-room area after Fran and Al had left me to have a few minutes to myself before coming down for the ceremony. I hadn't actually needed any time on my own; I'd just said that so I could hide the coke and be clear on how I could do it quickly and secretly later if Three ended up coming up at the same time as me, which he did.

As he went for a wee, I legged it to the dresser and grabbed the wrap, Tesco Clubcard and straw that I had shoved at the back of the top drawer under the hairdryer pouch. I made a reasonably sized line in record time and as I sniffed it up, in time with Three flushing the loo, I felt a feeling far away from my nostrils that didn't feel nice at all. But I pushed it away as this had been the best day of my life, and this feeling now was very tiny in comparison to the 19 amazing hours that had come before.

After a few of our other friends started getting married, conversations eventually revealed that no one ever had sex on their wedding night, like *ever*! On hearing from me that we had, they had all been quite impressed and it made me feel proud that we had been the only ones who had done it, like we were some kind of supercouple! I liked the thought of that.

The next morning we drove back to London to drop our stuff at home before going on our honeymoon (a part of the wedding shizzle I was completely onboard with!). We were both very tired and we pulled up at a Little Chef on the A35 next to a grass mound and lay on our backs, hand in hand, and had a little hungover sleep as the sun beat down on us. We were a proper family now and that made me feel happy. Lying joined like this made me understand something I hadn't quite before. Three was my home. He was the stable, loving thing I hadn't realised I absolutely had been needing and wanting to find.

Fake James

A month before our wedding day it was Al's hen do. She and Phil were getting married later in the summer so she had planned it for then so I wouldn't miss it when I was on my honeymoon. We went for a weekend in Manchester and did a spa and fancy lunch, and then later we had tickets to a super-club where we had a VIP area and all wore very short, tight dresses. The club was massive and we all spent large bits of the night separated, having lost each other coming to or from the dance floor or loos. After our second dancing session I lost them all again so went to stand at one of the bars to pretend I was doing something and a guy who looked just like James McAvoy came up and ordered a drink. He seemed sober and nice, and if it weren't for his Manc accent I'd have sworn it was him. We chatted over a drink that he bought me and my fanny went wild. He asked if I wanted a dance, and we did very close bum-to-dick grinding for all of JT's "SexyBack." Then, as Akon's "Smack That" came on, with my back still pressed against his front, Fake James moved his hand to the top of my right thigh and slipped his finger into my knickers and kept it there, wriggling it about around my clit until the end of the song, when he removed it just as I came. Then, from nowhere, Fran lunged at me saying she needed fresh air coz the weird plant-food thing she had sniffed was making her spin out and I got dragged away, leaving Fake James with his wet finger.

I'd never had an orgasm from someone without snogging

them. That thought drove me sexually mad and made me very wet for at least two weeks. It also meant that it wasn't too far from the rules—not ideal, and a bit of a slip, but we'd not kissed or swapped numbers or spent longer than an hour or so together. Plus, most men get strippers or lap dances at stag dos, and I'm sure with the latter their penises defo get rubbed and come probably happens. So really this was just a less gross version of that.

Honeymoon

Sex was a nightmare on the honeymoon. We had loads of time and opportunity to have it whenever we wanted but we were on an island in Greece so I had no access to my coke supply, and the Fake James wetness had dried up so I couldn't even use that via the Creepy Nick Method. Alcohol had become difficult to manage without doing coke alongside it; when I drank now it made me feel angry, like I was missing out on doing a line, so it wasn't a great help on its own and I had to cut back on drinking to avoid that feeling. Over dinner one evening, Three said something to me that made me have the saddest feeling I had ever experienced with him. "I feel like you don't always like spending time with me."

Ahhhhhhhhh!

"Don't be silly, of course I do!"

"You never want to stay out after dinner or have a cocktail on the beach."

I felt awful. I had been so totally distracted by my now-shite relationship with alcohol that I had been rushing to end the evenings. No way could I get into that with him . . .

"I'm just really knackered after all the wedding madness."

He looked less worried.

"Shall we head back and watch *Boardwalk*?"

"That'll be nice."

On day four we started a wakeboarding course. In my pre-honeymoon daydreaming I saw me on a board, elegantly surfing and jumping waves and expertly handling the tow rope with one hand. This was not the case. By the end of the first day Three was standing on his board fine and speeding around doing mini jumps, and I still had Andre, our French instructor, constantly in and out of the water trying to help me stand up.

The boat would slowly launch me, pulling me with the board turned up against the sea, and I was supposed to get myself upright and on it, but I'd spent most of the day being dragged around on my bum with the wrong side of the board sticking out of the water like a shark.

After lunch Andre got someone else to drive the boat so he could hold himself to my back to help guide me up on the board. It was all much faster and fiercer than I had imagined and it was very hard keeping hold of the tow rope as it felt like it was yanking my arms from their sockets. I kind of hated it, but with Andre looking after me it was also very exciting, because he was so, so, *so* hot and made things happen inside of me in a fizzling kind of way. I finally managed to stand and stay up, and as the boat picked up speed Andre dropped off, leaving me to my first solo go.

It was amazing—until the boat started going really fast and suddenly my board got flipped in a particularly awkward position, dragging me under the water. Which meant I should stop holding the tow rope, which I did, but it had got caught on the boot bindings, meaning I had to quickly unattach myself, which was actually a simple process since these were step-in bindings but in that position was really quite confusing and also my whole head was surrounded by water. I was starting to panic as the thought hit me that I might drown if it went on for much longer.

FUCKKKKKKK.

I wrestled with what I hoped were the right bits until finally I got free and let myself sink away from the board, which continued on its journey. Peaceful thoughts of jumpsuits and pain au chocolat and suntanning went round in my head. Andre suddenly grabbed me; he was out of breath from speed-swimming over to me and was so worried. It really felt like we were in a romantic film or an episode of *Baywatch* and should kiss. But we didn't, because a) I don't know if he even wanted to, b) he had to go and sort the board out and c) I was on my honeymoon.

Andre took me back to the board hut so he could make me some sugary minty tea, which is actually a lot nicer than it sounds, and as I changed from my wetsuit in the tiny wooden-cubicle changing room, hearing him clatter with the cups, I fingered myself and came before the kettle had boiled. With my actual finger, in that quick amount of time!!!

When Three headed in after his session and Andre asked him how it had been I suddenly felt a huge feeling of stress. I needed to leave the area as I felt like maybe Three could sense what had happened somehow. I went for a swim and spoke to myself underwater about the fact that I had accidentally broken one of the rules, as although Three didn't know Andre, he kind of also did, and I did not like the feelings that made me feel. I had a little underwater cry and then reminded myself that this had all come off the back of a proper almost-death situation and therefore, of course, my brain was a bit scrambled. I returned to the shore feeling back to myself, and that night, after cocktails on the beach, the Andre inside excitement was very useful for having a pain-free sex session with Three.

~

I met up with Fran and Al when I was back from honeymoon. Over bottle of wine number three I decided it was time to try to raise the coke-coping situation and how it had made me feel on holiday. Neither of them thought the quantity or frequency was a big deal. The month before Al had accidentally taken too much E and was rushed to hospital to come down from it there. Fran was six weeks into a broken ankle received while at a roller disco high on ketamine. In comparison my coke issues were small fry.

I went through the list of men with them that I had used as tools over the last few years. Including Andre, there had been 10! I had been starting to have creeping feelings of not-niceness and wanted to just get it out in the open with them. "Is this a bit extreme?"

Fran asked me a question. "What's the worst that came from it?"

"Just me frantically fingering myself over other men, I suppose."

I didn't want to be honest about the dance-floor Fake James incident.

"Exactly. It's no different to a man watching porn."

"Maybe."

Al agreed. "She's right."

I wasn't so sure, though. It wasn't just the Fake James fingering. The last few guys before him had seeped into my life beyond only seeing them in person. I had bent my rules and allowed Facebook flirty messages and exciting texts, with a bit of premeditated meeting on my part. Nothing that you would have read or seen and thought, "Fuck, they are up to something proper," but messages I got at unexpected times that would make my heart go a bit faster and cause me to smile with excitement. I was ignoring the original rules, which stated clearly that there was to be no outside comms carried on from the initial exchanges. It made me feel uneasy. And so I kept those details from the girls.

Al continued: "It is NO different to a man wanking over porn. Think of live porn chats."

"Porn's complicated too," I said. "I suppose because Three doesn't watch it, it makes that theory harder to justify. Why can't he be normal and just enjoy it?"

80

Fran is shaking her head. "I bet he does; he *must*—what kind of man doesn't use porn?!"

"I dunno, he is a soppy weirdo. When I watch porn it has to only be two women. I've tried to encourage him to watch that with me but even that he's not interested in."

"I don't watch porn. Never wanted to," Al said.

"Really?!! After all those years still with the same person?!!!"

"Doesn't work for me."

"Well, it's definitely odd if men don't."

Fran cuts in: "Hold up, you *only* watch lesbian porn?"

"Yeah."

Fran does her cheeky eyebrow-raise at me: "Interesting . . ."

"Shut up . . ."

"Maybe you need to explore THAT . . ."

"I don't. It's 100 per cent only men in real life that can make my bits tingle. In porn I just can't have any men in it. If there are, their shite acting and manhandling of the female porn people puts my orgasm back by double the amount of time."

Actually, I think my relationship with porn is more complicated than that. I don't want the heavy-handed men around with their giant and unappealing-looking penises, but I think that's also because putting dicks inside my hole did nothing earth-moving for me even before all this pain stuff, so why would I wank over seeing that? Plus, it's hard to be exactly sure, but I think, when in fantasy land, I like to objectify women in my mind, linking that to men getting all excited about my curves and shapes and wet bits and gasps. Basically, I think my mind becomes like a heterosexual man when I wank.

Fran's comments hadn't quite left me. "Anyway, I know I'm not properly into women coz of uni Licking-gate . . ."

I'd got myself in a situation where me and one of my uni mates said we'd do a threesome with a guy we both fancied, but it made me feel really uncomfortable when I had a go at licking her fanny.

"... I don't mind the thoughts in my eyes but not in my mouth, that I am certain of!"

The waiter came over to top up our drinks but quickly hurried away.

"But if this is worrying you, maybe you should do something about it?" Al suggested.

"Maybe."

I actually had bigger problems with Three because now he was desperate to move to a house rather than stay in our flat, and I couldn't quite explain to him in ways that would make sense to him why I didn't want to. I just knew I didn't want to leave our current place.

Upscaling

It's annoying why people always want something, get it, want to upgrade it, then do it all again. I'm immune. I never upgrade my phone in the month that I could and I don't care for new cars or big houses. I loved our flat; it had everything you could need: a garden that got sun, a tiny shed for storing dull stuff and spider eggs, room for bikes out the back, a big cellar for storage space, a kitchen and a big table and cozy lounge area, a bath tub and shower in the same room, and a spare box-room for all my clothes. Even when it came to clothes I didn't upgrade as such. I did buy an insane amount, always getting excited about the newest trend to wear, but that love and excitement for the new ones didn't take away from my love of the old ones, which I would always still wear—even some stuff from when I was 18. That's why it was great that we had the spare room.

We'd been living where we had for almost a year and things only just properly felt how they should. Like knowing inside out all of the roads and shortcuts around your street, and the places to go to when you needed the bum on a pair of jeans sewn up, and the right pub garden to get afternoon suntanning, and the postman's name.

But the flat had gone up massively in price even though we hadn't done anything to it and so Three had become almost obsessed with the idea of moving somewhere bigger. He mentioned it nearly every dinnertime, and tried to persuade me by implying that if we had a house I could have a proper walk-in wardrobe with sections and shelves and shoe bits and bag stands and its own lighting system, which was just the best thing I could imagine. But this would all have to be in Willesden instead of Hammersmith, so that took the shine off massively.

"People *only* move to places like Willesden if they are giving up on a fun and exciting life and settling down."

"That's not true, your hairdresser mate lives there."

"He's 48 and boring and my hairdresser, not actually my friend, so I don't see how that proves anything . . ."

"You're always like this about the thought of moving to a new place."

He had a point.

"You never wanted to move to any of the properties we've lived in and always go a bit sad and down on it beforehand."

Three and I had lived in three places now and I'd had proper mind problems when it came to having to leave each one. It made me feel stressed and worried and like, why change up a good home for something unknown? Home was where everything had a place and was safe, and if that was all being moved around to an unknown picture I couldn't see yet, there was no way I could be chill and calm about that.

"But once we're in, that afternoon you're always OK, and end up loving it more than the place we'd been before."

He was right.

Actually . . .

"That wasn't the case with the flat in Ealing. I hated it there, hated, hated, *hated* it . . ."

Three looked at me sadly and walked out of the kitchen.

I did hate that one. It was mouldy and miserable and the crazy witch lady who lived above us and owned the property would throw tuna and baked beans out of her kitchen window, which was above our bedroom window, so we'd have smudges of that all over our view.

Three came back into the kitchen.

"Maybe one day we'll want more rooms for other reasons . . ."

"What, rooms for people to sleep over?! You don't like your parents and my dad will always only stay in a Travelodge if he visits. So the sofa bed in the box-room is fine for any overnight guests. You know what I think about people who have houses full of unused nice-looking guest rooms. It's weird, all those beds waiting empty for most of the time. I don't want that."

"No. Children," he said.

Well, fuck me, so that's what's going on. Now that we're married it's like he's forgotten everything ever about me. I don't want children. I've never wanted children. I don't need a big house coz there won't be any children. This felt really unfair, and I could feel anger bubbling up, but I looked at him, his face all sad, and decided to be kind, not angry. "But you know I don't want them."

"We never properly know anything for sure."

"You have a point, obviously, but I feel so so so so so so so so so so so so so so so so so so so so so so so so so so so so so so so so so *so* strongly deep down that that version of life doesn't interest me. I thought you were onboard with that."

"Don't you feel like the weekends sometimes are just too long, and if we had children, we could go to the park with them?"

"Are you mad? Did you not hear what I just said?"

Nothing from him.

"I did not expect this from you!! No, the weekends are not too long, they are not long enough! You know I hate going on walks—why would having children make them any better? And I'm already never not in the park: I run there, I tan there—I don't need more park in my weekends. And WHAT THE FUCK, you want children??!"

Three had always said he wasn't bothered about having them, and even if he decided one day that he did, he had said he'd prefer to have me over them. We had that discussion again before getting married. I made sure we did. I had never not felt this way about not wanting them. I wasn't the one changing things here.

Hulk

Three started to feel down more often and he also began to get crap at communicating what time he would be home from work things because he'd get way too drunk and after about 9 p.m. he'd stop texting me.

His job had always involved a lot of evenings because they had to take clients out, but up until then Three had always been conscientious in regard to texting and what time he came home. He liked to have a run before work in the mornings and if he went to bed before midnight, he would have enough sleep to do that. And he'd always text to say he was on his way, even if I'd already texted to say goodnight.

But now work evenings would involve him texting around 9 p.m. to say he'd be home soon and then there would be hours of silence and no more updates. No replying to any of my texts or phone calls and no sign of him. I'd try to go to bed as normal at 11 p.m. but would always wake around 1 a.m. and again at 2 a.m. and, seeing that he wasn't in bed, check my phone, which would show that he still hadn't been in touch, so then I would try to call again or text and then, due to still being ignored, I would be a) worried that he was actually okay and b) fucking livid that the worry I now felt meant I couldn't get back to sleep. Which was really shit as not only was my job a bit more important now, but they had also changed the working hours to 8 a.m. to 4 p.m. so I had to get up super-early and my day often started with meeting and interviewing the scientists, since I now wrote the regular "what the scientists were up to" blog on the company's website. None of the science stuff had become any easier and I'd lie awake shitting myself about how I'd actually understand the things I'd be told the next day. These thoughts would make something inside me snap and I would stew on feelings of deep hate, so that by the time I heard the front door open, usually around 3 or 4 a.m., I'd be ready for a massive fight. I'd creep down the corridor, and on seeing that Three was so bladdered he hadn't locked the top part of the door, I would launch into all the reasons his behaviour was fucking unacceptable, transferring my sleepless anger to him.

Drunk Three could never understand why I was so upset, but by mid-morning the next day he always seemed to have caught up.

From: Three
To: Me
Subject: Bad Bean

Really sorry for making you worried and tired. Your note made me feel really bad, I will get better at texting.
Love you,
x

A few months after agreeing not to sell our flat, we had a really massive fight. I had spent the day busy doing Saturday things—went for a run, read a magazine in the bath, I'd gone to the shops, done some fashion planning and made some lush food for lunch (loads of homemade slow-roasted tomatoes on toast). Three had spent the day watching *Robot Wars* in his pjs, super-hungover from his work event the night before. It was now 7 p.m. and in 15 minutes we had to meet all our friends for a dinner he had planned weeks ago, somewhere 30 minutes away.

We were already going to be late, and I was ready to go. "Are you going to get ready? I don't want to be late."

Three was annoyingly in a state of half-undress looking for his spanner—apparently something needed tightening on the wardrobe door.

"Just need to find the spanner."

"Do you need to do this now?"

"Yes."

More and more Three was making us late by looking for stupid shit that didn't matter when we were supposed to be leaving. It always made us argue even though I would be quite fair about it.

"Come on, seriously, can't this wait until tomorrow?"

He didn't budge. "No, I want to fix it now."

"What needs fixing?"

"Wardrobe door handle's got loose."

"You've done nothing *all* day and now, when we have to leave for *your* friends' thing, you decide to fucking fix shit?!"

"Have you moved the spanner?"

"I haven't."

"Well, someone has."

"Well, then that's you, isn't it, coz it's not me. I've never used it."

"I haven't. Everything goes missing in this flat."

"No, it doesn't, you've just forgotten where you put it."

"You've moved it."

"NO, I HAVEN'T."

Three pushed past me as he ran into the bathroom and started randomly looking in the drawers.

"Can you just go and put your clothes on?"

He ignored me and continued emptying the drawers, which contained what they always had: neatly arranged medicines for every kind of scenario ever.

"Why the fuck would the spanner be in there? For fuck's sake, stop messing them up. Can we just go? Please??? We're so late . . ."

"You go, I'll catch up."

"NO!!! I want to go together."

I changed tack. Talked a bit more kindly. "Come on, if you can't find it, I'll buy you a new one tomorrow morning . . . Please, please, *please*???? Can we just go??"

"No. I don't want money spent on something we already have."

It was really hard staying in kind mode throughout this craziness, so I went back to my previous mode. "You're being a TWAT."

"Stop shouting at me."

"STOP BEING A TWAT THEN."

But he wouldn't and he had completely messed up all the ordering of the ibuprofen, paracetamol and aspirin packets. I pulled him away from the bathroom cabinet to try to snap him out of his weird search, but that fucked him off even more and he returned to full-on looking mode like a weird searching zombie.

"Please stop. I don't know why you always get like this."

Nothing.

"Don't ignore me!"

I hated him for caring more about a fucking spanner than our night out. I prodded him in his side, hard: "HEY."

"Don't prod me."

I shouted in his face, "HURRY UP!"

"I will not hurry up when you are being so unreasonable and impatient."

I couldn't handle this. I pushed him into the wall and shouted at him, "I AM NOT UNREASONABLE, YOU ARE!!" He roughly moved past me and then grabbed the brand-new shower gel, which was waiting to be put away by the bathroom door.

"DON'T BARGE PAST ME!"

He turned and squirted loads of the shower gel at me. It landed a bit in my hair, all over my top and across my face.

And that almost sounds quite funny, but it felt far from it.

I was so, so, *so* angry and upset as it meant that I now couldn't leave; he'd ruined my look, and my hair and make-up, and what it really properly meant was, because of that move, this fight was nowhere close to ending. I went livid. I became something else for a moment. I screamed words I can't remember at him, the loudest I have ever shouted at anyone ever. I ran to the kitchen and locked myself in there and threw loud things I knew wouldn't break, like wooden spoons, cookbooks and a rolling pin, hard against the floor. I needed to make noise. I needed to sound scary. HOW FUCKING DARE HE?

It was a fit. And I had to keep myself away from him as all I wanted to do was hurt or break things. I am not the kind of person you can do that to. I wanted to really damage him.

And then eventually I calmed down.

It's a weird time, the calm bit after the mental bit. You're sort of delicately borderline, and the slightest wrong move or thought could tip you back into it. It's also logistically tricky. Where do you go? You're not ready to be with the other human yet. How long do you stay in the kitchen? I wished I had thought to grab my phone en route.

After doing some tidying up in there and picking recipes for my next week's meals from Jamie Oliver's *30-Minute Meals*, I was ready to unlock the door. I had no idea how long I'd been in there—I should have reset the microwave clock after unplugging it for the Nutribullet. It must have been almost an hour by now. There hadn't been any sound on the other side of the door for a while and when I came out of the kitchen, the lounge was empty and the car keys were gone. It was a relief, and I was able to transition into normal mode more easily.

When Three came home, he approached first with an apology. He had gone out and bought a new shower gel, and instead of the Asda Basics one we usually got, he had got the Imperial Leather one, which was double the price.

I hugged him and told him I loved him, and he said the same and did a bit of a cry thing, saying how sorry he was.

Before bed we joked about how silly squirting shower gel on someone actually was, because from this distance it felt a bit funny now.

Three admitted he didn't need to find the spanner then but had just felt like he really, really needed to find it in that moment. I said that I was sorry and sad that I had started the shouting and swearing and I shouldn't have called him a cunt, but explained that I felt like he always did a version of this before we were due to go out and it did make me feel really stressed and upset. He said he would try to stop doing it.

The next morning I spent an hour searching for the spanner and found it in his old bike pannier.

We were very kind to each other for the next few days and both felt very sorry for our own parts in it.

TOP HUMPS

NAME: Ben
AKA: The Gun Man
AGE: 19 (him), 23 (me)
BUILD: Like a marine.
GENERAL VIBE: Soldier; he wore a bullet he was shot with on a chain round his neck.
ACTUALLY LIKE: Kind, bit thick, into guns.
SPECIAL SKILLS: Really fast at taking apart and putting back together pistols.
FANNY SCALE: 9/10
BRAIN SCALE: 3/10
OVERALL RATING: 5/10 = Short-term Pleasure
PRE-GAME: He was in London for a few months for a PTSD research group and was staying in the cheap hotel next to the pub. Mollie and I invited him to lock-ins and then after 1.5 wines I would start to flirt with him even though he was quite young and also a bit not-okay in the head.
THE DEED: One lock-in some of his solider pals joined us and they all had a competition to see who could undo and redo their guns the quickest. Ben won and my fanny went mental, so I went back to the shitty hotel next door with him and, even though his mate was sleeping in the other single bed, we had very quiet sex.
PLEASURE (me): No orgasms.
PLEASURE (him): No orgasms, because although the meds he was on massively helped his head-thinking, they made it hard for him to come.

Summary: It was hot but short-lived as a) he never tried to make me come and b) it did feel a bit gross knowing he was in London for reasons of his brain not being happy and my objective was only to have sex with him.

After this I met Three and retired the scorecard system as I was becoming a proper adult. No more Duff Humps—I'd met THE ONE!

Cufflinks

Three's losing and misplacing of stuff didn't improve and he didn't find better ways to cope with it, so it always became my responsibility to find the missing item. Which I hated. It was never me who had moved whatever it was he had lost, but in his searching frenzy he always blamed me and, in the end, whatever the thing we were looking for, it always turned up in a place that ended up being quite logical to him after all.

Once I had worked out it was a pattern, I did try to go in more calmly with helping him to look, but on the occasions when it happened while we were trying to leave the flat, I found it hard to stay patient and the fights would always go a bit mental. We had big bust-ups over his work pass, his special wedding cufflinks, a screwdriver, cricket tickets, his woollen tie and loads of other clothing.

He'd say he had lost something a few minutes before we were due to leave, I'd look in all the obvious places, when I couldn't locate it I'd tell him kindly that I'd find it as soon as we were home and remind him that the things he lost usually turned up and if they didn't I'd buy him another. But he'd then get wound up about that being a waste of money and go off about the usual "the flat has hidden my stuff" bollocks and then I'd flip. I'd shout at him and call him a crazy cunt and that he was ruining the night, again. And I was sick of it. I'd want to kill him. But I would get my phone and put myself away somewhere instead. Wait it out. But as this pattern went on Three would start getting more annoying and I'd get angrier and nastier and, in his frustration with it all, he would often throw something across the room or at the floor.

I found it very hard not to physically go at him when he had just broken one of my picture frames, or the laundry bin, or when he threw the TV remote into our newish and first-ever flatscreen TV and it smashed the screen, or when he broke the second and the third laundry bins.

The breakages felt like a personal insult. He would never hurt me, and he would always apologise afterwards and also state that he would never hurt me. But it was upsetting me. It made me feel scared and angry and powerless. And it was always me that would end up fixing or replacing the damaged items because he felt too embarrassed to, so I'd do it really positively the next day after we'd made up, which we were both very good at doing once the craziness had passed. But over time I really resented it.

Then, after fighting over another set of missing cufflinks, Three spat on me.

Isn't that strange? I'd been with him for almost five years and now, for the first time ever, he had spat on me.

I've actually been spat on two other times in my life. Once, when I was at uni, I was smoking a rollie sitting on the steps below Bluskey's and loads of pigeons were gathering in the shite water feature below. Four boys, all about 13 years old, were throwing their lit fag ends trying to get them to land on the pigeons' backs to burn them. I told them to fuck off or I'd get my bouncer boyfriend from Bluskey's (a lie) to come and put fags out on the middle of *their* backs. They legged it up the steps and I felt powerful. Ha!

Then the fuckers all leaned over and at the exact same time they all spat. A huge dollop of collaborative saliva landed on the top of my head. It was horrible. Little shits.

The second time was when I was seeing Danny, the LA exchange student, in second year. He was very melodramatic, and when I told him I no longer wanted to have sex with him (he had a rule of no kissing and it had started to piss me off coz it made me feel like I was in *Pretty Woman* but without the extra money) he spat his chewing gum at me in the student bar. In front of people! I was pretty shocked, but then Old Rob and Northern Sam—guys I played pool with in the year above who were on a film tech course (i.e. they were harder than the average humanities student)—followed him outside and gave him a talking to that didn't involve words.

Three spitting on me made something explode inside. Like the Hulk turning green. I went for him, pushed him hard into the bedroom door. Punched his stomach. Strangled my hands around his neck. Told him I was going to kill him. Meant it. He wrestled out of my neck embrace and we struggled against each other until we were on the floor. I dug my elbow deep into his neck. I wanted to separate it from his spitting head.

"GET OUT, GET OUTTTTTTTT!" I wanted him away.

He started apologising but it didn't feel calm. I got myself up from the floor situation and moved away from him.

"LEAVE ME ALONE GO AWAY GET THE FUCK OUT."

He was following me around. He was so stupid. I wanted him away. I ran into the kitchen and I grabbed our biggest knife.

That changed the atmosphere. It felt good. I liked holding the knife. It calmed my anger. I felt I had the control.

I said to him calmly, like in a film, "You go away now. Me and the knife don't want you any closer." Which was a bit odd, giving the knife some kind of existence like that, but that's what I said.

Three was in the lounge area and I was in the kitchen so there was a lot of distance between us. He was begging me. "Put the knife away so we can talk."

What the fuck was wrong with him? If there's a human pointing a knife at you saying go away, just go away.

"FUCK OFF OUT OF THE FLAT AND LEAVE ME THE FUCK ALONE!" I screamed as loudly as my body could and I moved closer to him with the knife pointing out.

It felt *really* good.

He shouted at me that I'd overstepped a mark getting the knife, and then he left the flat.

Knife in hand, I stood looking at the closed front door with tightness in my chest and wound-up feelings whizzing around inside me. I stood there for quite a while until I heard the old lady next door open her door to a delivery, which took me out of my daze. I hoped she was at the stage in her old age where she could no longer hear very well. That thought went to stress me out, but I let it go away from me. I felt calmer now, so I walked back into the kitchen and put the knife carefully back in its drawer. It had served its purpose. And I knew I couldn't pick it up in fights with Three again—I had liked the feel of it too much. Which worried me, as deep down I wanted to fight all the time now.

Micky's Gym

I started boxing regularly. Just punch bags in a proper boxing gym that I had cycled past a few times under the railway arches on Latimer Road. It was how I let my fighter out and it felt great.

And I also prepared to have sex with someone.

Dylan was a guy who was often at Micky's Gym. He was hot and had big arms and a dreamy Irish accent. He dropped into conversation that he trained on Wednesday and Thursday evenings. So I made sure I went those nights. Whenever I noticed him in the gym my punching got harder and faster. And even though it wasn't necessary to help me box better, I started engaging my pelvic floor. Fanny was back.

Dylan would come over and give me little tips. He would show me and sometimes touch my shoulders or arm, and even though he was actually quite short, these moments shot sparks of excitement all around my body, he was that hot! We started to flirt, with our eyes and mouths and cheeky bants. One day he told me how much he liked the shape of my teeth and I wanked as soon as I got home, with those words looping in my head.

Those teeth.

Those teeth.

Those teeeeeeeeth!

After a month he asked if I wanted to get a drink. I said I did. And after one and a half drinks I kissed him at the table, and after three drinks we kissed outside further down under the railway arch and I let him finger me until I came.

At this stage I had no intention of sleeping with him, but we texted and Facebooked and I loved getting messages from him.

I was breaking my rules and not even using the Dylan-lust to have sex with Three. I didn't care. I just wanted more.

We would meet and kiss twice a week after our boxing sessions, and on one rainy Tuesday as we sheltered in a bus stop he told me there was this song that he wanted me to listen to, and he put one of his headphones in my right ear and one in his left ear and he played me Tom Waits's "I Hope That I Don't Fall in Love With You." I had never heard of Tom Waits or this song and it completely and properly floored me and felt like the most romantic thing someone had ever done.

For the next few weeks I listened to it on repeat whenever I was walking anywhere and I also put it on when Three went on a mad one looking for the car oil, which helped me not react to him.

Dylan told me that he had to go away for work for a night to Bristol and asked if I would like to go with him.

Fuck. Fuck! That's all I wanted.

He told me to think about it.

I thought of only that. Wanked over it, daydreamed about the train journey down, sitting next to each other on the train all electric, what would happen once we were in the room. Clothes ripped off, the first time his tongue touched my fanny, the first time I would lick his dick slowly, the shagging, sleeping, shagging, sleeping, waking up together, morning shagging.

There was no way I could do this, but it was the only thing I could do.

I told Three I had to go to Bristol for work, which was a bit out of the blue and not the usual thing my job called for, but he didn't question me. I packed a bag and wore the only

99

pair of sexy knickers I owned; I'd had them since sixth form and they might not have actually been sexy but they were satiny shiny and that propelled them way above all my other cotton ones.

The plan was to go to work as normal and then get the 6 p.m. train from Paddington and find each other on the train. All day I was so excited. So, so, *so* excited.

At 4 p.m. Dylan called to ask if I wanted a bottle of champagne for the train ride. I did and I also told him I'd like some Percy Pigs, if he could find them. He would find some, he said!

It's interesting how great all the normal shit things are when you're massively overexcited about something, living in a thrill. The tube to Paddington was one of the best tube journeys I had ever taken. I felt incredible. The train for Bristol was on time and departing from platform two. I got on coach C as that's always the coach for people with no reservations. I texted him to ask him what coach he was in. He called me immediately, asking didn't I get his voicemail? His wife was ill so he had to stay home to look after the children; he had called me at 4:30 p.m. to tell me that. I hadn't received it.

I was gutted. And on a fucking train to Bristol that had cost me £65.

Of course this wasn't really going to happen—me getting on a train with a guy I didn't really know, lying about where I was going. That was insane behaviour.

I felt like a knob.

I pressed my head against the window and cried. I stopped crying when the train passed Kensal.

What a complete and utter twat. Me, him.

I got off the train at the first stop that I could, which was Reading coz it was a fast train. Fucking Reading.

Standing on the platform waiting for a train to go back to

London, I felt so shit. When the train came I couldn't get on it. I let it leave without me and went to the station loos and did some more proper crying.

Then I went to a phone box and used the special phone card to call Mum. By the fifth attempt it was ringing through.

"Hello, Bay Sanctuary, how can I help?"

"Hi, it's me."

"Oh, hello, darling, what a surprise! You just caught me on the hop, literally—I've got Albert, our latest intake, hanging from my foot!"

"What is he?"

"A very friendly squirrel! Are you OK?"

"I'm away for work in Reading and the evening thing we were supposed to do got cancelled and now I feel a bit . . . like a loose end."

"Oh, darling, Reading is a bit of a miserable place at the best of times! Why don't you pop along to the shops and cheer yourself up? I would love an evening of late-night shopping—those were the days!"

"OK, will do. I'd better go, the phone card is making beeps."

I felt clearer. It would be more suspicious to go home, so I was going to stay in Reading for the night and I would make something fun come from this.

I googled "Reading Topshop," and it was open until 9 p.m. I then googled "Reading Travelodge" and booked myself a single room for £57, which I thought was a pretty decent rate. Three wasn't expecting a phone call and I felt relieved that I could just have the time to myself.

I spent the evening shopping and also bought a new electric toothbrush in Boots because they had them all for half price and I'd been after a sonic one for ages. On the way back to the Travelodge I got a chicken pasanda takeaway from the Indian opposite, which I ate in my room watching a dodgy

Channel 5 film about lost sisters. And weirdly I felt like a proper adult.

~

For the first few times that I went back to the boxing gym after the Bristol no-show I was full of hope and excitement at seeing Dylan there, then really disappointed when I didn't. I felt so sad throughout that time. Deleted that stupid Tom Waits song.

I didn't see him again until four weeks after the night we were supposed to spend together. He was back at the gym.

I walked in and he was flexing and checking out his muscles in the big gym mirror, and seeing him made me feel physically sick. Was he always that vain and gross?!

It was in that moment that I was relieved we never had sex. I started going to another boxing gym after that.

Five Years

I decided to make more of an effort to have sex with Three. All the fighting pre-Dylan had made it not such a present thing, but now I was going to actively try to make us better at it.

On a Thursday at 6:48 p.m., as he came home from work, I gave him a blow job in the area between the lounge and kitchen, probably the first in a lot of years.

After he was done, I pretended to swallow his come but then left the room, spat it out in the bathroom sink, locked the door, ran the tap and then cried hard on the floor.

I put on my running gear and ran up to Ravenscourt Park, where I cry-ran for approximately 40 minutes. Once I had got all the tears out, I lay in the middle of the green bit and stared up at the darkening summer sky wishing for things to be different.

I wished I had normal, exciting sex with Three.

That my fanny worked properly and was wet by looking at him.

That I was up for the next adventure with him.

That I wanted to own houses with lots of rooms with him.

I wished that I wanted children, and wanted them with him.

I wished that he was less mental, and that we fought less, and that our fights were less scary.

I wished I could not get so wound up by him, and that I could have shitloads of patience and be calm and not shout and swear at him.

Why couldn't I be better or more normal with all of this?

When I got home from the run, Three had cooked chicken stuffed with Philadelphia cream cheese, wrapped in Parma ham, and over dinner we had a conversation about how we should celebrate our five-year anniversary, which was approaching.

Knowing how much I loved tanning, he suggested flying somewhere hot and flash, but I didn't want to go away.

Our last weekend break to Italy had been awful.

We'd had a huge argument about him not wanting to use the sat nav, even though we had gone round the same roundabout three times and one of those times he had driven around it the wrong way! When we finally got on the motorway we were both yelling at full sound levels. He then suddenly slammed on the brakes for no reason other than to express his anger at me, and the seatbelt, thinking it was in a crash situation, went stiff and cut into my chest and neck really hard. I stopped yelling and started crying. A bunch of cars beeped as they passed. What the fuck was he doing? He could have killed us.

"Can you just drive on?"

"Not until you stop shouting."

"You've stopped on a fucking motorway. OF COURSE I'M FUCKING SHOUTING!!!!!"

But as he continued not to drive the car, I stopped shouting and stopped being angry. He had purposefully stopped the car at speed without warning me. On a fucking motorway in a foreign country. It was fucking out of order and threatening, and I wanted to get out of the car immediately, so I did.

Following me, he drove over to the hard shoulder and threw the rental car keys at me through the open window and I ducked but they didn't make it through—they hit the part of the window that was closed and it caused a tiny shatter in the glass.

Five years.

Five years.

Five years.

I didn't want another five years of this.

But we were family.

And he was my home.

And long-term relationships were *supposed* to be hard work.

~

I'm not exactly sure what I bought him for all of his five-year anniversary presents. I love present buying and normally I'd get him a few little things and then one big thing. It was five years of being together and one year of marriage, but we'd decided that we wouldn't ever do the silly wedding-anniversary things of paper, steel or whatever. The big pressie I got him was a compass. Something for him to use on his long walks, which he had started to like doing.

I just can't remember what the other bits were, even though I know there were some.

I remember what he got me.

He got me a big bunch of my favourite flowers, old English roses. Light-yellow ones like the ones we'd had at our wedding. And a very delicate bracelet from a jeweller whose name I couldn't pronounce. I remember that clearly, because as he gave me the bracelet the flowers were lying knocked over on the floor and Three was on his knees begging me "not today," with the bracelet held out in the palm of his hand, pleading.

The roses made it harder.

They were such pretty flowers. They weren't for scenes like this.

The morning before our anniversary, I woke to a voicemail and a number of texts from Three—he was away at a conference and had forgotten a ticket reference number, so needed me to get it off his laptop. Which I did. It was in his emails. I'd never gone through Three's phone or emails; the whole time we were together I had never even thought about wanting to do this. In his inbox there was an email from someone called Alison, with the subject line ". . . xx."

I opened it, obvs. And then went on an hour-and-a-half detective mission. I found 12 emails in total, to and from them. Over a period of four months.

Looking at the evidence, it seemed that they had been having a little thing. She worked with him (I corroborated this on Facebook). She had mousey brown hair and was younger than me and very, *very* dull looking with a very average fashion sense. She appeared desperate in her profile pictures and boring. That's not me being a cunt, just accurate.

I felt a bit insulted that he had gone for something shitter than me.

They'd had walks and kisses in pubs. Their emails weren't explicit, but I was upset and angry and sick and really worried. He was a cunt and she was a cunt. She was a boring, dull cunt.

But then I became quite strict and didn't let myself go on feeling crazy shit about her. I didn't care about her. She didn't know me; this was not personal. I was angry at *him*. While I'd spent all this time having sex I didn't want with him, doing sexual things that felt uncomfortable and unpleasant, I hadn't fucking *needed* to! All those nights he didn't come home when he said he would and I'd woken up at 2 a.m. to his empty side of the bed with no messages from him on my phone and worried about him getting hurt or having fallen asleep on a bus, and he was probably with her. I'd never made him worry like that over me those last few years. The fights it had caused were another layer in our ever-more-toxic fighting style.

How could he? How fucking could he? I should never have doubted my equations on marriage = cheating. He obviously did have a bigger desire for sex than I thought, although their emails made it feel like something worse. Like the point of them hanging out was actually to spend time together. At least with my stuff I was doing it to help us, to get me wet and bring that home to him. Their thing was the opposite, and it made him into a cunt and made us fight all the time. I grabbed his laptop in rage—I could feel myself about to lose it, but then I caught my face in the lounge mirror and it stopped me. I continued to look at it. It spoke to me without moving its lips.

"Do you think what you did just then was fair?"

"What?!"

"Justifying your things against his?"

"Piss off."

This different part of me was annoying.

"You've had lots of feelings for other men over the years. Haven't you?"

I told it to butt out; that it wasn't the same because I did all that to try to keep the thing we had. Didn't I?!

But this different part of me wouldn't leave it. "THE DYLAN THING."

I held eyes with it for a while, like an angry staring competition, breathing deeply through my nose.

Standing there, staring and breathing, I felt something actually change inside of me. Calm washed all through me. I put the laptop down. I didn't really have a right to have a go at Three for this.

Three wasn't home until tomorrow morning, the morning of our five-year anniversary, and I had a work event I had to manage that night—a celebration of all the scientists we had created companies for over the last year. I needed to be there and in good work mode. So it felt like the best course of action was to get on with the day as normally as I could. Find a way to process it and work out a plan for when I saw him on Saturday morning, 24 hours away. Sophie, my favourite friend through work who sometimes helped us out with events, was around from the afternoon and I told her about it all over our Pret wraps. She put the shutters down over the meeting-room internal glass walls, locked the door and hugged me, told me everything would be okay, I'd be okay, I just had to be brave about working out what I wanted to happen next.

I didn't let myself drink at the work event, but I spoke to people like I was drunk. As soon as I could, I left and rang Al on my way home. I told her of the plan I had decided on, and that I was scared and felt so sick and didn't know if I could do it . . .

"Yes, you can. You are super, you are strong. You can do this hard thing." She made me say out loud that I could do it.

"I CAN DO IT."

The next day was a lovely Saturday morning—clear blue skies, great tanning weather. A perfect day for a five-year celebration.

It reminded me of the start of our two-year anniversary; Three had planned something secret in Ravenscourt Park and was so happy the sun was shining. After a morning of shopping, having been driven to the Westfield Topshop for an outfit-buying spree on him, Three had headed into town and said I had to be ready at home by 1 p.m. Which I was. I was never late for anniversary stuff. We walked to the park and he placed a rug on a mound bit and brought out all of these amazing Fortum & Mason treats, including champagne and real glasses. We sat and ate and drank and he told me the toilet was just over there because he knew I hated drinking in parks without a loo nearby. He gave me my present and it was in the most amazing packaging—a pouch, in a box, in a bag tied with a ribbon. It was a Tiffany's silver bean on a silver chain. I had never had anything from there before and it felt pretty epic. He said he had wanted to get it for me the year before, to go on top of the fake gold "Beano" one I had demanded for our first Valentine's, but he hadn't been able to afford it then.

"I love it, it will go brilliantly with Beano, and I love mixing gold and silver. I love it soooooo much!"

His eyes welled up and he said that he loved me more than anything he'd ever known, and I'd told him the same and meant it.

"You and me forever, Beano?"

"You and me forever!"

I had felt really, *really* happy. I knew he would never leave me. And I knew that I would never leave him. We came from the same place. We didn't leave the people we loved.

We probably couldn't even leave the people we didn't love.

Three came through the door at 10:35 a.m., smiling with the yellow roses. I asked him to sit down.

He said he needed to shower.

I couldn't handle just hanging around waiting for him to do that—he always took an unnaturally long time to wash for a man with slightly-longer-than-short hair—so I went for a run.

I listened to Cypress Hill on a loop. Music for bravery.

When I arrived back outside my front door I couldn't go in. Have you ever had that? A really strong physical pull away from the place you are supposed to be?

It was awful, very terrifying. Worse than getting a tattoo.

I finally went in.

Three was arranging some gifts on the table.

My gifts to him were already on the table. I didn't know why I'd done that and I didn't remember when I'd done it. There was the compass-shaped box and all the little ones which I had complete mind-blank of what they were.

Arranging them on the table seemed weird considering what I was about to do.

I asked him to sit down.

He did.

I had gone through the different ways of having this conversation in my head:

1. Make him tell me.
2. Ask him, "Who is Alison?" and see what he does.
3. Just tell him what I found out.

I went with Option 3. I was tired of drama. I just wanted to talk without any of that.

I told him that I had seen the emails on his laptop and knew about him and Alison, and that I thought it was time we ended things. All calm like, kind. No shouting.

He went really shaky and knocked the roses over in shock rather than violence.

Started denying it.

I went to the sofa and took a brown A4 envelope out from behind the cushion. Written on the front in a Sharpie was "You and Alison." I presented him with the photos I had taken of their email correspondence, in chronological order, along with images taken from her Facebook page. I had spent yesterday's lunch break printing them all out.

I told him calmly not to waste time. That this was going to be a conversation about what happens next. Now that it is over.

I told him this wasn't to do with Alison, but that she was the catalyst for change that we both needed. As we had both fucked this thing up.

I sounded so with it.

I told him he wasn't a bad person, that he was a good person, a person that I loved, but that we, him and I, us, were not a good mix. We had become bad together and it was time to stop.

"You said—you said we would never do that, that night in the car in Acton. That we would never leave each other."

"I know."

He had tears and snot and dribble on his face, and three hours later I had dried tears and snot and dribble on my face.

It's really shit, causing someone you love so much utter pain. But I was unmovable in my decision. It was over. I was leaving the person I loved.

I helped him towards a plan. He would go and stay in a hotel. He mentioned not knowing where to look, so I opened up his laptop and googled cheap hotels nearby. The one I found happened to be by the restaurant he had booked as a surprise for tonight's special anniversary dinner, and when I said the street name, that pushed him over the edge and he lay crying on the floor.

He kept repeating, "I've not been myself lately, I've not been myself."

I hugged him and told him I've not been the me I want to be either. This is why we were where we were. He got himself up and sat on the sofa and my eye was drawn to the bottle of pound coins on top of the shoe cupboard, and I had a very quick thought about spending it all in Topshop. And I think that's how I knew whatever upset and stress was ahead, I was going to be okay. I *was* going to be okay. That *had* to be the case. Even though it felt a very long way away from me in that moment, I would at some point be standing in a shop excited about buying new clothes. That would definitely happen at some point. Therefore, I was going to be okay.

And five years on from the exact date we met, Three and I ended.

Adapting

I hadn't ever had to worry about where I lived. Three and I had done all our home-thinking together, which actually was mainly him working it out and me agreeing and going along with it. And before Three, it had been very simple. I'd left home as soon as I'd finished school, moving into uni halls that you got allocated by filling out some forms. Living there morphed into living in a uni house with my course-mates, which morphed into two of us moving into the Red Dragon at the end of our final year when we decided to work there full-time for a bit before looking for "proper jobs."

And then I met Three, and after six months of being together he moved out of his mum's and I moved out of my shoddy windowless room in the roof of the pub, and we went into renting our very first (very witchy) flat in Ealing.

So those home-planning places in my brain weren't developed enough and I found it overwhelmingly frightening to have to do it on my own.

I also really, really, *really* didn't want to leave my flat. We had been so lucky to get it—well, a mixture of luck and Three being clever. Him signing us up to the flat-buying scheme with the housing association in Hammersmith and Fulham and them accepting us, meant we were granted our Shared Ownership flat. They wanted minimal deposit and you didn't need to have a big wage—it was amazing. I'd spent the first year of living there in buying happiness, picking and finding special pieces for it. Frames, cushions, coloured chairs, a giant knife and fork, which I nailed to the kitchen wall. The first time I had friends around to eat on the new garden furniture it had felt as exciting as the first time I had worn my red jumpsuit.

In the early weeks of ending things with Three we took it in turns to stay away from the flat, him in cheap hotels and me on Jay's sofa bed. I found it so hard leaving the flat for my turn. It was confusing to know the difference between the sadness I felt about Three and I being done, and the grief I was feeling about getting ready to say goodbye for good to the flat and heading into my new solo life. So I wrote a lot of lists detailing the difference between routine-change feelings and actual future worries, so my brain wouldn't confuse me, e.g., feeling sad about seeing food Three would like to eat in the supermarket. This was a routine-change feeling. Whereas not knowing who I'd go on holiday with was an actual future solo-life worry.

Moving away from automatic consideration of Three in my everyday thinking was, like changing any ingrained habit, very hard—but this hardness was not the same thing as still actually wanting to be with him. I didn't. I just needed my reprogramming to happen faster.

But Three wasn't making that easy.

From: Three
To: Me
Subject:

You said you'd always love me, if that wasn't a lie I don't understand why we can't put this behind us and try again?

I find it utterly paralysing leaving someone who loves me, because of the hurt-confusion they'll be left with. When I was younger, after Mum left, I felt that feeling regularly. It was horrible realising she loved me but not enough to be with me.

I never wanted to make any human I was in a relationship with feel that too. But this was what I had done to Three.

I felt constant worry for him, but there wasn't one minute where I thought ending it with him was a mistake. I didn't doubt my decision.

From: Three
To: Me
Subject:

I know how much you love me, can't that be enough?

Three wasn't talking to anyone, and he kept turning up at my lunch break at work and insisting on conversations that tied all our problems to the Alison thing, even though I told him over and over that the issues we had were around long before her. He wouldn't take it in, and I needed him to understand.

I felt strongly that after the length of time we had been together, we owed it to each other to be careful and caring and to find a way through this ending together, so I made us go to marriage counselling once a week to help us with that.

"I want you to be OK."

"But what does that mean?"

"It means we'd talk to her about why we are ending."

"What's the point?"

"Your brain keeps asking me the same things, so I thought the counsellor could show us how to have the right conversations to help you with this bit."

It was awful, and a bit of a tricky task for our counsellor, since usually she'd have the objective of helping couples improve things to continue a life together, but I had given her the strict brief that this was over. The goal was to get Three to a better place of understanding, to get him to actually listen to what I was saying when I spoke.

Three saw the problem as being that he had cheated and therefore I had ended it. I used the weekly sessions to make it clear that there were some pretty major other reasons that all existed long before his cheating, which meant it was over and that it was both our responsibilities, and that the cheating was just the trigger to give me the bravery to call it.

Because I could see now that I had wanted to end things for a while.

Throughout the first session Three continued to tell me I was wrong, that it was just this Alison issue. He broke down, did a weird hair-pulling thing, hit his face a bit—which I'd never seen him do before—and then started crying, saying to himself that he was such an idiot. The counsellor didn't do much about it, she just let him carry on, but I was relieved there had been someone else there.

Three just kept repeating, "Why have I ruined everything?"

I wanted more than anything for him not to leave this relationship thinking he was an awful person. He was brilliant, one of the best men I had ever met.

In week two, I explained to him the contributing factors in why our relationship was over. I wrote them down on a piece of paper so I could keep on track.

1. I have lost respect for you. There's not an exact event to link it to, but basically all the mad losing stuff fights over the last year and you always flipping out means I just don't look at you in the same way.
2. I don't want to be in something where there are crazy toxic fights that make me want to be violent and where my partner's actions make me feel scared.
3. I don't want children and you actually do.

4. *I can't face having any kind of sex or physical sexiness with you ever again. My love for you is strong but only platonic.*

It's really, *really* hard having to tell someone that you no longer like the idea of having sex with them. But I thought it was very important that this was said. I didn't want him to have any hope of something romantic ever being salvaged between us. The thought of anything like that with him made me feel *very* uncomfortable.

I didn't mention anything about my coping tools. Maybe that makes me a cunt? But I just couldn't. Our thing was over and I didn't want to be honest about that part of things with him. Ever. Plus, I'd only just been able to have those conversations with myself—that actually what I had been doing was proper cheating. I really hadn't considered it as that when I was doing it, but it hit me just after I ended it. I had been a cheater. I felt tricked by myself. I had always been adamant that I'd not do the things I found appalling about my dad, but I had spent the last bit of time with Three doing exactly those things. What a fucking idiot. I didn't want to ignore this major fuck-up but I knew in this setting, with the counsellor and Three, I wanted to remain very, *very* private about all of that. Which is why reason number five for me on the list couldn't be said out loud.

5. *I never want to be in any kind of committed relationship where I ever do something inappropriate with someone else.*

For now and forevermore, this would be my guiding rule as to whether I should be in or out of something. It was etched into my brain now.

I'm not a complete cunt though. The deal I made with myself was that by keeping this stuff secret, I was not allowed to be mean or angry with Three about his Alison stuff. And I would be patient and always kind even when he was speaking absolute bollocks, which he had been doing a lot of.

After three weeks of going to marriage counselling, we stopped. During the first session the counsellor had asked Three a lot about his losing-stuff feelings, and after hearing him describe it she referred him to a psychiatrist.

He was stressed out about how much a private appointment would cost, because the NHS wait was ages, so I gave him the bottle of pound coins to put towards it.

He got his official diagnosis through just before that third and final session—cyclothymic disorder. Which is sometimes referred to as bipolar III. He was put on different mixtures of medication to treat it, and went on his own counselling journey with someone who specialised in the problems surrounding it.

The diagnosis was the best and worst thing to happen to Three. He felt relief that it explained years and years of problems he had been battling with, but it also made him incredibly sad, because he told himself that if he had been treated for this sooner, things would have worked out better with us.

"If I'd got this diagnosis before, I'd have not been such a dick."

My mind drifted to last Christmas, when he had punched his wrapped-up present to me in a rage. On Christmas Day when I opened it, even though it was the dark-brown fake-fur jacket that I had wanted for over a year, I didn't feel excited because the box was completely fucked. I had asked him then to go and see someone about his breaking things in fights. I had said I would too, for my anger. But he wouldn't do it. I did, though—I did 12 sessions with a free online NHS counsellor. He wouldn't.

He continued with his new theory, "I'd not have been frightening or out of control in fights if I'd been on the medication. I wasn't able to compute, or move on, or back down. It wasn't me, it was the disorder."

I got it, I understood. But it didn't change anything for me. I just felt sadder for him.

Walthamstow

Three's new narrative of why I had to give it another go didn't let up. He regularly told me, through notes left around the flat after his turn there, how cruel it was of me not to even consider trying; how the medication he was on was already making him feel better, that the guy I had struggled with was not him, and therefore I owed it to him to try with this better-brained version. And I started to feel trapped, slowly sinking.

I spent a lot of my pre-teenage years absolutely shitting myself about quicksand. Me and my friends all did. When we'd be running through woods, or cycling our bikes across fields, or especially on visits to the beach, it would be at the front of our minds, making us screech and freak-out even though none of us had ever encountered it in real life or known any real people who had either. In primary school there had been a particularly dramatic episode of *Lassie* where one of Lassie's pals got trapped and died in quicksand, and that may have been what triggered it. Either way, I was petrified it might play a part in the end of me, the scariest bit being how slowly the sinking bit would happen. Slow, slow, sinking, trapped.

I needed to move forwards.

I would not let myself feel any responsibility in Three's years of being undiagnosed. Sadness, yes, but guilt, no.

So I did what I had been putting off, and moved into a new home properly.

I hadn't told many of my London friends what had been going on, so I set about doing so, asking if anyone needed a flatmate, and within a week I had three offers of a room and moved into the house Sophie rented in Walthamstow. Her flatmate had suddenly lost their job and needed to move back home. I'd been just about to take a place I didn't like the smell of in Wandsworth when she rang me to tell me. I went to check it out.

Sophie:
Just popping to the shop, should
be back before you arrive. It's
the turning after the
hairdressers, Google Maps can
pin it wrong! Xx

I had honestly never heard of Walthamstow. I had assumed it was in Essex, not London. A far-away and not-of-interest place. But it wasn't far away. It was on the Victoria Line and only six stops from King's Cross, but that didn't make me feel happier about moving there as it was still a very dull place to live.

Sophie had made cake and tea for me and her other friend George, who was also coming round to see if he wanted to take the other room, because her old flatmate's girlfriend lived in the third room and she didn't want to stay on without him.

Sophie had rented there for the last few years and she'd had some pretty shit past roommates, so she was excited to be able to shape the house she lived in with people she actually wanted to live with. The first step was an industrial clean, which she did herself as she flipping loved cleaning things.

My room was £100 more a month than George's because it had an en-suite bathroom, which I felt was going to be key for surviving the change from having a whole flat with all my stuff in it, to suddenly only one room. Obviously I felt quite stressed about this, but at least if I didn't ever have to wait for the shower, or to have a wee, or feel rushed having a poo, I was pretty sure I would get used to it more quickly. Plus, I could put extra cabinets in my bathroom for breakout clothes storage. I was quite worried about how to store all my clothes.

The house had a big garden area where Sophie said I could bring my sun lounger and garden table, and a huge garage in which she said I could store lots of my stuff that wouldn't fit in my room, meaning I could pack and move out all of my things from my actual home. I wouldn't be needing my plates or ornaments or cooking utensils at Sophie's since she had it all completely stocked out, so I was pleased they could wait for me in boxes in the garage for whenever I needed them again. Sophie said we could buy a big clothes rail to put all our coats on in the hallway and she said I could even bring some of my furniture if I wanted to. She thought there was room for my metal cabinet, and we could probably fit in a second sofa so I didn't need to rush to get rid of mine. She said she'd hire a van and drive it all over with me. She was everything I needed, and actually, this house was a pretty lucky offering.

And I would get used to having to live in Walthamstow. As Three said, I always hated all the new places before I actually moved in.

The last time I had lived with friends was when I was at uni, and friends was a bit too strong a term as it was just the people I had been grouped with in my first halls flat. At the time it was fine, but none of us stayed more in touch than having a nice conversation at a reunion thing. And actually, Melissa—the one I ended up moving on to my second uni place with—was actually a proper nightmare to live with because she was a wreckhead and also maybe a prostitute, although we never had hard evidence for that last bit. But we were pretty sure. She would always pass out, leaving the front door open, and she was fucking messy and didn't do her share of the tidying, with her washing-up always piled in the sink. So one day, Jane, the quiet English-lit girl who also lived with us, and I put all the dirty dishes in her bed, under her duvet, and then threatened her with her own hockey stick when she came in later that night.

I was very much aiming for a more mature and actually nice living-with-proper-friends vibe this time.

After being shown around, George and I sat down at the kitchen table with Sophie, who asked if we definitely wanted to move in. Yes, we both did. She opened some Prosecco in celebration. And then I started crying, saying I never imagined myself living in Walthamstow, it was just so far away. I just kept repeating that like a mad person, totally ignoring the fact that Sophie had obviously specifically chosen to live there!

George looked a bit awkward; I had massively brought the move-in excitement down.

I promised him that I wouldn't be a nightmare housemate/ emotional saddo, as generally I was a very positive person, and that I did really think this place was amazing and was looking forward to living with them both. He smiled and gave me a hug, saying, "Don't worry," but in his eyes I saw proper dread, poor guy.

Sophie:
Just gonna make a coffee then
I'll buzz ya once I've got the van
x

The next weekend Sophie helped me move all my stuff in. She was tiny and looked like a doll but was the physically strongest thing I'd ever met. As promised, she'd hired a huge van and driven it herself across London. I was seriously impressed.

Three had purposefully gone away for the weekend because he couldn't handle being around while I was doing the move-out. He was going to stay living in the flat until we sold it, and even though he was still unable to have a conversation without getting really upset and asking me the same things, he was being kind in other ways and had agreed to split my new rent with me until we had got rid of the flat.

As we came into the lounge/kitchen area there was a note on the table written in capital letters with a small box.

PLEASE TAKE THESE I DONT WANT TO SEE THEM AGAIN.

It was the special wedding cufflinks that he loved. Sophie asked if I was okay, but I couldn't talk and my nose got that tingly upset thing. This felt like the saddest thing ever. Why do humans always want to give back things given in love? Why couldn't he keep them until he was okay? I put them in my bag and hung it off the shoe cupboard. Sophie followed and pulled at my arm.

"Hey."

I kept my back to her and pretended to look in my bag. "I don't want to do lots of crying today, we've got too much packing to do."

"OK."

We went into the kitchen, which was full of dirty dishes, and this brought feelings of annoyance, which helped to move the tears on. At Three's worst, he was unable to do any helping in the cleaning/tidying departments. It used to make me really upset having to do it all. Sophie went to start cleaning them but as there were no plates I wanted in the huge pile, I told her to leave it.

The week before Three had agreed to all of the things I had suggested taking, which actually didn't include that many joint things because Sophie's place already had stuff like a telly, table, chairs. He had said I could take the Nutribullet but as I went to pack it I couldn't, because I knew he used it as regularly as I did, so I thought I'd leave it for him. I filled my bumbag up with the spice jars he'd never use and then left him a note saying I had done that and telling him to try not to be too sad and left it poking out of the bread bin.

We were ready to load the van. I had so much stuff the flat now looked quite nice and minimalist, but I knew seeing it like that would push Three's feelings over the edge, so I reorganised some of the remaining frames on the walls and the items on the bookshelf to spread them out so it didn't look quite so gappy when he came home.

Sophie and I were equal in van-packing skills and we organised that motherfucker better than any van's ever been loaded. As I locked up the front door for the final time, the old lady came out from next door and said hello to me for the first time since living there. As soon as we turned out of my street I cried until we reached Paddington.

Sophie held out her hand. "You're going to be OK, you know?"

I squeezed it hard. "Thank you."

I felt very emotional towards Sophie; watching her drive me and all my stuff across unknown parts of London made me feel huge love towards her. What an absolute legend she is. Only men had done things like this in my life before. She was saving me. And she could lift an IKEA six-drawer chest with the drawers in without any help. Sophie was being my actual hero.

Security

I was definitely a bit of a weirdo those first few weeks after moving in.

At night I would fall asleep just fine but then wake a few hours later worrying if the front door was locked. I'd been so used to being in charge of that kind of thing with me and Three that I couldn't handle the stress of not knowing if Sophie or George had locked up properly on the nights they came in after I'd gone to bed. George was a musician and currently doing the music in a musical, so had very different hours to me. And even though neither of them was at all as bad as Crazy Melissa or even very drunk Three, I had noticed that they only ever locked the top Yale lock and never did the bottom mortice lock. This seemed insane, security-wise. I could have easily kicked in our front door. So for the first few weeks I'd sneak downstairs in the middle of the night to check the door was shut and to lock the bottom lock, which was making me pretty tired. So I asked if they'd mind if I got a lock fitted to my bedroom door. I didn't want it to seem like I didn't trust Sophie, so I said I'd get her a spare key, which she could use whenever she liked (so long as she remembered to lock up after, ha!), and that it was only about me needing to feel secure. They smiled and said sure, but it was obvious they thought I was mental. I know because later that night I had been on my way downstairs to say goodnight when something stopped me, and I sat for ages at the top of the stairs listening. After some time I heard them talking quietly about it in the kitchen.

Sophie said something about me having a hard time readjusting, telling George that Three had been a bit careless and she was sure I'd relax into things. I hoped so; I didn't want to be the kind of person who had to be whispered about in kitchens late at night. That was a bit depressing.

But also, away from break-up brain, I think I would always have a high bar for security on any property I lived in. I had a bit of a bored stage when I was 15, which tied in with us all trying poppers for the first time, and we got into the habit of doing a bit of minor breaking-in to places. It was more in the same vein of when you're young and would find a hole in a hedge and then make yourself a den out of it, but this time we were nearing adulthood and making dens in actual people's homes when they were away, while helping ourselves to their ice cream and booze. The point is, I know how to case a joint and find the vulnerable places to get in. Security weak spots are my specialist subject.

After the locksmith had fitted my new bedroom lock, later that night I did a Prosecco and cutting-of-the-ribbon moment with George and Sophie to make it all a bit less weird, which it did. Having the lock calmed me massively and I started being able to sleep through the whole night again, getting my usual eight hours.

I would just like to stress that I've not broken into anyone's home for at least 15 years. I think it's important you know that.

Sophie:
Morning! Was late for a shoot
this morning so took one of your
yoghurts, I'll replace when I'm home.

126

This text made me feel confused. I was pleased to know my yoghurt was being replaced, but not sure why it would have been touched in the first place. A panicky feeling came over me—I don't know if I can do this shared flat thing. My general living routines were so different to how they used to be. Now they seemed to constantly involve logistical conversations about things being taken, and how best to use the fridge and freezer. Three would never have taken my yoghurt, and we didn't spend any time discussing the arrangement of the fridge as it was clear I was expert at putting things in the most suitable place for them.

Unlike now. We had a shit system. George was the tallest so he had the top fridge shelf. Sophie was shortest so got the bottom, and that meant I had the middle. Now the problem with the middle shelf was that I was only an inch taller than Sophie, so the middle shelf was too high for me to get to the stuff at the back. It was a very tall fridge. Plus, there was no logical place for shared things like condiments. Currently there were three separate mayonnaise jars on each of our shelves. Which is insane. The whole situation was making me feel sad, and as my emotions were still a bit raw I spent a lot of time crying after coming away from the kitchen. It was hard enough that all my weekly food only had one shelf to live on; not being able to reach it all pushed me over the edge.

I researched getting an extra fridge for the garage that could be just my fridge, but after speaking to Al about it she thought it might be a step too far and that I needed to just learn to adapt to this one. I tried, but it was hard—I had done weekly food shops from the big Asda superstore for the last four years; I didn't want to become the kind of person who wasted their money doing numerous trips a week to the one really shite, tiny Tesco Metro that was at the end of our road. It was really expensive and it never stocked any kind of herbs or aubergine. But who am I kidding? You can't be a weekly shopper anymore when you're living with only one fridge shelf. Those days were over. I cried some more.

By week three of living there I was still getting teary whenever I encountered the fridge. Sophie came home to find me having a meltdown in the hallway.

"What's happened?"

"I can't handle it—I don't think I'm ever going to get used to the fridge."

"The fridge?"

"Yeah, it's been really upsetting me."

"You should have said!"

So Sophie helped me come up with a solution, which was that we'd get rid of the two vegetable drawers and this would become the new bottom shelf (which was much bigger, so Soph was happy). I'd then get the old bottom shelf, which was now shelf number two, George would keep the top shelf, and shelf three could be for condiments and veg. Which everyone was pleased about. It was a huge relief and meant I rarely needed to cry when exiting the kitchen, which made a nice change and meant I could focus on my second-biggest new-living problem—my commute.

I've always cycled to work but it had always been relatively close. My new route was eight miles, the old one had been three and a half. It was quite a change. My current tractor bike, which I had inherited from one of the scientists at work, couldn't handle that kind of distance in a sophisticated manner, so I got a better bike through the Cycle to Work scheme, which basically means you pay nothing and it comes off your wages a bit at a time over a year or something.

I had really wanted to discuss all this with Three as he was very good at knowing bike stuff, but we weren't at a stage where I felt I could ask for anything, because although I knew he'd want to help, it would then be followed up by his latest point about us, which was currently, "I don't understand/was it all a lie?"

The new bike I chose didn't weigh more than a truck, and so I properly committed to it. I bought strong front and back lights, mud guards and two pannier bags just like a full-on cycle twat. Whenever cyclists tried to chat with me at traffic lights I would pretend I hadn't noticed them, and if they carried on talking I'd inform them I wasn't in this for the lols, but to save my travel and gym money so I could spend it in Topshop instead. No one would do this route for pleasure, even on a half-decent bike. On a good day, if all the traffic lights were green, it took 54 minutes. The cycle home was even longer as there was a fuck-off massive hill that I had to ride up at the very end part of my journey.

For those first few weeks, halfway up The Hill I would start to feel really, *really* down, and it would make me cry. This isn't what I had hoped for in life, this fucking long, hard hill. It was too high—I couldn't do it every day. They didn't have hills like this in Hammersmith. It was so steep I'd have to get off and push my bike up the last bit. I wasn't the kind of person who got off and pushed. It would make me feel embarrassed, having to get off, and then this would upset me more, and by the top of the hill I'd be proper angry-crying. One day, just before I was about to have to get off and push, I shouted at the hill through angry tears, "FUCK YOU, YOU FUCKING CUNT!" An angry man shouted back at me, leaning out of his upstairs window, "You fuck off, you little cunt!" and threw a not-even-empty Coke can at me. He looked really rough and I felt a bit scared and suddenly had the adrenalin to make it up

129

the rest of the hill. This finishing of the hill changed something in my cycle muscles, because I was then always able to do that final bit, very, very, painfully slowly, and still with the crying, but I wouldn't have to get off.

The confusing thing about the hill-crying pattern was that once I'd made it to the top, the rest of the route home was all downhill, which meant that by the time I got off my bike my tears had dried from the wind and I actually always felt pretty great. There's nothing nicer than freewheeling all the way home! But it did make me feel a bit like I was mental, the rollercoaster of emotions my daily cycle would cause.

Al rang to check in on how I was getting on with the fridge and I filled her in about how things had improved with that but how I now had this awful hill.

"Find a way of cycling around the hill. There will be another way."

I hadn't even considered that. I got out my paper road map, as I always prefer to do proper plotting on a physical one rather than Google Maps. There was a better way—of course there was. I'd hang on the road instead of turning off right at the usual spot and come in from a slightly longer but flatter direction.

Life suddenly became a lot easier.

Gossip

Sophie:
You home for dinner?
Xx

          Me:
          Yes!

Sophie:
Great I'm doing squash
curry xx

          Me:
          YUM xxx

Sophie:
PS can't wait to tell you
what I found out today!

          Me:
          !!!

Sophie was into gossip. She knew the shit that big-time celebrities were doing, as well as so much stuff about people in our industry. I don't know who or what her sources were, but she was never not talking to someone on the phone. Coming home, I would become loads more knowledgeable about things famous people I didn't care about in America were doing, or receive serious intel on a scientist. She would know the new joined-together couple name of any celebrity pairing before the gossip pages would put it out. TayTo was a particular highlight since not only was she mad on Taylor Swift, but she was addicted to Tayto crisps. Tonight's gossip update—told over her "classic" squash curry, which definitely was full of squash but definitely didn't have anything curry-like about it—was about some pop star who had been caught out lying about being pregnant to try to keep her cheating fiancé and how awful that was and what kind of girl lies about that kind of thing?!

My cheeks went red and I changed the subject.

I had lied about being pregnant.

Sometimes girls at school would lie about having abortions for extra sympathy. I was never into any of that. I was always hugely relieved I had never been pregnant. It scared the shit out of me.

Even though there is an easy solution, I didn't understand what actually happened during abortions and therefore the thought of getting preggers petrified me. Especially as, thanks to really shit sex education, most of us did often panic that we had got pregnant in the most unlikely ways.

In Year 10 Fran thought she was pregnant after letting Jonny C finger her coz she thought she had seen something wet on his finger before it went in her knickers—and back then, fingering meant jamming their fingers up our holes.

We got her a Boots pregnancy test. She wasn't pregnant.

That same summer I wanked off Stoner Si and made him come, which got onto my hand. And then afterwards I went for a wee and wiped my fanny as usual with loo roll, and then spent the days up to my period freaking out: what if I'd had sperm on my finger that I had put on the toilet roll, and then used that exact section to wipe with and it had got up me?

Al got me a Boots pregnancy test. I wasn't pregnant.

In Year 11 I had a pants-on dry-humping experience that worried me massively because my knickers were lacy and therefore weren't a complete material barrier and his dick had made his boxers wet with sperm patches, which could have leaked up into me.

I got a Boots pregnancy test. I wasn't pregnant.

In Year 12 Al panicked after a no-pants dry-humping experience because she was sure she got pregnant from it. We all worried about that one for her—it felt so likely.

We got her a Boots pregnancy test. She wasn't pregnant.

We were all a bit thick. Of course none of us got pregnant from those things! But that shit felt real.

My pregnancy lie was just after moving in with Sophie.

I'm not sure it was a proper lie. I just never told Three that I was pregnant. Or anyone. Coz if I didn't tell him, I couldn't exactly let other people know. That wouldn't have been fair. So when people had conversations involving knowing what it felt like to be pregnant, I keep quiet like I never had been.

Three months before Three and I had ended, Dr. Butt had made me come off Microgynon, the contraceptive pill I'd been on since I was 15. It worked brilliantly for me, but I'd had two migraines that year, which I had gone to him about, and when I went in for my pill prescription renewal he said they weren't allowed to give it to me anymore. Something on the computer had flagged it—because of the migraines I was now at risk of a stroke or something. He asked if I wanted a prescription for another kind of pill, but I hadn't been prepared for this and since Three and I rarely had sex, and on the occasions we did I made him also wear a condom (as I didn't want to only rely on the pill for not getting me pregnant), I didn't want to commit to another type right then. This was a huge life change and therefore I needed to do a serious amount of research about my options—checking which ones caused more spots or could make you fatter—not just take the quick description from some old-man doctor.

After I left the doctor's, I forgot to give my new birth-control situation any thought. I was 29 and had never been pregnant, and I planned to have as little sex with Three as possible, and since when we did he wore condoms, it didn't seem too pressing. Plus, I'd learnt a lot of info since school—some of my friends were actively trying to have their first babies and were finding it hard. They'd be full of sperm many times a week and not be getting pregnant.

I only took the pregnancy test as I felt massively heavy and like I had put on weight. Most Januaries, in denial that my extra pounds were just from heavy Christmas eating, I ended up doing one. It was always a bittersweet moment—relieved to not be pregnant but gutted that I had actually got a bit fatter.

Finding myself pregnant after our final time, two weeks before we ended, was a bit of a joke. I'd been on the pill for over 14 years and it was supposed to take your body a long while to get back to a normal cycle. Mine had worked it all out in three months. Stupid body.

I didn't want children.

I didn't want Three. We were over.

I needed not to be pregnant.

I wanted an abortion. And I didn't want to have to explain that decision to anyone.

It didn't make me sad or sentimental. It made me certain.

From my research about NHS abortions I found out that they happened through having a pill and then the pill made you have something like really bad period cramps for hours, then you passed bloody stuff out and then you were baby-free.

Because I'd been on the pill for so many years I hadn't actually experienced any period pains ever, and I rarely bled. This absence of blood and pain along with the deep certainty of not wanting children would often make me wonder if I was perhaps not completely a woman—or maybe just a very lucky one, not having to deal with that monthly mess and pain.

Sophie got both, and badly. Her periods would make her face move into pained expressions, and she'd have to lie in a dark room full of painkillers with a hot-water bottle on her belly. I had no idea what that actually felt like, but I'd had all that internal physio so hoped it couldn't be much worse than that.

I went to my old doctor's surgery but got someone I didn't know, Dr. Afral—they often allocated a random doctor when booking appointments. I don't think London doctors believe in an ongoing doctor–patient relationship. I should probably have swapped to a medical centre in Walthamstow now that I lived there, but something in me needed some things to stay the same, so my dentist and doctors remained in Hammersmith.

I told Dr. Afral I was pregnant and didn't want it. I had expected her to take over from there, like with all my other referrals. But she just gave me the name of a Marie Stopes abortion services helpline and told me to call and speak to them.

It was after leaving the surgery that I had a proper cry about it all. I think I would have kept my shit together if she had just been like, "Great, come back on this date and we'll sort you out." But I'd had to get her to repeat the name of the service three times and spell it out for me, and then she hurried me out. You'd think she would have shown more care, what with her being a woman, but she treated my situation with less interest than prescribing antibiotics. What a waste of time. What was the point of going to the doctor for them to just tell you to ring somewhere else?

I got my phone out. I really, really, *really* wanted to ring Three, but I couldn't. He just wasn't in a place in his head where he could handle any part of this, and the thought of having upset-not-processing-him adding to it all made me feel even more stressed. Aside from him, in terms of panic/upset, Al or Fran or Sophie were the ones who always answered and always made me feel better. But in this instance I decided it was better if I just got on with things on my own. If you want a secret to remain secret, the only way that works is by telling no one.

I stood at the side of the road until I felt calmer and rang the clinic number. They made me go through a lot of details. Dates, birth control, questions about the person whose sperm was in me, that kind of thing. I wished I'd picked a less busy street to call from, but my bike was leaning against a lamppost so I couldn't move along.

After about 15 minutes, they gave me a time to visit their White City clinic. And I cycled on to work relieved.

On the day of the appointment, walking into the clinic I kind of felt like a proper independent grown-up woman. I didn't mind that I was on my own. I felt empowered.

Even though I had been told I had an appointment at 11 a.m., they took hours to see me. Everyone else there was with someone. Mainly female companions, a few couples. The receptionist didn't seem to know much about the order of appointments, and I felt like I kept getting missed. I asked her to check when I'd be seen.

I was always prepared for waits so had my notebook planner, four-in-one pen and snacks. For the first bit of any wait I found it quite pleasing as it meant I could go through my notebook of life-admin lists, crossing off, colour-coding and re-listing. Planning made me peaceful.

There were loads of signs in the waiting room saying eating was prohibited. I've no idea why. It made the wait more annoying, not being allowed to eat. I considered taking my Crunchie bar to the loo to eat it there, but there's something a bit depressing about eating food with a toilet bowl looking at you, plus I didn't want my turn to come and miss it. It felt the kind of system where they said your name once and quietly, and if you didn't hear they immediately moved on to the next patient waiting. That was why I wasn't listening to music, and also why I wasn't drinking my water bottle even though I was really thirsty. I was desperate for the loo. I wished I had the ability to just let a cheeky dribble out but I don't have that kind of control; it's all go-go-go as soon as my hole opens.

An hour and a half in, finally the nurse shouted a name that sounded vaguely close to mine. I was claiming it. "Yes, here!"

"I'm so sorry for the delay. Follow me."

She led me into a room with a bed.

"If you would like to put your stuff down there and go next door to urinate into this."

She gave me a plastic container and I headed to the loo to do my long-awaited wee. I massively over-filled the cup. It wouldn't stop. My right hand was completely wet. There aren't a lot of options when you're overflowing a little container held between your legs mid-flow. I just kept it there till I was done. My wee had soaked the paper name label on the pot and made the ink run. It was mega embarrassing.

I cleaned it up as best I could in the sink—made it not smell of piss at least—and went back to the room with it. The nurse got out a strip that looked like the ones we used in GSCE science for pH testing. I had never seen a pregnancy test like that. It wasn't clear what made the strip confirm if I was pregnant or not, but the nurse knew, obviously. After looking at it, she whacked down some kitchen-roll sheets on the bed. "Right, up on here, trousers and knickers down."

She was going to do an internal ultrasound.

"Let's see how far along it is. Ah, only six weeks."

Thank fuck. It would have been awful if I'd been like those girls you hear about who had somehow not noticed being pregnant for nine months or something.

"You'll need to come back in two weeks."

"Two weeks? Why?"

"It's too soon."

Too soon? What the fuck?

"Are you sure? I thought you had to get it taken care of quick?"

"No, the optimum time for taking the abortion pill is weeks seven to nine. So you'll need to come back then."

Seriously, why didn't I know these things?! It sounded fucking bonkers—that actually you want to be a bit more pregnant to then get rid of it. I didn't want to walk around having to be pregnant for the next bit of time. That was too weird.

I'd taken the day off work as annual leave and felt a bit stressed that it was for nothing. So I went to the Topshop in Westfield and shopped through lunch and also through dinner, stopping for a duck wrap and salt-and-vinegar crisps in the Pret next door once I was done and my hands full of bags.

When I went back to the clinic two weeks later I'd been able to get a Saturday slot, which had been very hard to negotiate with them. I was also better prepared about what to expect.

I'd be seen by a nurse, have the pregnancy checked, then be given a pill to take.

Then, and this bit I found very surprising, I'd have to come back between 24 and 48 hours later to take a second pill, and it was after then that the abortion would happen.

For the first pill you came as you liked and didn't have to prepare anything specially, meaning I could cycle there. For the second pill, you had to have not eaten that morning because an empty stomach was needed, and they made you have someone with you as it could be a bit full-on 30 minutes after taking it so you needed someone to help you get home.

I didn't like the sound of that.

After taking the first pill it was life as normal. I didn't feel anything out of the ordinary. I wasn't allowed to have sex but that wasn't on the cards anyway—I'd not been having any kind of feelings down there at all.

Sophie and George had organised a barbecue party that evening and I was planning on doing fake drinking by leaving the gin out of the gin and tonic, because I didn't want to risk feeling at all emotional and then having alcohol-tongue letting slip to Sophie about the abortion. It was very important to me that if Three didn't know, no one could.

Also, I didn't want to chance any drunk anger or fear, which gin could cause, as either option might make me crack and end up ringing Three. Away from whatever emotions he might have felt about me being pregnant and his current break-up state, normal him would have been brilliant in helping to arrange it all and he would have made the whole thing feel so much easier.

I cycled past Wilko on my way home from the clinic and picked up loads of party decorating supplies—big paper lantern things, battery-powered fairy lights and bunting chains. George and I spent the afternoon decorating the kitchen and lounge and garden, while Sophie made the food supplies. The theme was sausage and potatoes, so Sophie was cooking 40 sausages and making five different kinds of potato dishes, because she really knows how to do exciting things with them. We had loads for leftovers all week. It was one of the great summer barbecues.

Mad Men

On Monday morning I was back at the clinic. I had a longer
wait for my second pill because even though they saw me on
time, when I got into the treatment room the nurse spun out
when I mentioned a course of treatment I was on that she
didn't know anything about. She had been describing what
would happen—I'd take the second pill by putting it in my
cheek, and before that I'd need to take some antibiotics to
head off any infections during and post-abortion, as the pill
makes your cervix open, which is apparently dodge for catching
infections. I hadn't expected I'd need antibiotics. She then asked
if I was taking any other medicines, so I flagged that I was
halfway through a course of steroid injections for some pain in
my lower back. It had started hurting last year after I skidded
off my bike, but then never got better. A scan showed there
was some inflammation on my SI joints, so Dr. Butt arranged
for three rounds of hydrocortisone injections over the year. It
was such a non-thing I shouldn't have bothered disclosing it
because by bringing it up, the nurse said that as she didn't know
anything about it, she didn't think we could continue.

"Are you serious?"

"Yes, I'm afraid without knowing what reaction it may have
we won't be able to proceed."

"Can't you just look in that book that the doctors look in
when they prescribe me something new?"

"I'm afraid I'm not aware of any such book."

"It's a reaction reference book—you look up the medicine name and cross-reference it in there."

"We don't have one here."

"Well, can't you check with one of the senior members of staff, or the manager?"

She seemed really reluctant to do that.

"Someone here will know about this book. Even the pharmacists in Boots have it. I don't understand why this is all suddenly a massive problem. Why the fuck was I allowed to take the first pill? Why would this all happen now?" I had started to raise my voice because she was being very standoffish.

"We do not tolerate swearing or shouting at staff."

I changed tack and pleaded, " 'I'm sorry, I'm just worried, please can you just go and check?!' "

She left the room and I was so upset I kicked the closed door really fucking hard. So hard it dented. A steroid injection in my back fucking up my abortion was fucking ridiculous. I wanted to ring Three so badly. He'd always been with me for all my other health-related dramas—the time I got stung by a wasp and my whole leg turned into thousands of blisters and the hospital wouldn't give me the treatment until I'd sat for an hour with some cream on them, even though they were doubling in size really fast, or when we got stopped in transit in China when the security guards wanted to confiscate the contact lenses I had with me. He was always so calm in those situations and always got us out of them. But my anger had dented the door. What if they saw it and kicked me out? I needed to not look like a person who had kicked the door when the nurse came back in. And I needed to remember not to swear. Or raise my voice. I got my four-in-one pen out and wrote "voice" and "swear" on my hand so I had a visual reminder and stared at it until the door handle moved.

She returned with a senior member of staff who explained

they couldn't continue until they had word from my hospital consultant that it was okay to do so.

"I don't have a hospital consultant. It was a one-off thing. Are you not able to ring and check with my doctor?"

"No, you'll need to arrange this."

"I'm not sure I'll be able to in time; they often don't answer the phone and have a 24-hour answerphone line so they don't usually reply until the next day."

"I'm sorry, but we're not able to get the information for you."

"Could you not just speak to any doctor? They would all have the medical reference book and be able to confirm that it wouldn't react."

"No, it would need to be the medical professional in relation to your treatment. And we would need to receive this via fax."

Fax?! I mean, for fuck's sake. I had worked in an office for over five years and we hadn't ever once used a fax.

"Would you accept a PDF?"

"No, fax only."

This was really stressful. I had taken the day off work and I needed it to happen. Plus, I only had a small time gap left to take this second pill.

"If you wouldn't mind stepping back into the waiting area and then letting reception know once you have that documentation."

The fuckers couldn't give a shit.

I got quite upset and started crying.

I asked them if I could remain in the private room so I could try to make all the phone calls I needed to in there.

They reluctantly agreed and left me to it. Cunts.

I calmed myself down and got a piece of paper out to write out my options.

— *Phone the doctors*
— *Go to the doctors*

If I couldn't work it out on the phone, worst case I could get a taxi to the doctor's surgery in Hammersmith, get a letter or something from the staff there and come back. Reckoned I could be done and back in two hours.

I rang the surgery. There was no one picking up on reception there, and I tried all the numbers on the website. As I was searching for an email address, I remembered that the receptionist had once given me the phone number for the surgery's manager as Dr. Butt was going to be away and I had wanted a copy of my back scan. I searched the folder in my Gmail account titled "NHS/Back" and found it in an email I had sent myself.

The surgery manager picked up after three rings, and I asked if she could urgently get Dr. Butt to send a letter via fax explaining that it was all okay for the abortion to proceed. I made myself sound like I was having a totally professional conversation and was fine using the word abortion, but I had to pinch myself really hard to stop myself from crying.

Thankfully the manager was able to help, and she emailed me 50 minutes after we spoke to inform me that the letter had been sent her end, so I could wait by the fax machine. She had also attached it as a PDF and, because the fax took a while to arrive, I showed that to the receptionist, but he said the nurses would only proceed with the fax version. Twats.

After the fax finally arrived I was then allowed back into the private room. Before getting on to the final bit I had to agree to a new birth-control method. I was about to be angry about this, thinking *this* is *not* the time for this shit, but actually maybe it really was. So I agreed to an appointment to have the implant put in my arm as I defo wasn't interested in having the coil and I still wasn't allowed to be on the pill. The implant would give me three years of not having to worry.

The nurse finally handed me the mixture of pills to take and said that as long as I wasn't sick within 30 minutes of taking them that it would all work okay.

She asked me where my person was, and I said he was waiting in the car as the ticket had run out due to all the delays. She gave me a bunch of leaflets in a bag with loads of sanitary pads, and then I was told to place the second pill in the bit between my gum and cheek. Which I did, and then I set my stopwatch.

I was now free to go.

I ordered an Uber and it took me to a hotel in Bayswater that I had booked for one night. I hadn't wanted to go back to Sophie's because I didn't know how I'd be, so I had told her that I was at my brother's for the night. I'd picked a hotel only a 15-minute drive away since all the hand-outs had said it starts working after 30 minutes.

Six minutes and 43 seconds into the taxi ride, I felt really queasy.

It was such a bumpy journey, and I was so hot. It was unbearable. I had to pant-breathe like you see women doing when they are in labour. Every turn, corner, traffic light made my face squirm in stress. I must have looked mad. The driver finally got me to the front of the hotel and I felt I would be okay once I got still. Check-in was quick, and I got the lift up one floor.

I still felt very queasy. It had been 25 minutes and 16 seconds since I took the pills.

My body really needed to get rid of something; I couldn't tell if that was out of my bum or mouth.

I took my coat, trackies and knickers off and stood hunched over, partially naked, in the bathroom, desperate for time to pass more quickly.

I placed a towel on the floor around the loo and then sat on the toilet seat making a weird moaning sound as I tried to hold whatever this was off. And then very quickly I moved to a kneeling position and was massively sick into the toilet bowl.

Shit.

I checked the timer. It was 28 minutes and seven seconds since I'd taken the pills.

What the fuck did that mean?! Had I yakked up all the medicine I needed to make the abortion happen and/or stop me getting infected?!!!

I felt really stressed. And I couldn't stop being sick.

I needed to call the helpline, but all my hands were busy.

I hate being on my own when I'm sick. It feels like the most unnatural thing your body can do, all the stomach and throat bits working in reverse; it makes me feel this is what death might be like. Things not working in the way they're supposed to. And no one wants to die alone. I had not factored this sick element into all my research. Oh God, I hope I'm not some weird case where my abortion happens by coming up and out of my mouth. I know that's stupid, but it felt unknown and scary.

After about 10 minutes of puking, the sick seemed to stop. I checked my fanny and there was no blood and I felt no pain, and my belly felt much better. I put my knickers back on and lined them with one of the giant pads the clinic had given me, which was like three times the size of a normal sanitary towel. I was to monitor the blood amount and if I was soaking through more than two pads an hour I was supposed to ring and let them know, as this was obviously bad.

When I got through to someone on the helpline she asked how long after taking the pills I was sick, and when I said 28 minutes and seven seconds she said not to worry, that it would be fine. I asked her if she was sure, as the leaflets had made it seem otherwise. She said that the pills would have been in my bloodstream after about 15 minutes and they put 30 to be extra-cautious, and that being sick was quite common and okay.

Thank fuck!

I stopped worrying and put on the first episode of *Mad Men* on my iPad. I intended to watch the first series as I had never seen it and there were seven of them to get through, and my favourite podcast constantly referenced it and it was annoying me that I couldn't share in their jokes.

By the end of the first episode nothing had happened to my body. I continued watching. I ordered room service—got a burger and chips and Fanta Orange, which felt like a nice treat. And then I carried on watching. I was enjoying *Mad Men* very much. The main guy, Don Draper, was extremely hot and after episode five, feeling a bit sleepy, I had a wank over him. Which surprised me as a) I hadn't been feeling things with fanny lately, b) I don't usually fancy people I've not met in person and c) I never imagined I'd be up for doing that kind of thing after an abortion. I would have assumed you'd not want to look at, touch or think about that area for a good while, but it actually felt extra-exciting and a bit different because I didn't want my fingers to go anywhere near my hole for fear of what might come out, so it was a unique style of delicate fingering.

As I still hadn't had any blood or cramps, I was interested to know if the fanny wetness from my orgasm would have other stuff with it. After I came, I got some tissues to investigate. It didn't. It looked completely normal.

After a snooze, I had a cup of tea and a Crunchie with 10 almonds. It was my new fav combo, the sweetness with the crunch.

Then, around 7 p.m., I started to have some tummy pains. Like muscle squeezings.

I felt some stuff come out of me and went to the loo.

There was blood, like a fresh period.

This continued in an easy way for the next few hours. The pad had barely any blood on it, but I changed it each time more came out as I had been given 20 so it seemed a shame not to use them all.

I slept great through the whole night and in the morning the pad had the amount of blood on it that you'd expect from a heavy period.

I had been worrying I might wake to find something more foetus-like in there. It would have grossed me out. But thankfully I never saw that anywhere.

That morning I went back to work as normal, and it only took a 20-minute walk as the hotel was much closer to the office than my home. So that was nice.

After leaving the hotel I didn't feel badly affected in any way about the abortion. Even the initial stresses at the clinic had floated off. I felt so happy and relieved that it was done, I considered sending them a thank-you card!

Two weeks after pill day you had to take one of their weird pregnancy strip tests and ring in the results.

Mine said pregnant. The woman on the phone said not to worry, that this was common as my body still had the pregnancy hormone floating around it. I wasn't worried.

She said to take another test in another two weeks and call back with the results.

I did, and it said I was still pregnant.

The person on the other end of the phone said I had to go back to that shitting clinic.

I asked for the earliest slot on Saturday and I guess I was considered more of a pressing case now as I got it without any persuading.

Abortion Number Two

After an internal ultrasound, the nurse told me that part of the pregnancy was still in there. It hadn't passed completely from the medical abortion. I would now have to have a surgical one. And I'd have to have someone with me.

I was very nervous the day of the surgical abortion. You had to have a general anaesthetic, and even though that would mean I'd not feel anything during the procedure, the thought of being put to sleep made me scared. Too many people who weren't me being in charge of keeping me alive without me there to coordinate? I didn't like that.

I wanted to talk to someone about it, but I couldn't without explaining why I was needing to have one.

I had to arrive at the clinic for 8:30 a.m. and I wasn't allowed to drink or eat anything for 12 hours before. Being thirsty is so shit. So I brought the water spray I used for cooling my skin off when I'm tanning and squirted it on my lips and tongue to trick my body into feeling refreshed. It worked quite well. It would be in the top 10 of my "having a surgical abortion" tips.

They led me out of the waiting room, and on my way past the loo, seeing that the door lock said "Occupied," I leaned close to the door and said, "Sophie, I'm going in now. See you after!" so the nurse thought I had someone with me, as she had been hassling me about it. They kept stressing that it is really important you have someone to take you home. I disagree—I think it would be really important to have someone with you before, to help your nerves, but I don't think it's a big deal getting home, because the mega advantage of this kind of abortion is that once you're awake you're fine, no bad tummy or bleeding stuff. You're just a bit drowsy, which couldn't be any harder than getting myself home from Fran's sixteenth birthday, navigating dark country lanes having smoked three shotties and downing loads of vodka. This would be a piece of piss.

They led me through a door that said "Outpatients Only" to a changing area and told me to pop into a cubicle and take all my clothes off and put on a gown, badly fitting paper knickers and some NHS sliders, which were waiting for me inside. I was then directed to a locker, which I had to put all of my belongings into. I was then taken through a door and made to wait on my own on some chairs outside three doors. It wasn't a proper area; it felt like a passing-through place. There were no posters and I had nothing on me, so nothing to distract me. I sat there just waiting. Waiting with my nerves.

Suddenly I could hear lots of screaming; the surgery room must have been on the other side of the nearest door. It surprised me, the closeness—made me feel a bit rude. I could hear lots of muffled voices trying to calm the screaming lady. It sounded fucking horrific. Why wasn't she asleep? Maybe it was like that film when the guy was put under for a major operation, only he wasn't put under properly and even though he couldn't speak his brain could feel everything. Only it couldn't be like that as she was using her voice.

I wished I had my phone on me. I would have cracked and called Al.

I was getting quite anxious.

The screaming didn't stop.

I couldn't sit down any longer.

I had to move about.

I put my ear to the door. She was saying, "No, no, no, what's going on?" I wanted to open the door. She wouldn't stop—she sounded quite annoying. I felt like I would sound a lot cooler if I was screaming about whatever she was screaming about. Why didn't they just fucking sedate her? Isn't that what normally happened to hysterical women in hospitals?

She was scaring me and it was making me angry.

It was going on for so long.

Should I open the door?

I didn't want to have to wait there and hear that shit. My anger was boiling. How dare they put me through this bullshit? How dare they fucking scare me?

I went back to the door that the nurse had brought me in through and poked my head out into the empty corridor. I was wearing a backless hospital gown with the badly fitting NHS knickers on; I was at a massive disadvantage. I needed someone to walk past so I could get their attention. I shouted, "Excuse me!" a few times and finally somebody came. She looked annoyed and old.

"Hi, I'm just in here alone and a woman in the other room is having an awful abortion and screaming loads and it's making me feel stressed."

She looked at me, doubtful. "I don't hear anything."

We listened together for a moment to the silence, and then the woman continued yelling. I saw something change in her old eyes.

"I'd like someone to look after me properly, please. I don't want to be left in that horrible holding area on my own. It's like the start of a shit horror movie . . ."

"I'm very sorry, I'll go and find someone."

Shortly after that, the clinic manager, Belinda, came and waited with me.

"Hello my love, are you doing OK?"

The woman was still screaming. I nodded my head and went to speak but annoyingly tears started coming out of my eyes and my voice wouldn't work, which was stupid as I'd got the thing I'd wanted—some kind company. She went to give me a hug but I moved my head to the side so I had a bit of privacy for my wet face. But I let her hold my hand.

"Oh, yes, that can't be very nice to hear. I checked in with her team before coming to see you, and that lady in there has already had her abortion and it all went smoothly and painlessly, but she has woken from her general anaesthetic a bit disorientated and upset about having to have it. That's why she's screaming. The doctors are trying to calm her down in the room before they wheel her out to the recovery ward."

"OK. Thank you."

That made me feel better. I wanted my abortion, so this was all going to be okay. I couldn't imagine a situation where I'd be sad about waking up and not being pregnant.

Belinda also told me some nice details about the team who would be managing my procedure. Christina was the nurse, Michael was the anaesthetist, and Dr. Webb was very experienced and would lead it all. She had known him for years and he was a very capable surgeon. I had a forceful urge to ask her about the state of his fingernails—men who have long ones gross me out—but I stopped myself.

"What happens in recovery?"

"Basically just tea and biscuits, and making sure you are OK before leaving."

"What kind of biscuits?"

"Custard Creams."

"Oh, that's a shame, a Custard Cream does not excite me as a biscuit choice."

Belinda laughed, thinking I was joking. I was being serious.

"You've survived almost-death and all you get is a basic Custard Cream?" I continued. "I think a chunky chocolate-chip cookie would be more appropriate to hand out."

Finally, it was my turn. Belinda apologised again and said she would come to see me when I was in recovery. I liked her and felt looked after. I let her hug me goodbye.

Lying on the bed for the surgery, Michael injected me with something and Christina asked me where my next holiday was going to be and, sensing I didn't have long before I passed out, I said, "I don't have time to answer this properly; you should have asked me earlier . . ."

Then I woke up in recovery. It was a really nice waking-up feeling, like I knew exactly where I was and what was going on, while also seeing it from a very far-away, gentle distance. Like waking up after an amazing massage.

I felt fine. No part of my body felt weird or fiddled with, which is a bit strange considering it had been!

Belinda came by as promised and she gave me some Bourbon biscuits—they had some leftover from their stash in the staff room. I kept the truth from her, which was that I considered Bourbons to be in the top three of shittest biscuits ever, worse than Custard Creams. I was starving, though, so I ate them all with my cup of tea. I had a fake phone call in front of Belinda with Sophie, who I said was waiting in her car. And then they discharged me after 40 minutes with two more pregnancy-strip tests and I was free.

I was free!

And this time I really was.

I wish I had known to ask for the surgical procedure in the first place, because it was so easy. And aside from the freaked-out woman beforehand, it was actually all really fine. But also I was just pleased it was all done. I would write Belinda a thank-you card.

Afterwards I did a lot of reading about places in the world where women didn't have access to free abortions and it really got me upset. I didn't do anything about it, though.

Admin

Things felt so much lighter after the abortion. Not just physically, but mentally too. I hadn't been in emotional turmoil about it or anything like that, but I realised I had actually been continually worried during that time. When it went away as a problem, with all the time that had passed in between, I realised I actually felt much better about the new solo-me situation too.

I'd done some thinking, reassessing some of the theories I'd previously held. I'd been through the proper adult love stuff. I knew what was going on now: 1) My fanny needed to be happy for my brain to be too and 2) I'm someone who can't leave very well.

I don't mind the things that went before, the wrong turns, if going forward they inform my future ways. So to ensure that I didn't accidentally fall into something wrong for me again, there would be no rushing and no lying.

I wrote that down on a Post-it note and stuck it to the corner of my mirror. I wasn't looking for anything right now, but if something came along I felt hopeful that if fanny and brain were both happy then maybe a long-term love could work!!!

My eye moved to the Post-it stuck in the other corner of the mirror:

Sort divorce.

Which I couldn't start doing yet as we needed to wait for the flat to sell first.

From: Me
To: Three
Subject: RE: the flat

Hello, did you see the below? Is it ok to confirm the two viewings on Wednesday with Foxtons?
Hope all's ok?

From: Three
To: Me
Subject: RE: the flat

Your Mum rang the home phone last night, I didn't know what to say so I said you were out. Have you not told her? Does that mean there is a bit of hope for us?
Can we meet?
x

Urgh. No. He knew full well that my mum was the last person I'd tell if anything big happened. There wasn't any secret hidden meaning in her not being told.

From: Me
To: Three
Subject: RE: the flat

Sorry you had to do that. I'll let her know the situation.
I'm happy to meet but would prefer a lunchtime, and only if you don't ask the same things you always ask. As everything I've explained before is the same.
Can you please reply about the Foxtons viewings? And please can you make sure it looks tidy?
x

So frustrating that he kept ignoring Foxtons.

I typed the kiss at the end, then deleted it, then put it back in and then deleted it again. And then put it back in. I didn't really want to sign off with it, as I didn't want to include anything that could be misinterpreted. But then not putting one in felt like some mega-awful statement, so it was probably better to whack one in to prevent further "you've turned so cold," "how could you?" and "was it all a lie?" When Three said the lie stuff, that really, really, *really* fucked me off. I'd written him a letter the month before laying out clearly again the reasons for us breaking up that I'd gone through in our marriage counselling, explaining why it was definitely over for me. Telling him how our relationship would always be very important to me and how my love for him was real and would always be there, but only in a very platonic way now. But even with the words written there for him to reference, Three still wasn't taking it in.

Two days after the letter, he had turned up at the house. Sophie had answered the door. She came to get me, "You'd better come down." As I grabbed a jumper to put on over my pyjamas, she added, "I didn't know what to do so asked him to wait outside."

"That's OK."

"He's completely wet and crying."

"Oh. You OK if he comes in?"

"Of course."

He had walked all the way from his office to ours, which was *a lot* of miles, and even though he was the kind of guy who loved walks, this one didn't seem to fit with that vibe. Firstly, he was wearing his smart work shoes, which he would never normally do walks in; secondly, it had rained the whole way and he wasn't wearing a rain jacket, and lastly, it was 10:30 at night.

Three didn't seem like he'd had a drink, but he really didn't seem like he was in a normal state of mind either.

"I wasn't planning to walk here."

"What happened?"

"I was on my way to a meeting and then just carried on walking."

"That's a lot of rain walking."

"I know."

"Did you let the people know who were expecting you for the meeting?"

"Yes. Can we talk about the letter?"

"We can, but not now. I'm not good at big things at bedtime."

"I know. I'm sorry. I've ruined my life."

He started crying. I made him a cup of Horlicks and listened to him for ages continue to not make sense of the situation, and eventually got him in an Uber. I texted Jamie and said although Three wouldn't admit it, he was struggling, and I asked him to check on him over the next few days. I hated seeing him in this state and although there was nothing at all threatening about Three's behaviour, it made me feel massively stressed that he had turned up like this. I didn't want surprise late-night desperate visits.

I emailed a follow-up to my "to-kiss-or-not-to-kiss" email asking him to please not take anything I had written badly, and asking if we could concentrate on selling the flat so that once that was out the way, we could see what kind of friendship could develop. If he wanted it. I did, but I also knew that, as the one who had ended things, you had to wait till the other person was ready, which Three might never be.

I then emailed my mum, and sent the same email to Dad (with Jay copied in—as I had told him not to mention anything to Dad until I had):

From: Me
To: Dad
CC: Jay
Subject: News

Hello, just some news from me. Three and I broke up a couple of months ago and it was my choice and I am now living with my friend Sophie in her house in Walthamstow (address below). We don't have a house phone so am on my mob obvs. I don't actually want to talk about it over the phone but you can email questions if you have any, although I'd prefer not to have to answer those for now too.

Please don't say anything about us being married or any of that. We are working out how to sell the flat, etc.

I am ok. Been going to work, eating, etc.

Feel free to pass this news on so I don't have to but also pass on that I don't want to talk about it.
Love, me x

Great, family break-up admin complete.
A few months after that, I met X.

Part Two

Fanny's Back

X was unlike any man I had ever been with. Physically. He was older, had a beard, loads of deep forehead lines, and all his hair was grey. He looked a bit like a bearded Gordon Ramsay, who I had watched on the telly loads and never once had hot thoughts about. But bloody hell, I ended up fancying X like mad. Not immediately. At first, I wasn't interested at all, what with him being old and grey and full of creases.

I kept X quiet from Sophie. Initially I think this was because I was a bit embarrassed about what my fanny had decided to crush on this time. I assumed, as with the Creepy Nick Method examples, that my excitement for X would fizzle out after a couple of weeks. I was up for sex, but I was not looking to meet someone serious right now—I'd only just started feeling okay from the big Three change, plus I had all the dating sites to try. I'd been too busy to sign myself up on them the last few weeks because I had got it on with an actor after meeting him at the after-party of George's show.

George had already warned Sophie and me of the perils of having sex with male actors. He had done so a few times, and said they were very fickle. They fall in love fast and by the time they have a new job they are on to a new love.

Charlie, the actor, had played the main part in the play. He was a soldier, so had spent the two and a half hours in uniform, which he looked fucking good in and which got my fanny going. In real life he wore too-tight jeans with slim boots and a lot of necklaces, and looked in mirrors a lot when he passed them: my brain scale slid down and I knew there could be nothing serious for us. But he went to good parties and was pretty charming, so I got it on with him a few times. I noticed that after the seventh occasion of seeing and having sex with him, even though his personality pretty much repulsed me, my body did something very odd, which basically made me feel like he was the most amazing human ever and I needed to see him all the time. He wasn't and I didn't, and the sex was pretty average as Charlie did have quite a small penis, which maybe was what my hole needed post all the Three painful sex, but it also meant that it didn't excite me. At all.

Being shit at leaving things, I continued to get it on with him until he told me he had landed a film role in LA and wasn't planning to come back for a while, and he would miss me and I'd impacted his life massively and, as he wished me great love and luck with whoever I met next, he took off one of his horrible crystal necklaces for me to keep. Charlie had fucking dumped me—what a cheek, and also what a relief! I put his crystal cast-offs in my present box as I was pretty sure Fran would love it.

I went into the X thing totally expecting my body to try this shit again, so I decided it needed to have some boundaries and they would be that I would see him only six times.

The first occasion we spent time on our own together, he took me for dinner to a small restaurant that had tall wooden booth seating, meaning the dinner was very private. He ordered chicken on the bone and ate it like a caveman. It put me off and I didn't feel any kind of sexual excitement towards him, but my brain found him interesting. At the end of the meal, he picked up the bone and sucked the meat off it, and even though I did that any time I ate meat on the bone, I didn't appreciate seeing him doing it. He didn't go and wash his hands after finishing, which meant if you were to sniff his fingers they'd smell meaty and of gravy. This final detail was what really made me feel certain I'd not be doing anything hot with him that night—it made me feel a bit queasy. I can't stand food particles on people's fingers; it makes me wonder what else they might be all right with having on them.

But before pudding came and after my second glass of wine, X told me a story about how he had stopped a man from drowning once. He told it matter-of-factly, like he wasn't boasting or anything. After hearing that, something relaxed in me. He moved on to the bench seat next to me to share the pudding as the table was quite deep and hard to stretch across, and once he was next to me my fanny started going mental. We snogged throughout the rest of the pudding, which they called "burnt milk" but which was essentially a crème brûlée. It was at this point I realised that X's kissing was very, *very* good. Big amount of tongue but not in a too fast or sloppy kind of manner.

When the bill came, it was shitloads. He had picked the place and asked me out so even though I offered to go halves, twice, I still very much expected him to pay. It was £75 each. That was the amount I spent on my yearly special winter heeled boots.

He let me pay half. I was a bit gutted.

When we left the restaurant, my previous excitement about his kisses had evaporated and we were both planning to head home. He lived west and I lived east, so this was where the night would end. He snogged me again against a lamppost on a side road, and the excitement came back. We pressed our bits against each other hard; his bits felt very there! And then he put his hand down my jeans and I let him finger me on the street. I was pleased I had worn my stretch jeans so it meant his hand had no problem slipping in. I didn't give it a second thought that his finger probably still had chicken juice on it and what that might mean for a potential UTI or thrush. It should continue; it was doing incredible work. As I came, I saw someone adjust their curtains and didn't even care.

X and I had met when he'd spent a few months in a corner of our office while our company finalised the paperwork for his own company and its office space. And although I had seen him at work regularly for that bit of time and we'd had polite conversation at the water dispenser, we'd not paid any major attention to each other. He then moved into the proper start-up space we leased out in West London and, as with all new additions, after a month I'd go and interview them. X had developed some kind of facial-recognition thing, which was of interest to the police and also other random places like wine shops and plant shops. He was away on the day I had to interview him, so his business partner took the meeting instead. At one of our regular "thank you to the scientists" parties, I decided X was the least boring person there, so we ended up chatting all night and that was when my fanny took over. He had emailed me the next day to tell me he thought my thinking on how "ASOS could utilise clothing recognition" was interesting, and he would be up for discussing this further over dinner or on the phone if I'd prefer.

I liked that—that he was respectful while also asking me out.

This after-dinner pavement fingering also occurred at the end of the next two dates. Being a girl is really amazing: you can actually have orgasms in public pretty easily. The second one was under the tunnel to the IMAX—he made me come in the time it took to order an Uber and wait for it to arrive. Four minutes and 45 seconds!!! The third one was behind a tree in a bushy area in a locked square. We found a gap in the railings and squeezed through into the crowded bushes. I had been touching him too, but not to the point of making him come—he must have been having to do that once he got home.

This kind of pleased me—me getting off and leaving him to sort himself out. I felt like I was back.

Although it is less exciting, it feels important to point out that our conversations prior to the street orgasms were pretty incredible too. I liked him. X was hot and kind and clever and rough and smooth and knowing and open and thought I was brilliant. But best of all he was very calm. Stable. I could tell when he talked about work that he dealt with things in that way too. He was very reassuring to be around.

Weirdly, each time we met I would have a frosty 15 minutes where both my fanny and brain would suddenly go into reverse. My fanny would shout at me through its Morse code that I didn't like him at all and my brain would ask me what the hell was I doing there?! But then, usually after approx. 1.75 glasses of wine, that would all float away and I'd suddenly want him to kiss me. And flipping heck. As I said, they were *very* good kisses. He gave incredible kisses.

After a few hours of spending time with him I would leave thinking X was a 10 on both my fanny and brain scale, but then after not seeing him for a bit he felt more like a 6, and if I googled any pictures of him it went down to a 3 as he was not at all photogenic.

We had an eight-day gap before the fifth date due to it being my thirtieth birthday and all the various celebrations I had planned. I had always assumed that my thirtieth would be massive—some kind of festival gathering with everyone there and loads of presents and all food and alcohol covered by me, and probably a band that were semi-famous who were there because our paths had crossed somewhere and it was their birthday gift to me. This was not the case, because it turns out that 30 was not the age when me or any of my friends had any kind of impressive earnings or regular encounters with those kinds of exciting people. So I postponed this plan for my fortieth and instead had a number of small gatherings across the week. A lunch with Dad and my stepmum and Jay, followed by an evening in the pub with just Jay. An afternoon tea with the work people I actually liked, ending with a trip on the London Eye (I don't know why). A four-meat meal that Sophie and George cooked, and a karaoke night with my London friends, which Al and Fran came up for. Three had asked if he could drop something off and I felt relieved that I knew in advance. He came by before the dinner night and stayed for a beer, and although it felt much easier than his rain-soaked visit, it was still a bit awkward because Sophie and George were being nice but trying to focus on cooking, and I could tell Three thought they were being weird with him. He told me so in long, late-night emails over the next few nights.

This break in seeing X meant I felt less bothered about meeting him again and so I decided I would actually end it ahead of the six-date deadline. It had been great but I didn't feel it was a good idea to have sex with someone if I had to have a 15-minute warm-up before the fancying feeling came; surely that was a sign? I'd spent five years ignoring signs, and my new thing was to listen to all of them, always. I'd promised myself that. So I decided to wear a jumpsuit for date five. A practical solution to making sure he couldn't finger me in the street as I had no power over saying no to that, it seemed.

As he brought the beer and crisps over I informed X that this would be our last date, and then we spent the next hour snogging in the pub, during which time I hugely regretted wearing that stupid jumpsuit. I went home and had a record-time wank—three minutes and 20 seconds!! You might think it's weird that I know the exact timing, but since leaving Three and getting to know my fanny again I wanted to do it properly and so kept records of its progress in a little notebook by my bed. I owed it that.

Orgasm Tally

from me   from him

卌 卌 卌 卌 | ||||

So far during this new X stage I had given myself 21 orgasms morning, night and some other times, and he had given me four. Which equalled 25 orgasms over three weeks. That was more than I'd had in total over the last few years! Who was I kidding? We needed to have sex. I'd see him one more time.

For our sixth and final date I booked a hotel. It all felt so adult and exciting. I hadn't told him. I made him meet me in the pub opposite the hotel and I got there first so I could have a beer before he arrived to see if that prevented my usual Frosty 15 Minutes. It did. I was very excited and I looked very hot, or I felt very hot, which I think equates to the same thing. He arrived looking great. He had really good dress sense and I don't think I've ever been with someone who has had that kind of style before. Not labels or flashy stuff; he just knew what clothes to wear that made him look good, and the best part was that he didn't even care—it was all by accident. God, he was so hot. And big. He was big in the right places; upper arms, hands, willy.

After sharing a packet of salt-and-vinegar crisps, a line came out of my mouth that I totally hadn't prepared: "Shall we talk about the sex we're going to *that* hotel to have?!"

It was so slick and I felt like I was playing the lead in a steamy movie.

He said yes—of course he said yes!

Walking across the road I was so, so, so, *so* excited. I had bought a see-through lingerie body suit from ASOS, the first exciting bit of underwear I had ever purchased, and I couldn't wait for him to discover it, as well as being relieved at the idea of finally taking it off because I'd been wearing it since I got dressed that morning and it was not the most practical or comfortable of items to wear all day sitting at my desk at work. It also didn't support my boobs properly, so annoyingly I'd had to walk at half my usual speed so they didn't bash about in a painful way.

When we got to the hotel room, we snogged standing up and then I took my T-shirt off and displayed the low-dipping see-through top part and X almost lost his shit. The underwear inconvenience had been worth it. He sat on the edge of the bed and we kissed and touched some more, like the most frantic, best kissing and touching in the world kind of thing.

Oh shit, it was a nice feeling. Pure, full-on desire. And finally to be set free on each other's bodies without the restriction of hiding by a bush. I felt amazing.

We started doing sexy stuff at 8 p.m. and hadn't stopped by midnight. *Four hours!!!*

I did not know sessions like this were possible. It was easy and amazing and never-ending. Our bodies were very compatible, and when his dick went inside me for the first time, him looking into my eyes while it hovered above the area before I moved into it, all slow and easily, his pupils got bigger and I did an actual gasp. Like seriously, looking into his eyes I actually gasped. Ha, what a douche! It was just all so connected.

He was about the size of the second-largest NHS dildo but it didn't hurt at all; it felt amazingly good—it was unlike any sex I'd ever had. I fucking loved it and I actually really, *really* enjoyed the going in and out bit—there was no pain at all! I thought I had never cared about that part of it. And I had thought the noises I usually made were put on, but with him I had no control over them. We did it over and over and he came three times and I had three orgasms!! The moment his tongue slowly touched the tip of my clit I almost exploded right then, and it was like that the second time too, and then the third time he did something with his teeth (at least I think it was his teeth) that was unlike any licking out I'd ever known. Prior to this I had never had more than one orgasm in a 12-hour time period! I didn't know my fanny was capable of such things. To be clear, they were all clitoral orgasms; my hole was still unable to find that feeling even with X's glorious bits, but still my vagina was a fucking legend and it was definitely not broken or being ignored anymore. It worked really, really well!!! I had never been so excited or enjoyed anything more, ever. It was quite tiring work though, and I was relieved I had two Gold bars in my bag to eat in between all the sex.

At 1 a.m. I thanked X for the last six dates and told him it had been nice getting to know him and wished him well with his future plans, then got a cab home so that Sophie wouldn't worry.

I slept amazingly that night.

The next day, completely sober and at around lunchtime and after an unsatisfactory Zara shopping session, I rang X.

"Hello! I'm going to ask you something and you must say no, OK?"

"Er, OK . . ."

"I need to say what I'm about to say and you have to say no."

"Right."

"Do you agree?"

"Yes."

"Good. Will you meet me tonight?"

". . . No?"

"Thank you, goodbye."

Urghhhhh. I'm a dick.

He rang me straight back. "I obviously really want to see you tonight!"

I was so happy. I silently punched the air like a complete loser!

"Well, you can't be trusted to follow simple instructions . . ."

Not the Plan

What happened over the next few months was an education, only one I was actually keen to get.

I learnt so much. Way more than I did throughout all of uni.

I was never not horny for X, and all my dirty (and also non-dirty) thoughts always included him. I had never experienced this kind of thing for such a long and concentrated period of time. We did soppy shit too. Every day we sent each other a song; he'd mostly send me country, funk and soul, and I'd mostly send him gangsta rap, hip hop and cheesy pop. Sometimes the songs were to express something we felt, or as a response to an earlier conversation or in anticipation of the meeting ahead. Neither of us were that up on the other's favourites so it meant there was no crossover of sending the same artist, but our tastes were quite similar so it meant we both enjoyed the other's selections and now had an abundance of new music to enjoy. I did not know I liked Merle Haggard, Bob Dylan, James Carr or Nick Cave until I met X. The age gap meant that when I would send him some of my favourite gangsta rap, he would then in return send the original sample as that had been one of his favs back when, lol. When he sent me Mtume's "Juicy Fruit" in response to Biggie's "Juicy" it sent me crazy and made me so wet listening to it I had to have a wank in the work loo!

My Orgasm Tally

from me	from him
ﬀﬀ ﬀﬀ ﬀﬀ ﬀﬀ ﬀﬀ ﬀﬀ ﬀﬀ ﬀﬀ ﬀﬀ ﬀﬀ IIII	ﬀﬀ ﬀﬀ ﬀﬀ ﬀﬀ ﬀﬀ ﬀﬀ ﬀﬀ ﬀﬀ ﬀﬀ I

I'd never sent anyone naughty pictures of myself before, but bloody hell I was on fire with that too. And I definitely had never craved getting dick pics from anyone ever, but when I asked X to send me some naked pics of him I'd zoom in on his penis and just look at it adoringly for a seriously long time. It was the first dick I had ever in my whole 30 years thought to be incredibly handsome. I had always assumed I wasn't actually into the look of a penis, that they held no beauty and deep down they weren't really for me, but his was just so lovely and strong-looking!

Part of what made this all even more exciting was that neither of us had ever done anything like this with anyone else before. Even though I was 30 now and he was in his forties, we had never thought to share content like the pictures and the song swaps before meeting each other. Maybe partly because when we had both last been single smartphones hadn't existed. But still, sharing these technological dirty firsts together felt special.

We also, strangely, sent each other personalised limericks. I don't know how this first happened; neither of us are poets or Irish. I guess this is one of the effects of really wanting someone—strange, unexplained creativity. We didn't always obey the proper limerick syllables and rhyming structure, but we did keep to the five-line AABBA formation.

X:
There once was a girl who lived for food
Until discovering something more lewd
Kisses in bushes
With deep intense pushes
Oh she loved getting screwed

Me:
There was an old man from West London
After a good session with him I felt done-in
Flipping hot sex
Always the best
Leaves my head in a bit of a spin-thing

Objectively his were probably better in terms of the language used, as he held a lot more words in his head than me due to a) being older, b) having gone to one of the good universities and c) because he read at least a book a week—on average I read five a year.

My Orgasm Tally

from me	*from him*
ℍℍ ℍℍ ℍℍ ℍℍ ℍℍ	ℍℍ ℍℍ ℍℍ ℍℍ ℍℍ
ℍℍ ℍℍ ℍℍ ℍℍ ℍℍ	ℍℍ ℍℍ ℍℍ ℍℍ ℍℍ
ℍℍ ℍℍ ℍℍ ℍℍ ℍℍ	ℍℍ ℍℍ ℍℍ I

I was orgasming on average about 15 times a week. A week!!!! That's actually flipping insane, right?

We had undertaken sexual activity in nearly every borough of London. I didn't want him coming to Sophie's as I was trying to keep us secret, because I wasn't entirely convinced we were going to be a proper thing. So we'd meet for a drink or food, and then things would always get sexy and urgent so we'd head to hotels, parks, bushes, pub loos, dark alleys, shops—nowhere was off-limits as long as it was very close by!

In Kensington and Chelsea we had sex in the Harvey Nichols department-store loos on the sixth floor, as well as fingering action in a couple of pubs, and a bush. If anyone was ever waiting outside the disabled loo in Harvey Nics and we needed to exit, I would make noises like I was being sick, flush the chain, and then when we walked out together I'd stick my belly out like I was a pregnant person having a queasy moment and he, my caring partner, was helping me with tissues held in his hand. X being older and me also looking like a proper respectable adult meant we could totally get away with this act.

In Lewisham, we had sex behind a giant bin down an alley; it was a recycling one, so not as gross as it sounds.

Richmond upon Thames was a fingering under a picnic blanket in the park while dogs ran past and the chilly sun shone down on my face.

Lambeth was sex in the loos of a medieval-themed restaurant. This was the first time I had ever had front-on, looking-at-each-other-in-a-mirror sex, which was very enjoyable and very hot.

Southwark was where we visited most hotels, as a lot of them near Elephant and Castle handily did half-day or hourly rates. In the hotels, we explored EVERYTHING from tying up, spanking and biting to gentle whole-body licking. Sex while sucking a lolly. Sex with chocolate spread around our holes. Slow, teasing top-of-the-willy sex, eye-to-eye romantic sex, dirty, hard pin-down sex, and tightly-holding-his-neck-when-he-came sex. Sex with furniture moved and mirrors positioned strategically so we could stare at ourselves. Erotic lap-dancing sex and stainy, wild period sex. Sex where I told him I was his and he was mine, and sex where he told me he was mine and I was his.

On the escalators going down into the tube station after a session, I slipped my knickers into his coat pocket for an over-night sniff loan, and told him so just before I legged it onto my tube. I then spent the whole journey feeling mega-embarrassed that I had actually taken my (slightly wet) knickers off and done that. Also, my jeans' crotch hem was making things feel not-nice and itchy. By the time I got to King's Cross, I had convinced myself it was a step too far. I had actually said the word "sniff" to him . . . When has that been sexy, ever?!! But as soon as I got reception, my phone beeped with five hot-fire emojis and two aubergines. Phew!

One evening in the City of Westminster we did some very cunning standing-in-old-tree-trunk-shadows shagging on the perimeter of St. James's Park. The shadows of the trunks meant no one could see us from the road!

In Islington we had the most exciting and rewarding sex I have ever encountered. After a nice dinner we went down a cul-de-sac for a snog and there was a parked-up crane. There was a small gap between its framework and the wall. We slipped behind it and then he slipped in me. After he had come he fingered me until I did, still standing, from behind. Near the end, just as I was about to come, my eyes fell on two unopened Mars bars just resting on the frame, level with my eyes. They were king size. It was a glorious moment. We ate them on the walk to the tube and life felt pretty amazing. The workmen must have stashed them there for their mid-morning snack. It made me laugh thinking of them looking for them the next day.

He fingered me in cinemas in Brent, Camden and Tower Hamlets. On a bus as it went through Greenwich and on the train as it passed through Kingston upon Thames.

In a pub in Hammersmith and Fulham, in order to look like we were actually talking and not just doing inappropriate dirty stuff, I created a sex-related word-association game inspired by *Wacaday*'s Mallett's Mallet, while he fingered me under the table. We just looked at each other in the eyes and took it in turns to say one word . . .

"Hard."

"Nipple."

"Skin."

"Lick."

"Tongue."

"Wet."

"Moist."

"Suck."

"Hard."

"Mouth."

"Teeth."

"Hold on, 'hard'?! We've already had 'hard' . . ."

Never mind—I was at the point of coming so I let it go.

And in Hackney on the way to work I gave him a blow job hidden in the bushes around Hackney Marshes at 7:42 on a Monday morning.

We were unstoppable. Insatiable. And throughout these times, I often stopped wearing knickers under my dresses and skirts for easier access. It was all so flipping exciting!!

I don't know what would have happened if we had met during not such a mild winter in regard to all the outside bonking. Maybe we would have persevered; the pull between us was very strong.

My Orgasm Tally

from me	from him
℔ ℔ ℔ ℔ ℔	℔ ℔ ℔ ℔ ℔
℔ ℔ ℔ ℔ ℔	℔ ℔ ℔ ℔ ℔
℔ ℔ ℔ ℔ ℔	℔ ℔ ℔ ℔ ℔
℔ ℔ I	II

By the end of month three I'd had 163 orgasms—we had been seeing each other at some point most days and were talking non-stop. Before we went to bed, as soon as we woke up, and sometimes in the middle of the night if we had both gone for our wees at the same time. On the way to the shops, in Ubers, on loo breaks—basically any minute we weren't with other people. I knew the movements of his day-to-day as well as I knew my own.

Without planning it, we started calling each other "Guv." I'm not entirely sure how that came about, but I think it was from an old police TV programme we had tried to watch before sex took over.

Also, the limericks had started to get more romantic on both sides.

Me:
You are still so so cool
The sight of you makes me drool
Your body I desire
The smell of you sets me on fire
And pursuing your happiness my only rule

X:
There once was a girl who liked milk
Whose skin was softer than silk
Her eyes they did gleam
Her mouth was a dream
There was no one else of her ilk

I do *really* like milk. Had to look up the word "ilk."

When he had to go away for a few days, on his return I presented him with a record and he gave me a pretty little bracelet with a treble clef on it. In honour of our daily song swap. Pretty soppy stuff. And quite all-consuming.

Sophie:
I missed you again! Will you be in tonight/tomorrow? And want to do a party next weekend? Xx

People whose company I normally loved and had fun with, I now found I could only handle for a couple of hours at a time, as after that I was bored by them—or more accurately I was too distracted thinking of X. Either wanting to rush off and see him, or rush off and get home alone to my bedroom so I could pore over any emails or messages he had waiting for me. My friends couldn't now hold my attention for long, but I could happily stare at X's hand holding my knee in the cinema for hours without a thought about how shit the film was. It was bonkers!

Romantic love happens to me in what I think is a normal and healthy time period. Not too quick, but soon enough to know and not be wasting time. For me, three months of seeing and being with someone almost every day, and being only happy and excited during that time, while neither of us is holding back or doing any game-playing, meant I was now in love. Which pissed me off, as this hadn't been the plan.

I don't think saying "I love you" is particularly big or scary because I feel it quite a lot in terms of my other normal, non-romantic relationships. When I first met Sophie, I knew I loved her after about six months (it can take longer with friendships depending on how intense the beginning hanging-out is, and instead of sexual action these kinds of loves are sealed with an intense drinking session together). With Al and Fran I knew I loved them after sharing a whole bottle of vodka neat with them in the cattle market at the end of Year 11, voicing all our fears about being split from our usual tutor groups for the new ones that had been decided for us when we started sixth form next term. I told them how much I loved them *all* night. I've always been very open with telling my friends when I knew I did, even though back then that meant momentarily having the piss taken out of you.

It was inconvenient that I was now in love with X. I hadn't been wanting or hoping to be with someone and I hadn't even really been bothered about him before I got to know him. I'd had big and exciting plans about what my dating life would look like once I was out of the fog of leaving Three. I felt sure that I would very much win at online dating as I loved eating and loved meeting new people, didn't suffer from nerves *and*, most importantly, didn't really have a type. I thought I'd go on loads of dates and have hot one-off sex after eating amazing meals and then they'd do something cringe or slightly psycho, which meant I couldn't see them again (which would suit me so I could move on to the next one). I'd then recall this all to Sophie over a midnight glass of Baileys (that was our thing; she and I both love drinks that taste like milky pudding) and she'd gasp and laugh and tell me that I should start a dating blog as it was all so hilarious. Which I would and it would become massively successful and ground-breaking and I'd get an award for talking about my fanny and heart so openly and also get shitloads of money. And then eventually, quite far in the future, when I did go into love again with someone, Three would be better and happy and hopefully in love too and we'd be able to be those things together but with different people.

Instead, it was 6:08 p.m. on an almost-raining Wednesday and I was sat in a pub being really weird with X as I was secretly moody that I was about to tell him I loved him for the first time. He'd brought the usual beer and salt-and-vinegar crisps over for us and I was definitely giving him more back-and-shoulder than front attention. He noticed. "Are you all right?"

"Oh yes, great."

"Do you want to turn round a bit?"

"No, no, I'm really comfortable and . . ."

He interrupted me. "It's hard to hear you."

I made myself louder, "I need to tell you something and it is much easier for me to do so from this position."

"OK . . ."

Then I turned my back completely, so that the back of my head was all he could see, and continued. "Look, it's slightly inconvenient, but I love you now."

I don't know how this news landed as I didn't turn around. That fucker better say it back in the next few seconds.

"Did you hear me?"

"No, you're facing the wrong way. Turn around . . ."

I actually couldn't. My body can be so stubborn sometimes. So he slowly pulled my shoulders round the right way and said, "What did you say?"

"I said that thing that people say when they need to say the thing they're feeling at this stage of things."

He then smiled and kissed me and said, "I'm just teasing. I heard you. I love you. Obviously."

Obviously!!!!

I felt all the feelings that could ever possibly be felt when someone you are completely obsessed and in love with confirms they feel the same, and we snogged—deep, long and very connected kisses.

And this made me *very* wet, obvs.

To celebrate I took him down an alley near the pub and gave him a blow job in the bottom corner, which, halfway through, I realised actually smelt quite pissy as I think it is a popular spot for tramps to wee unseen. But we both loved each other, so woohoo!

Once the love words had been spoken out in the open, it was a very exciting progression for our limericks.

Me:
My creamy dreamy gangsta Guv
Touching me gently or giving me a shove
I want it
You're fit
Then, now, next Thursday, forever my love.

X:
We go together like a hand in a glove
Like it's been decreed from far up above
When you're wrapped around me
It's mind-blowing you see
There's a word for it, Guv. It's called love.

Yeah, he was better at making them up than me. And yeah, the Guv thing had properly hung around.

I loved getting limericks from him, and other messages and love letters. And I loved that our becoming in love happened this way, through written declarations, as we spent quite a few nights apart.

We really wanted more of each other but we couldn't spend all our time together as he had two children and still lived in the same house as his wife.

Loving X

At first I hadn't minded at all; it suited me. I didn't want things to move fast and I had liked that X had proper commitments elsewhere. Plus, it was such a relief to have no pressure on me about the future and children. Before meeting X, even though I hadn't managed to try out Tinder, I had been on two other set-up dates with two guys who had been around my age, and it was clear that children were in their life plan and marriage too. It made me feel immediately stressed. I couldn't give them those things, so no point in seeing them again. X posed no such threat; I guess that's why it all happened so easily with him—there was no pressure at all; it felt simple.

But now that we were In Love I didn't want him to continue living with his ex. I hadn't felt bothered about her existence at all before, but post-Love I had started to get a bit jealous about him living with another woman. I didn't want to live with him either, I just wanted him to a) not live with her, and b) have a place of his own that I could visit when I liked, as even though I now loved X, I still wanted to keep us a private thing until it became clearer what it was. I didn't want Sophie to know, and I definitely didn't want Three to know. Therefore, X needed a flat, somewhere we could cook and have baths and naked dances.

I had never sat in a bath with anyone I had romantic feelings for before meeting him. I've always enjoyed solo baths and on average would have two a week, but being in one with him and with alcohol was amazing! We'd have Prosecco and long talks and then normally some kind of awkward bath sex. It was a great way to wash.

Back when we did the I Love You exchange, before the pissy blow job, I told him it would be hard to progress if he remained living with his ex, and he agreed and said it was time for them to make their separation more official—i.e., tell the children and their parents, and live separately. He and his ex had been together 13 years, and although they didn't argue and genuinely liked one another, there was only platonic friendship there now. I could totally relate to that. We are all such a stupid, thick bunch, bumbling along in whatever not-quite-right versions of relationships the long years have created. If I had wanted children, their situation could have easily ended up being mine and Three's.

That night after the Love exchange, I told X I had cheated on Three—words I hadn't even let myself say out loud before. Told him what I had created to cope: the drugs and the Creepy Nick Method. I went through all the men. Even the ones I couldn't tell you about earlier, like the ugly footballer I had met in a club on a girls' holiday in Spain two months after my honeymoon. I slow-grinded against him while snogging his face off by the wall at the back, until I noticed Fran heading my way. As we left he slipped me his mobile number, and when I got back to our hotel I called him from the bathroom of the shared bedroom and we spoke dirty to each other until I came—even though my phone company didn't have a deal with other countries in Europe, meaning I knew it would cost me shitloads of money!

X confided that he had done a similar thing with his ex— one-off moments with a couple of strangers over the years to give him something sexually that for whatever reason he and her no longer shared together.

We were both very ashamed and relieved to be able to be

completely honest about it to someone at last. And we spoke at length about the fact that neither of us had felt any guilt about doing this while in the things we had been in, but how it had caught up with us now.

In the months immediately after leaving Three, I had done a lot of internal thinking and stressing. The "what kind of person actually am I?" kind of thing. It worried me that I seemed to do what I wanted when I was with boyfriends. Was I inherently selfish because I was built that way? My dad had cheated on my mum and maybe it was just something passed on like his good skill in maths and his ski-jump nose? It worried me that with Three I had genuinely felt like I deserved to follow through on my attraction to other men. That it was in me and I had no say over it—it could not be changed, and therefore it was a positive thing that I used for good by helping me manage my life with Three. And that taking the time to set up the rules made me feel different, more thoughtful than my dad.

But these talks with X made me realise otherwise. Cheating and being selfish wasn't decided by what kind of parents I had been given. It was decided by what kind of truth I wanted to have with myself. What level of denial I was unwilling to accept. Normal, nice people cheat, coz normal, nice people just have to get by in the version of life they've found themselves in. But I was now out of that and free and could live only in truth with myself. It felt like *such* a relief!

X and I realised there had been moments in our last relationships, way before either of us cheated, when something had changed and not worked for us, but sadly neither of us had mentioned this to our partners. He could pinpoint the moment he should have said something to his wife, and I could with Three. His was after their first child was born and she took some exciting job that meant she had to spend weekdays in Paris and he didn't say the truth of how that felt. Mine was the first time I had found sex difficult, two years in—if I had brought it up then, and continued to talk about it, we would have either fixed it or broken up sooner.

Sharing these new thoughts and realisations, stuff I hadn't even told Fran and Al, felt easy with X. After the huge download, we were very excited about a new way to be. Honest. We declared that we would communicate all things, always, meaning we'd be a step ahead before whiffs of problems or cheating could take over.

I felt sure this was the answer.

The talking.

Three months turned to six and the hotness of us, the sex and orgasms, they didn't calm down. At all! With both of us coming at least three times whenever we met. There was no exact routine to this but often I would end one orgasm and then immediately afterwards X would continue and I would get another one from a different position of licking. The first would happen quite quickly as I was usually in such a state of excitement. The second would be pretty quick too, especially if we'd had sex in between, as it *really* turned me on that he would lick me after coming inside me. There was something about knowing that he was taking in his own come that just drove me crazy, like I had tricked him or something. It made me feel empowered that if I swallowed it, then so did he. Previously, whenever I had been licked I would need the tongue to leave the area as soon as it was done. But with him I would want it to linger and explore the areas around my clit, my hole, my other hole, the bridge between them! Which he did without me having to ask. And, when in the right position to do so, I would look him straight in the eyes, something I had never wanted to do with anyone before. It felt sooooo naughty. Which is silly, coz I looked him in the eyes all the time over eating food and other normal stuff.

But I'd had them so tightly shut before that this felt new and erotic.

He would lick me even when I was on my period, adapting his style to be less hole-focused, but still being so up for it, which really turned me on as I loved that he didn't care. He loved my smell whatever stage my fanny was at, from the more metal-y times to the hard-to-explain onion one that would occur once a month. Watching him take enjoyment from sniffing it was just the best feeling in the world.

He also introduced me to a finger up my bum while being licked, as well as stuff like holding my arms tightly as if they were tied, and then sometimes he would actually tie me up, teasing me for ages before eventually making his way to my clit. While I was tied and trapped, he loved licking my whole body, and I mean every bit—even in between my toes, which actually wasn't so hot for me and made me feel a bit stressed. Also, if I thought about his saliva drying on my shoulders or knuckles it would take me out of the moment because dried saliva, no matter how fresh your breath is, always smells a bit rank. It made me want to move away but, being tied up, he'd interpret my extra wriggling around as taking pleasure in the situation.

He licked me out in every kind of position humanly possible: standing up, half-crouching with one leg up on the bed, kneeling, flat on my front, bent over in a roly-poly, and positions where my body had been held in such an awkward way that I couldn't straighten up for five minutes after. I got an incredibly strong core at this time and wondered if a lot of what I was doing was basically expert-level yoga.

I *really* enjoyed licking his dick. Even the days when it smelt super-strong, on him that just got me going more. I also licked him in every position and created naughty scenarios and outfits that would always make him get that pre-come dribble, which

I fucking loved licking off. I actually liked the taste of his come and even liked tasting his bum—my first ever bum-licking experience—I'd been a bit one-way with that street before X. It wasn't as bum-tasting as I had feared, and I *loved* how excited it made him. No one had ever gone near that area before; I liked being the first. One particularly hard-core session, I tied him up and put my vibrator up it. It was one of the lipstick-sized ones, so nothing too intrusive, but it made me feel so powerful entering him in some way. He was a bit nervous, which added to my enjoyment.

I wanted to make videos! So we bought a tripod and discussed angles and rough story notes before we filmed it. These were videos I wanted to watch, not all that shit, hard-banging porn bollocks. Slow, sensual fucks with close-up licking out to climax. Knowing I was being filmed made me prickle with excitement, and after completion we would watch them back together while he was inside me, gently stroking my clit. That's weird, right? Two people looking at themselves naked and getting off on it?! In one video, where I was doing what is apparently known as the reverse cowboy, I was mesmerised by the back view of my body; the curve of my back, how tanned and smooth it looked, and my hips—I loved how curvy they looked. I had never seen myself from this angle and I liked it very much. I actually looked good! I knew without heels I was shortish and had a biggish bum, which I did wish was a bit smaller or that I was taller to balance it out, as with clothes on, whenever I had looked at the behind of me in the mirror, I wasn't overjoyed with the view. But now, with no clothes on, I looked beautiful and felt proud. Our homemade pornos had given me a sense of confidence I'd not had before, as well as being an excellent aid for me to use to wank over when he wasn't around.

My Orgasm Tally

from me	from him
HHT HHT HHT HHT HHT	HHT HHT HHT HHT HHT
HHT HHT HHT HHT HHT	HHT HHT HHT HHT HHT
HHT HHT HHT HHT HHT	HHT HHT HHT HHT HHT
HHT HHT HHT HHT HHT	HHT HHT HHT HHT HHT
HHT HHT HHT HHT HHT	HHT HHT HHT HHT HHT
HHT HHT HHT III	HHT HHT HHT HHT I

Sex continued to evolve. One session while he was inside me, we even came at the same time. It took fucking ages but was incredible. It was still a clitoral orgasm, but he had been practising and perfecting being in me from a side position while reaching round and stroking my clit. It was interesting, coz if he moved too fast or did the normal dick moves that I usually loved, it would take my brain away from the pleasure of the clit feeling and then we'd be a few steps back. It was apparent that anything too large or fast-moving in my hole was not going to help me come. It was a fine balance for him between not coming and not losing his erection. But we persevered, and coming together meant everything to me. It was the first ever time I had achieved this, and it made me feel like I had won and I was properly in tune with my now working-ever-so-well fanny. We practised this method, and within a month I was able to have more rigorous movement in the hole and also a quicker climax by using my lipstick vibrator instead of his finger. It was fabulous. On one of the tries, I said to him, mid-session, how I would *love* it if somehow his tongue could be down there at the same time as his dick being in me. This thought drove me crazy, and it was the start of our talking aloud about fantasies where we had extra, make-believe people join us in certain imaginary hot situations. We tried out talking about both genders but neither of us would get turned on with any extra male involvement. Which is a bit weird considering I'm into men. But also, my porn preference was always only women so maybe it wasn't that odd.

So for our fantasy talk it was always women who would join us. It would drive me crazy asking him to describe her and what she was doing to me and then him. He was unsure at first. Had never done this and nor had I. Over a pint we had a clear conversation about the rules, as I had also got a bit confused wondering if I actually wanted a threesome. If I did, this felt like something I could totally explore with X.

I asked him. "So who would she be?"

"The simplest option would be to pay someone, but I don't think I feel comfortable with that."

X didn't watch porn and had proper morals around those things—more than I did, for sure. I continued, "It would need to be someone we didn't know, though."

"Yes. I agree, no one familiar."

"Yes. But we'd want to be able to trust her."

"Yes."

"Especially with sexual health; imagine if she gave us cold sores forever?!"

"You can only catch them if they're active."

"I wouldn't want to risk it, and also we would need to ensure that she wouldn't turn mental or fall in love with you."

"Or you."

"Or you with her."

"Well, that wouldn't happen from one night."

"You told me you knew after one night with me."

"Yes, but that was different."

"But it happened. It could happen again!"

My face felt hot.

"Hey, don't get upset."

"I don't like her and I don't want her around."

188

"I don't even want to be with another woman, I only want it if you want it."

"I don't want it."

"Neither do I."

"OK, good. Are you getting ready salted or salt and vinegar?"

"What would you prefer?"

"Salt and vinegar, please."

Talking about it clearly, away from that heady desire place, it was clear that neither of us wanted an actual real-life threesome. We loved the fantasy but practically it wouldn't work for us.

I guess that's the point with our brains and fantasy scenarios—it's okay for some things to only ever remain in them. Like sometimes when I walk over Waterloo Bridge, my deep-down-in-my-brain voice would say, "Why don't you jump off?" Not in a sad, end-my-life way—normally it would occur when I was in an excited mood; it was saying it to dare me, make my heart beat a bit faster. I would consider the thought properly for about two seconds and then my brain would move on. Which seems to be the actions of a normal and healthy mind (I googled it). In X's and my fantasy talk-out moments, we were staying in that brain place for longer than normal, which is why I think we got confused about if we wanted it to become real.

Clever

Sophie:
Do you want to come to the
Proxo opening with me tonight? I
never see you anymore!!!

I rang X. "Sophie will be out tonight, so you can come to ours!"

"Actually, I was going to see if you could do tomorrow instead—one of the dance parents is ill and they need someone to drive them after practice. Do you mind?"

"No, that actually works better. Sophie invited me to her thing."

"Do you think she'll be out tomorrow so I can still come round?"

"Not sure, I'll suss it out later!"

X and I spent our evenings together either at hotels he'd paid for or at ours when Sophie and George were out. Which was actually quite a lot as George was always working and Sophie was normally doing something. He'd either leave before they were home or creep out quietly later when they were in their bedrooms, or sometimes he'd have to sneak down the stairs when they were watching *Homeland* in the lounge. He had practised avoiding the stairs that creaked and was under strict instructions not to whisper as he left, as no man can whisper successfully.

Me:
Yes that would be great!

Sophie and I decided not to meet somewhere before, since there would be free everything at the Proxo opening, so better to head straight there. She had a new friend with her, someone she had started hanging out with who did something at Proxo, and I couldn't tell if she was being weird with me or just doing her new-friend-nerves thing. When the friend, Toni, went to the loo I asked her what she was doing tomorrow night.

"I don't know yet."

She *was* being weird with me.

In the taxi on the way home, a bit upset, she informed me that she knew about me and X. Not it being X specifically, but that I was seeing someone.

"Why have you been lying to me?"

"What do you mean?"

"I know you're seeing someone."

"I was going to tell you, I just . . . How did you know?"

"It was pretty obvious. You've been spending hours in your room apart from water breaks where you come into the kitchen looking like you've played a rugby match, and then we'd hear heavy footsteps leaving."

"Oh, sorry, I told him to be quiet!"

"It's not really on, not letting us know there's someone in our house."

"Sorry. I honestly hadn't thought of that."

"I'm actually pretty pissed off about it."

"Oh no, I'm really sorry. I wasn't thinking."

"And you didn't want to tell me?"

"Not you personally; I didn't want to tell anyone. Not yet. I just wanted to see how it went. And I took up so much of your time with all my Three upset, I thought you'd be sick of me going on about another man. Honestly."

"I wish you had trusted me and told me."

"I'm sorry. I do now too. I just knew how intense all the

Three stuff had been, him turning up a few times, his diagnosis fallout. I think I decided that I couldn't have both conversations with you—the utter joy with X and the deep sadness for Three—like that would have been greedy, or that I was wrong to have these two conflicting feelings at the same time and it made me feel a bit weird. So I just hid it."

"So it is something with him?!"

"Yes!!!"

"I actually met him at a conference—he seems nice."

I mean, this is the best news you can hear from a friend who is actually upset and pissed off with you.

"Are we OK?"

"Yes. Of course. Just don't keep things like that to yourself again."

I wouldn't, I wouldn't. I felt like a really shit friend and I wouldn't be again.

At home over a full, large wine glass of Baileys (the only way Sophie served it), I told her what I'd learnt since meeting X—that my fanny had actually not been broken, just the thing between me and Three. The months wasted at the NHS gyno department. And, in the spirit of being honest, I told her about my cheatings and how they had helped to keep me living that life for longer. She was shocked, but also not judgy. She got quite teary when I recalled how it felt when I had to have actual sex with Three; that it made me feel stressed and in pain. And then I got teary too. Even though Three was a great person, it's insane how quickly sex can turn into something that feels like a punishment.

I explained why I no longer did coke on our big nights out and she said she thought that was the saddest part. Not that I no longer racked them up with her, but that I had used it to cope. And for the first time, something affected me in a way I'd not experienced before and I got very upset. How could I have treated myself so badly for so long? What kind of dickhead was

I? I was thick. Sophie comforted me and told me I wasn't thick, that I was brave. "Some people never change their circumstances; you have!"

I had.

She also said, while being careful to acknowledge how much she had liked Three and could see he was a good one, that what he had done in fights and his behaviour was emotional abuse.

When she said those words I had the automatic feeling of wanting to punch her, but I didn't let myself, obviously. Instead, my head got very hot and my face turned red, like how it would when I got caught stealing sweets from Woolworths' pick 'n' mix and Mum made me apologise to the shop person.

I pretended to get a cushion and moved further away down the sofa. I couldn't agree with that; that felt really over the top. Three's behaviour was bad, yes, but I responded with as bad, maybe even worse. I told her about the knife. She still insisted what he did was emotional abuse. She was speaking kindly, but it felt like she was being a cunt. Luckily the pudding-like nature of a full, large wine glass of Baileys means you can't actually get drunk off it—if I had drunk that same amount of white wine I might not have coped with my feelings in this moment. Might not have been able to control my anger. I moved the conversation on. I told her I would think about *that* another time. I reminded her that this had a happy outcome; I was now aware and living properly in truth with myself, no coping-drug-taking, no making my fanny do things it didn't want to do, and I had found my new way, one person at a time!

To be clear, my new lifestyle choice was in place to make sure I did the best by myself. People can do what they want. I just knew that me cheating did not lead to healthy places for my body and brain.

10 Out of 10

As the months moved closer to a year, the sex continued to be spontaneous and adventurous and my fanny was always mega-excited by X. Although I did notice a small pattern with him. The first shag or coming situation would normally be quite easy to make happen quickly, especially if I was in full tease mode. The second one would normally be a bit more fantasy-based with us talking aloud about stuff, and the third one, which was a little harder for him to get to, would normally involve a wilder and rougher kind of sex, normally with him dominating me in some way—the classic being me, face down and lying flat, with him just fucking the hell out of me while maybe holding my mouth shut or pinning me down. Which I flipping loved.

We still saw each other most days and continued treating the whole of London like it was our bedroom, even though now we were openly able to be at mine whenever we wanted. We just couldn't always hold on till then!

It was amazing and slightly unbelievable. I couldn't understand why, this long in, we were still so into each other and doing it at such a prolific rate. But bloody hell, I was pleased that we were. And now it seemed I had only one type: him. Still a 10 on the fanny and brain scale.

Extraction

X hadn't found telling his children he was moving out easy at all. They were aged seven and eleven. Telling their mum had been okay, kind of—he had done this quite quickly after our being-in-love conversation three months in, but he had been very worried beforehand. He rang me from the Pets At Home carpark, quite nervous, which was a side of him I had never seen before. He asked if he could tell her that it was because he had met and fallen in love with me, as that would make things so much easier for him to explain why he was leaving now, but this panicked me and I just didn't think it was fair, because he had said it was already over with her, so why bring me into things?

At that point I was still having quite a hard time with Three; he was being difficult with our flat sale and we hadn't even got on to divorce stuff. I didn't want to hurry him and cause fights, but it had been over eight months and having everything still tied up in "us" made me experience on a low level the sinking-sand feeling. I just didn't have the head space to be part of X's break-up too. He understood and found a way to tell her, but he was unable to tell the children that day. He was dreading that. He didn't want them to worry and be upset at the thought of their dad not being around. She had said they could wait and do it together but that he should be the one to lead. She didn't seem in too much of a rush, I guess coz they had been bobbing along in this way for so long, and with her not knowing about me, why not take time? That had been my instinct with Three.

It was later that month after telling her, four months into our thing, that they had both planned to tell the girls. He rang me just before he was doing it and again he sounded very unlike his usual self. I was doing some pre-spring tanning in the most sheltered corner of our yard, and he was pacing around Hyde Park looking for something in the fresh air to help give him some strength. That old classic. X's voice kept cracking; he was so worried what this might "do" to the girls. And although I told him lots of positive things, like "it will be okay" and "fear is always worse in our heads," and I gave lots of examples of my friends who had very happy upbringings after their dads had moved out, by the end of the phone call he didn't sound any better. After our conversation had ended I had a really sick and worried feeling in my stomach and chest. I couldn't tell if it was because I wanted this to be all right. (I really, really, really wanted this to be all right), or if it was because I knew I had slightly lied to him. By omission. That I wasn't okay after my mum left and it definitely affected me for a long time on and off. But that was different as a) she was a mum leaving and b) she went really far away, whereas he was the dad *and* planned to see them *a lot*, being as much in their lives as he was now.

I'd always held back on telling X the feelings I sometimes had in response to his fear—that even though he was planning to be only a few streets away, that he was petrified of what damage this may do to the girls. I didn't let him know how hurt that made me feel, to see him as a parent putting that much thought into something not half as big as what my mum decided with me. I think I instinctively knew having that conversation might not help him with all this.

I texted X telling him to listen again to the song for the day I'd sent him, which was M.O.P.'s "Ante Up," because it would help his brain not go to worrying places. Then I rolled onto my front and cried over the situation and my left contact lens rolled out of my eye with my stream of tears. It was because it was a toric lens; the right one was normal and never got cried out, but this stupidly shaped one couldn't keep its grip when things got too wet.

X told me he'd ring me after, and an hour and 27 minutes later, my mobile rang. He had done it and I felt so relieved; it hadn't been a nice feeling, having it hanging over us. He said the girls were confused and sad, especially the youngest one—she had been very upset and said some random stuff about worrying she wouldn't see her grandma as much, which was a bit thick as she didn't see her that much anyway, but she was only seven and I obviously didn't say that out loud to X. He and his wife agreed that he would continue to stay in the guest room for a little while longer to give the girls time to get used to the idea. X checked with me that I was okay with this, which I actually properly was. I didn't like the idea of little people being upset over there, and I wished to myself that he had already sorted this out before he had gone on that first date with me. But I got it. I really did.

X said things might be easier with working out the next step of flat stuff if we were able to think about it as a place to live together, and he asked again if he could now mention me to his ex. Deep down inside me where all my major life rules were created, away from the Three stuff, I felt it *very* important that X didn't rush this process or mention me to any of them at this early stage. That the children should be allowed to get used to their dad living elsewhere, and for a while, so that they didn't have to experience too much change all at once and they could see that their lives wouldn't be that much different and that they would still feel happy and okay, coz crucially they had two very decent people as their parents (which, from what I had observed about X and the things he had mentioned about his wife, they were).

I was six when my dad moved out and in with his new partner, so I think that had all been relatively easy for me in terms of not missing him, because I'm pretty sure the only thing I was into back then was eating. However, the one thing I did know for sure was how shit having "step-parents" was. Even the nice ones—they were annoying and crap at getting it right and basically it would be better if they could just not be around. I hate the term "step-parent." I think it's a bollocks title and puts a lot of pressure on something that should just happen gently and organically, and which should have no official parenting rights. Too many of these "step-parents" abuse powers they don't actually have or haven't earnt yet. And it made the "parent" part of the word confusing when you were young, because mostly none of the natural things you felt happy being like and doing with your actual parents were applicable to these "step-beings." It really pissed me off when Clintons started making a range of cards for them.

Even though I didn't want children who had come out of me, I actually loved being around them and found them much easier company than most adults I knew. At the right time, I knew I would make an excellent non-step-related-adult to the girls. But they needed a good amount of time first.

X agreed.

Not mentioning me at this stage wasn't just about thinking of the girls, it was for me as well. I told him that only being halfway through my current rental contract at Sophie's, as well as not being further along with the flat sale, meant I needed more time to work my stuff out. Which he understood. Plus, until he had moved out and was in his own place and things were actually more proper with us, I wouldn't 100 per cent know how things really, truly felt for us as a couple. I didn't communicate that part with him, though, as he had enough to be worrying about.

And so that was the beginning of the slow steps of X extracting himself from the family home. His wife was very private and asked that they keep this between them for a while. She was five years older than him and X said they never communicated hard things openly, which is why I guess they were both in the mess that they now were in. I find it hard knowing how to refer to her here. She was his ex in terms of them both knowing the relationship was done, but then legally she was his wife. But wife sounds like such an active word, plus even when I was married I never referred to myself as a wife, so it feels extra-weird calling her his one. Ex-wife isn't accurate either, because you needed the actual divorce to make that a fact, which I knew would take ages—Three and I hadn't even got through the initial registration admin for ours yet. So I think the best thing going forward is to refer to her as Almostexwife.

Even though I had no plans whatsoever to move in with X, I helped him look at rental studio flats near where Almostexwife and his children lived, as it did feel exciting knowing he would have a place where we could be completely on our own together. I couldn't wait!

When X had bought their house, it had been in a part of London that no one wanted to live in, but now the area was in high demand, which meant the nearby offerings he could afford were a bit dismal. I suggested looking further away but he was adamant that he needed to be within a 10-minute cycle of the girls to make sure that taking them to school every day and being at their sports matches and swimming training, etc. wouldn't change.

I never thought I would live a life where I gave one shit about these things, but seeing how X factored all this into his planning made me love him so much more. Regardless of how he had dealt with his and Almostexwife's situation, he was a really good dad, and even though him being a bad one would have initially benefited me much more during this time (i.e., I would have seen him loads more, he would have been less sad, and I wouldn't have had to trek to West London), I was so pleased to see that he actually gave huge thought about the girls. Maybe you're a parent and you're reading this thinking, "Of course." But I've not had children and I've only had quite selfish parents, so it was genuinely quite eye-opening to witness this kind of behaviour first-hand. I honestly hadn't realised it could be this way. It made me feel hopeful for life in general and proud of the man he was. And just sometimes it made me feel really angry for a split second, but I would remind myself that wasn't X's fault.

The Manifesto

Two months after the I-love-you conversation, and a month after telling the girls, X had found a grotty studio flat to rent. I was pleased but also sad for him as it did look like a tiny pile of shit and he was getting well into his forties! Still, it meant he could move things on. He signed with the letting agent and was able to move in at the end of that month. We went out for dinner to celebrate, I ate a whole ball of burrata to myself for a starter, and in the taxi home he fingered me.

As the move-out date came closer, X started dreading telling the girls that he was actually leaving now. I tried to really understand, but I couldn't completely. And it was, on a small level, pissing me off.

After my dad left my mum she tried her best but was the kind of person that was only okay if she had a boyfriend. She dated some cool guys—a tennis player, a racing driver, a man who owned his own swimming pool(!!)—but in the end she settled with Bobby and his animal sanctuary in San Francisco. Which was ironic as she had played a big part in our first dog's death by keeping and using slug pellets that weren't safe for pets. Mum had been way more okay with leaving me with my dad to go and live all the way over there than X was being about moving five minutes away. And we didn't even have the internet properly back then.

X needed to get a grip. He would get teary if he focused on things like knowing he wouldn't be in the same house as their daily teeth-brushing and other non-exciting, normal girls-related life stuff. I suggested all kinds of practical bits of help, but really this was way out of my experience. I told him I'd be there for him and have the best new-flat move-in survival pack ready for him on the actual day. I couldn't wait. I knew he'd be okay once it was all done, but I had to keep my excitement under wraps while he went through this worrying stage.

He got upset after sex one night, that this was all going to be too much for me. "Are you sure you want this?"

"You? I love your body!"

"No, everything I come with. Children. Cruddy studio flat. I'm 50 in nine years!"

That *did* sound old. "Well, you don't look a day over 45!"

He looked depressed so I squeezed his cheek. "The shitty flat is just a stop-gap, and I'm pleased you have children. I don't think I'd have loved the version of you without them as much as this one. Plus, with the age-maths it makes more sense to round down, not up. OK?"

He pulled me to him and kissed me and told me he loved me and my insides did all the same tingly things that they now always did around him and almost an hour later we came up for air.

"Seriously, please don't worry about me and my feelings for you in all this. I'm here and I'm not going anywhere. *And* I'm not in a rush. I know the girls need to come first and I want them to. I'm relieved that you're not going to be a dad who leaves and isn't around for his children, and I'm relieved that your time won't be all mine!"

And I honestly was. I had been with someone whose time was all mine, and look where that got me. It excited me to be with someone who had other things to keep him busy. I think that's what I needed.

X had asked me once if I ever thought I'd change my mind

about wanting children. I normally felt annoyed when people asked me this but with him I didn't and took a moment to really think before replying. "Change is the one thing we can all rely on, but I'd be very shocked if that happened to me with this. Are you worried I'll want them?"

"Not worried, no. I know I'm not bothered about having any more, and ideally wouldn't have any more, but I would consider it if your feelings ever changed."

That felt really special. I might not want them, but I did want someone to love me *that* much that they'd want to have them with me. Fuck, I loved him and I didn't want to fuck this up.

While X concentrated on finding the right time to tell the girls he was actually moving out, I concentrated on creating a manifesto. Something that would safeguard us and all the sexually exciting things we had discovered and which I knew I now needed in a relationship to ensure previous dodgy ways didn't creep in. Since leaving Three, and getting the brilliant knowledge that hindsight gives, plus all the information I had learnt about X and Almostexwife's relationship journey, I had expanded on some of my theories:

— Having children makes your relationship suffer and they are often the thing that then keeps you trapped in something you'd rather not be in. So dodge at all costs.

— Humans tend to tick off all the "normal" relationship steps without properly considering what they really want. Move in together/get married/have a child/have another one. Lame.

— There is no guide for those who don't want to do the "normal" relationship steps. And if you're a woman in your early thirties who knows she doesn't want children, 99 per cent of people say something along the lines of "that'll change, you'll see." Fuck you, pal.

– Full-time living together makes domestic boredom come on quicker, and this domestic blandness is usually covered over with something from the "normal" relationship steps.

– Waking up together every day makes you take each other for granted.

– "I love you" seems to be said too much and its impact lost. And it's also a completely useless guide to where you are in your relationship, as it appears many of us still tell the other person that we love them right up to telling them it's over.

– It's people's actions in the relationship that matter the most. Nice ones, bad ones. Clock them.

– Sexual ways easily become lazy, boring and formulaic. Especially if you have followed the "normal" relationship steps.

– Bad behaviours and patterns are very hard to break once set.

– When respect is lost it's very hard for your fanny to get wet. And a dry fanny = painful sex. And if the loss is from deep within you, even lube can't help.

– Not communicating true feelings is the slow start to relationship doom.

I intended to use these theories to create my Manifesto—a set of rules to support the things I knew I didn't want in my life in response to a relationship, i.e.:

Marriage
My own children

Toxic arguments
Dry fanny and dull sexual routine
Fanny pain
Addiction to anything (i.e., something I relied on for longer
   than three months to aid a relationship)

The addiction thing sounds a bit extreme as it's hard to think
of in such small quantities, but that desire to need something
to help me through was the thing that scared me the most, and
I couldn't afford to let it back into my usual ways.

The Manifesto would ensure I kept these things away. And
most importantly, it would help my fanny operate, with the
man it loved, in the best form possible, i.e., wet. It was a guide
for the unconventional, long-lasting, monogamous love and
exciting sex I wanted.

I came up with the following to start it off:

1. Monitor fanny wetness.
2. At least once a month, a fingering should occur in a
   room that isn't a bedroom in the primary living place,
   and also somewhere outside of the primary living place.
3. Licking should include more than one position a couple
   of times a month, and should occur outside of the bedroom at least once a month.
4. Blow jobs should take place outside the bedroom more
   than once a month.
5. Sex should continue to be sought in rooms that aren't the
   bedroom at all times of day (minimum once a month).
6. Continue finding new ways to have sex.
7. Dirty texts should be sent at least once a week (more
   frequent during time apart).
8. Phone/FaceTime sex to be engaged in at least once a
   week when away.

9. Agree on sexual-fantasy-world ground rules for role-play (no describing of people we have seen/known).
10. No wanking over real people.
11. Create own porn videos (more crucial for times apart).
12. At least once a year take time together to reassess and update the sexual aids, which make things hot (e.g., an outfit/tool).
13. Naked dance once a month.
14. Communicate any change of feeling in regard to sexual stuff.
15. Prosecco in the bath at least once a month.
16. Make sure you treat each other how you would have during the first few months (i.e., in terms of politely tolerating gross food on mouth, bad breath, lateness, etc.).
17. Be wary of feeling urges around all "normal" relationship stages. Question everything and come up with at least four other options before committing to one.
18. Ideally don't live together full-time. Or sleep away from the home separately at least once a month.
19. Clean teeth at different times in an evening to prevent the habit of bedtime ritual, which leads into dull bed-only just-before-sleep sex.
20. No flossing in front of each other, ever.
21. Sleep on different sides of the bed once a month.
22. Domestic bills should be agreed and divided up prior to some kind of serious shared living arrangement, meaning each person is only responsible for that and no dull conversations should be needed concerning them.
23. No joint accounts.
24. Don't have children.
25. Years in, still continue to meet for lunches, etc. during the working day.
26. When apart, write letters.

27. When bad patterns occur, clock them, monitor them and set up a reward system over a period of time to help break them. Apparently most habits take 21 days to change.
28. Communicate always, even the hard stuff (ideally as close as possible to feeling it).
29. The only promise you are allowed to make is that you will always communicate honestly.

It was a bit repetitive in places and maybe too long. I googled "average size of a manifesto" and a link to the Labour Party's PDF came up. It was 122 pages and had lots of subsections. Maybe I would consider headings for the second draft. As it was, my 29 bullet points felt like a good start to ensuring long-term sexual desire and general good health in the relationship.

X and I had actually discussed a lot of the above and he seemed as excited and into my theories as me, although he did always point out that he thought rules, in general, were not a helpful thing in life, that they created pressure. Which I agreed with, but also every human has rules—especially those who don't think they do. Better to have something agreed upon and out in the open so you both know where you stand. That's all rules actually are. Two people naturally and honestly communicating what does or doesn't work for them. X had agreed with that.

Taking on X's thoughts around "rules," I would amend my terminology so that my Manifesto was more a set of guidelines, a starting point to be checked in with, like you would with an MOT. And just as equipment modernises and exhaust pipes become extinct, this list too might evolve and adapt to our changes. Maybe in 10 years' time I will suddenly stop enjoying being pinned against a wall and fingered, coming as my legs go weak. Maybe I'll find that g-spot in my bum which everyone goes on about and then that becomes the thing I'll need weekly. In which case I would add it in.

I added another point on the list.

30. Set a yearly date to check in and adapt any points where needed.

Prior to our next stage of his studio-flat move-in, and after he had moved on from his current stressful state, I decided I would present my guidelines to X. Even though they were mainly for me to ensure I would never accidentally tumble down a wrong-for-me relationship road again, I did want his buy-in also. It felt like the most important "contract" I had ever cared about. (I wouldn't call it a contract to him, obvs!)

X picked a Tuesday to move into the grotty studio flat. I was due to visit him there after work. At 11:39 a.m. he rang me—he was having trouble breathing. "I can't . . . it's my . . . something's wrong . . ."

"Hold on, it's OK. Just stop trying to talk for a minute and breathe in and out slowly a few times."

I could hear him slowing his breathing down.

"That's good. And sit down if you aren't already."

"I am."

"Good. It's OK, this will pass. You'll be OK . . . Are you OK?"

He calmed back to normal after about five minutes. Said he didn't know what was going on. I think it was a panic attack. It was hard to tell as I couldn't see him, but I had seen someone at work have one and it sounded the same.

"I can't go to that awful flat."

I felt sick hearing this, and accidentally dropped my phone coz my hand had turned completely cold even though the weather was lovely spring warm.

"Don't you kind of have to? Isn't Almostexwife wanting you to just get on and do it now?!"

"She's fine with it taking as long as it needs. We're both worried about Tammy."

Tammy was their youngest. X started to cry. "I know this is related to fear, I just don't know how to overcome it."

"Don't worry, I know this is super-hard. Could you maybe talk to someone about it? Someone proper. Next week perhaps?"

If he didn't go and speak to someone about it, I didn't see how I could continue with him. I knew where that non-talking version of stuff led to—what it had meant for me and Three. I can't be with someone who doesn't take the appropriate steps to get help. But he agreed to straight away.

"Yes, yes, good thinking, I'll do that." He sounded like himself again. "You're amazing. I'm so sorry for putting you through all this. The longer it takes me, the more I feel I'm letting you down."

"You're not letting me down."

I did feel quite let down. But I knew it wasn't personal. Therefore I didn't feel upset at him. But I did feel very upset. "Do you still want your future to be with me?"

"Yes."

"And are you trying to move towards that?"

"Yes."

"Then that's that."

"You're amazing!"

"I am!"

"I love you."

"I love you too. And seriously, I am in no rush. I love you. I want everyone to be OK, especially the girls. It will take the time it takes."

"Thank you."

I went back inside to my office and shoved the Sainsbury's Bag for Life that contained all kinds of non-perishable survival move-in treats that I had prepared over the weekend for him behind the boxes under my desk, and then sent him a limerick.

> **Me:**
> Not sure if a limerick is right
> But thought of you and your plight
> Hope that your day
> Will work out ok
> I miss being in your sight

He replied with a song, Eddie Hinton's "Cover Me." I rushed to the loo to listen to it. Fuck. I listened to it another five times in my lunch break. It's so weird how the combination of music and lyrics made by someone else can be everything you've ever felt inside for the person you're in love with.

Later that day, X forwarded on a reply to an email he had sent to a Martin Williams, who was a solution-based counsellor. X's email had explained that he was having difficulty actioning something he wanted to do and would be taken over by mini-panics when he came close. I thought that was a very accurate way of describing it. And it made me feel lucky that I was with someone who seemed to be so in tune with themselves.

Martin Williams had replied saying it sounded like X would benefit from a couple of sessions, but that solution-focused therapy is only ever intended for the short-term. He explained that it consists of asking simple questions, which, if they can be answered, often lead to the dramatic change the client has been unable to achieve.

In the email, I could see that X had signed up for a session that week. I felt very hopeful that this would be the thing he needed. He was definitely a man of action. He just needed some help.

During the next few weeks it made me feel good supporting X and letting him know it was right that he be extra-careful over this. He would send me sentences upon sentences declaring to me how wonderful and brilliant and surprising I was. And I cherished these words, printing them out and re-reading them until the paper they were on got thin and crinkly and faded like a letter from the olden days.

His limerick game was still strong too.

X:
I want to give thanks for your love
You're the best, my girl, my Guv
You help and you heal
And if he was real
I'd be thanking the Big Guy above

After four weeks of having solution-based counselling, X was ready to finally leave the family home. He told me the date and plan of how he was going to talk to the girls, and I wrote the day in my diary with the words "X moving" and covered it in loads of colourful borders like you'd do if you were 13 and in love and owned a 10-in-1 pen. Is it awful that all through his hard and painful journey I just couldn't flipping wait for him to be done?! More because I just knew it wouldn't be as bad as his brain was making him think. I wanted him to have the relief of it, which I knew would come. I told him about that day, on mine and Three's five-year anniversary, when I didn't think I could go in the front door. He thought he couldn't go out of his front door. But he could. I sent him the Cypress Hill song I had listened to for good luck.

After the first session with Martin Williams, they had worked through a lot and discovered that part of X's fear was to do with the actual grotty studio flat. Mostly solution-based therapy was about visualising what your life will look like once you have achieved the thing you are trying to do (I did a shit-ton of research on it all and am now a semi-expert). X would feel panic visualising that tiny, awful place, and in his mind he couldn't even see where the girls would practically fit. So he had pulled out of the flat and lost the deposit, but felt much more positive looking for a one-bed flat.

He and Almostexwife had no spare money since it all went into setting up his company. But X's dad was a thatcher and the family business earned his parents better-than-good money, so they were in a position to lend him some. X always joked about the summer he had worked for his dad after school but had been hopeless and accidentally set fire to part of a roof, and how relieved his mum and dad were when he got into a really good university to study engineering. X borrowed a few thousand pounds to cover the first six months' rent on a new one-bed, and the lost deposit on the studio. He hadn't told them what it was for; he had said it was for work on the house, which he said he and Almostexwife felt bad lying about, but he didn't want his wider family knowing before the girls knew what his new living situation would be.

By the second session with Martin Williams, X had found a one-bed flat in the same area, and it was available to move into immediately. So this became what they focused on in their sessions. Step one, he agreed to the flat. Step two, he signed the contract, paying the deposit and the first month's rent. Step three, he scheduled the move for a Wednesday, and this time the plan was for him to pick up the keys a few days before and for me to go with him for the keys collection, the idea being that this would change any patterns of previous worries and blocks around a new flat. I was pleased we had a solid plan.

Sold

From: Three
To: Me
Subject: RE: Flat sale

Hey,
Sorry for last night. I was trying to not get stuck on the same points but I find it confusing when you won't consider the options we might have together.
How do you know being with someone else will be better than what we had? I'm certain you'll meet someone but they won't love you as much as I did or look after or care about you in the same way.
I worry you'll end up with someone who doesn't deserve you and I feel sad that now I'm better you won't even let me try.
I know you've said it is too late for that now but I just needed to write and say it because I wasn't able to express these thoughts clearly before I started on my medication.
Sorry, I probably shouldn't be sending this.
X

From: Me
To: Three
Subject: RE: RE: Flat sale

Hi,

Thank you for apologising. I find it really hard and stressful when you go into computer-says-no loop/repeat mode. And you say you're better but then in those moments it feels like you're not.

I don't want to talk about people I may or may not meet or of them not being nice to me. Please could you not talk about all that again as it makes me feel a bit stressed?

I think it's big change feelings this week with the flat going through and I think we should be careful to let that pass before we meet up again. And of course it makes me feel sad. I loved that little flat and living there, but that feels like a different world now to me.

Sorry, I know you hate it when I say that.

Please think about seeing someone to talk to?

X

Keys

On the Monday before X's Move Attempt Two, we had planned a swim-and-key-pick-up afternoon. While we were drying off in the family changing room, X was acting weird and didn't finger me. He *always* fingered me in any private spaces we were in for slightly long periods of time. Something was up, and by the time my hair was dry I felt a bit anxious.

Instead of going to a café for some food X suggested we sit on a bench in a square near the pool. He was being really quiet and it felt like he was taking me there to tell me something awful. We sat on the bench and he put his hands over his face and head. He wasn't comfortable and was definitely delaying things. My body had gone into panic mode and I did something really, *really* bad and not at all like me.

I told him I was really worried and had been for a few days but had been trying to be brave and not talk to him about it because I knew he was preoccupied with this flat business—but my period was late and I had done a pregnancy test and it said I was pregnant.

He straightened up and reached for my hand. "Are you OK?"

"Yes. No, I just needed to tell you."

What the fuck was I doing?! I was now the kind of person who lies about being pregnant, and in the worst way.

"I'm glad you have. You know I'll support whatever you want to do?"

He was so brilliant.

I was such a cunt.

"Oh, God, thanks, but no, no, no, nothing has changed there. This is bad news, of course."

What a massive, ridiculous lie.

I started to cry like it was all really true. I actually started to feel like it was a real problem I had.

"It'll be OK, we'll do it together. It won't be like last time."

This made me cry more. I'd told him about the shit double-abortion experience I'd had before meeting him, and keeping it from Three. He was being so kind. What the fuck was wrong with me?! I was actually lying about being pregnant— something I never for one moment would ever have thought I'd do. Especially not at this age. And I didn't even really know why I was saying it.

"I'll go to the doctor's tomorrow and take it from there. I feel better about it all now, thank you. Are you OK? You didn't seem your usual self before . . ."

"I've not been feeling too great about picking up the keys. I've been having the panic feeling again."

I KNEW IT.

He looked like he was about to go into a worse state, but then something stopped him. I held his hands and pleaded with his eyes and said, "Please, please just go and pick up the keys, don't make it a big deal. Don't overthink it. Just pick them up and then talk to Martin at your next session. Forget about moving in on Wednesday, just get through today."

Part of me wanted to offer to pick them up for him, but something deep down stopped me—he needed to do this himself. He agreed with my suggestion. He had to collect the girls from school at 3:15 p.m., so he thought he would quickly beforehand, all normal-like, pop into the estate agent and get them. One step at a time.

An hour later, X sent me a photo of him holding the keys; huge relief and happiness flooded through me. And then a shiver of awful about my pregnancy lie. I knew what that was now: it was some kind of emotional distraction/blackmail. But I had made it clear I didn't want it, so it wasn't the worse kind, I suppose . . .

A week later I got out of it by saying the pregnancy test I did at the doctor's came up negative and I had spoken to Dr. Butt about it and he had said that sometimes the home tests showed a false positive and I had nothing to worry about. Which X bought.

I vowed never to do anything like that to him again and started a new note on my phone:

Lies to admit to X
—Lying about being pregnant

At the right time, I would own up and tell him. I wasn't going to be like Old Me and brush any un-ideal behaviour away. This plan made me feel less like a cunt.

X and Martin Williams had another session, but then they couldn't meet for three weeks as MW was away on holiday, so they had their final session in August, and eventually a new move-out date for the first weekend in September was agreed.

On the day of his actual move, X asked if it was all right if the girls came with him instead of me. It was something he and Martin had discussed, and I thought this was a really positive idea. I was also a small bit glad I didn't have to trek to West London, because the Central Line was down. He sent me a picture of the boot of his car loaded with his stuff and I wanted to send back all the fun and exciting emojis but instead opted for a low-key "love you x."

After he had moved in he sent me another photo, this time of Tammy standing inside his empty suitcase, with the follow-up:

X:
Helper!

I scanned Tammy's face for signs of misery, but she looked happy and sweet.

> **Me:**
> Tammy looks happy and also v, v cute
> hair cut!!

X:

> **Me:**
> There was an old man who finally moved
> Into a flat and his love now proved
> He wasn't all bad
> His situ not so sad
> Looking forward to making the bed used

That might have to wait—X's money situation meant he couldn't afford a proper bed for now.

After he had dropped the girls back home he sent me a picture of his new room with a single camping-bed-like thing.

X:
I know you wanted to come over
and cheer the place up, but it's
been quite a day. Can I just come
and sleep at yours?

When I had moved in with Sophie, she had convinced me to get the same bed as hers as it was THE MOST COMFORT- ABLE THING TO SLEEP ON EVER. Our friend Mia had a brother who had a friend who had a cousin who dealt in dodgy beds. Sophie and I had each purchased a memory-foam "not from John Lewis" mattress that should have cost £1,300 for only £100 including delivery (i.e., Mia's brother's friend's cousin's mate hiking it up to our rooms with it slung over his back).

Of course X should come and sleep over—sleeping on my mattress was dreamy! Also, being at my place made dressing and fashion decisions much easier in the morning. I was actually dreading how this new West London sleeping arrangement would practically work. I have *a lot* of stuff. I had got myself in a bit of a tizz the week before trying to map out the practicali- ties of how I'd coordinate the logistics of things like hairdryers, straighteners, hair protector, running trainers, contact lenses, etc., etc. It was a lot to carry with me, as well as the emotional pressure of having to plan my outfits days in advance before knowing what my taste would be for that day and being unable to factor in the weather. I would wake up on one day and want to dress in a totally different way to the day before. From scruffy sports style to a smart sixties mini-dress, there was no pattern to what look I might choose for the day ahead. It's one of the funnest things about waking up, lying there deciding what version of clothes I'd be that day.

If we had been living in California I really think this would have been so much easier, as I'd only be wearing light dresses and flip-flops and my hair could do that cool, salty beach-wave thing it did when I went in the sea. Our crappy, erratic start- of-autumn weather meant I needed a shitload of stuff. Sophie agreed—it was a rubbish thing about being a stylish female.

She helped me work out some initial things I'd need as back-ups at his:

X Flat Essentials
Straighteners
Hairdryer
Shampoo, conditioner and Moroccan oil
Deodorant
Contact lens solution and holder
Toothbrush
Face wipes
Face cream
Shaver
Running trainers
One pair fashion trainers
Leather jacket
Warmer jacket
Running jumper, shorts, tee, socks and sports bra

I planned to get the clothing clones and hair equipment on eBay and then, once I had them all, I'd leave them at his. But for the first bit of time after the flat move I encouraged him to sleep round at ours. He was up for this as he said it felt more homely there anyway. Which made me happy.

On average he would stay at mine about three nights a week. My favourite nights were when he'd cook for me and Sophie and we'd all sit around drinking nice wine and talking all kinds of shit, which always included heated discussions around Tom Hiddleston, Sophie's current favourite celebrity to be annoyed about. X was the kind of guy who had spent no time wine-learning, but just had that natural skill of knowing which one in the Sainsbury's fridge selection or on various drinks menus would taste the best. When he picked wines for me in restaurants and they tasted amazing, it would always make my fanny go a bit mad for him, and that probably explains why in the early days we would often end up having sex in the restaurant's toilet before pudding came.

On the other nights that he didn't sleep over at ours he

was mostly with the girls, helping with their homework at the family home and then doing bath time and bedtime. Almost-exwife would let him have dinners with the girls, and then he would always ring me on his drive back to his flat. Another good thing about being only a few streets away from his old house: his car permit extended to his new place!

I was pleased that X had as much access to their family home as Almostexwife was allowing him, because this all meant things felt less weird for the girls, and easier for him. And I loved having those nights to myself, to do fashion, watch box sets with Sophie or just have an early night wanking.

I was aware that I didn't want his continued weekly sleepovers to become annoying for Sophie. George didn't care; he was never in, so it made no difference to him. But on the nights X came round, I made sure we didn't spend too much time in the kitchen clogging up the area. And anyway, we mainly spent all our time in my room having sex, so it wasn't a major drag on the rest of the house. X was always around less at the weekends due to the insane amount of time having two children takes up, so actually, during the important non-work times, our house space still felt totally like it had before.

I had started to want more of X at the weekends, though, and this felt a bit hard. But between the two girls one of them always had some early-morning football/dance/swimming related thing on a Saturday and a Sunday, and then quite often matches or parties later in the day. X was never not heading to or from the park. I actually couldn't believe he had chosen this life. Imagine all your weekends for-almost-ever being full of all the activities your children needed to do. What a completely dull way to live. Sometimes on my weekend morning runs I would do my stretches near the football spaces in my park and look at all the parents and little children kicking balls around and feel quite weird that he was over on the other side of

London in another bit of green living that life right then, and it would sometimes make me cry a bit.

X was good at helping me not get too doomy about it all, pointing out that at some point, once things had settled and proper childcare-sharing arrangements had been established, he would have a version of free time on some weekends. And then I reminded myself that I *loved* my own space, and that I mustn't let my brain forget that in times of self-pity! This was all part of the plan. I made a note of this to myself:

Don't forget
—You want and like your own time at the weekends

And I added a line in the Manifesto about it too.

Typical Girl

I hadn't spent any proper time with Al or Fran for nearly a whole year. It hit me as I was showering and En Vogue's "Don't Let Go" came on the radio. I'd done that thing girls do when their new boy thing takes over. What an absolute failing of a friend I was. But also, where they were in Bournemouth was a ball-ache to get to now that I lived in almost-Essex and Three had taken control of our car. Al and Fran had stayed the weekend for my birthday stuff last year, and with that approaching again I guess I'd just not been keeping track of time. Normally we'd always see each other for our birthdays—theirs fall in April and May so often this would be combined with me going down to them sometime in the middle. This year's celebrations hadn't happened as Fran had been on holiday with her boyfriend and Al was away for work. And I was so into being me I'd not suggested an alternative time to come down instead.

I rang them both to apologise for my shitness and we made plans for them to come up to London for my birthday the following month. Being born in November I can never not feel total and extreme excitement about that time of year. The fact that my birthday and Christmas Day are contained in the same six weeks means I lose my shit and get delirious about it every year from around the beginning of November.

After uni, Al joined a netball team and they would hold their annual Christmas party in November, which is absolutely mental. Twice it was on the same date as my party meaning she didn't come up for it. When she eventually broke her wrist and gave it all up, I was only pleased.

This year's birthday plan would involve those guys coming up and sleeping over, and then we and Sophie and a few other pals would go for dinner at a cool new place that had opened in Wanstead. I *never* would have thought I'd do any birthday thing in Wanstead, mainly because I had assumed it was also in Essex. Turns out it's only a five-minute drive from Walthamstow, and now had this super-cool meat place where you ordered huge legs of lamb or beef and then ate it all sharing-style. I had to pick the menu ahead of the event and was deliberating with X over huge lumps of lamb or huge lumps of beef. I loved lamb slightly more but thought overall beef was a slightly safer choice for others. He agreed, and then asked if he could come.

"What, meet all my friends?!"

"Yes."

"Oh!"

My brain did a quick calculation of how many degrees of separation there would be between Three and the people there. I felt certain I didn't want to be letting him know just yet that I had met someone else, not until things were more sorted with us, and I definitely didn't want him accidentally finding out from someone else. My brain arrived at this group being safe. "OK, yes, sure, ha!"

X would be meeting Fran and Al and my brother. Jay was three years older than me and we were tight-ish, but coz he was a boy and I was a girl he was never the one to suggest hanging out, and we also didn't really go into the deep and intense sharing of things that I imagined sisters would. Sophie had four sisters and she spent nearly every second of her day when she wasn't working either FaceTiming, WhatsApping or conference-calling them all. Sisters took up time in a way my brother didn't. When I told him about me and Three breaking up, he said, "You'll be OK," and bought me a pint. I would *never, ever* in a million years discuss *anything* close to sexual things with him *at all*. For Jay there would be no deep significance about what X was for me; he would just be a guy I was now with. So them meeting was both big and also really small.

When I first moved in with my dad and step-mum, Jay and I were both at the same school—me in Year 3 and him in Year 6. I loved having an older brother there, and it got even better at secondary school, especially coz he was quite cool and could be hard. It made me feel a tiny bit like being in the mafia, having this powerful thing over my shoulder that people couldn't fuck with.

X mentioned being a tiny bit nervous of meeting him. And I got the good mafia feeling.

He needn't have been, though, because my brother had grown into a very considerate and softly spoken person who spent his working day caring for grass and trees and other living things. So not much of an actual mafia threat these days.

My birthday weekend and the dinner were amazing. Everyone loved X, and even Jay said how good a fit he thought we were. Which was the deepest thing I think he had ever said to me.

X had bought me the new Dyson hairdryer; if I had been told 10 years earlier that my boyfriend would buy me a hairdryer for my birthday present, I would have told them no way and they must be on crack as I'd never be with someone that dull. But X knew me even better than I did. I wasn't one to ever get excited about hair-related electrical products but I'd wanted one for a while. I'd made Sophie watch the advert for it with me. Initially she wasn't so excited, but after I explained how it could dry long hair in under four minutes she was on board. Can you imagine? I've had long hair all my life, and the heaviest of shite hairdryers. Every other day I'd get arm ache and lose minutes of my life to the necessary evil that is drying long hair. But the Dyson was £350, so no way was I going to spend that kind of cash on that myself. Not when I could picture what that amount of money would get me in Zara. So when I unwrapped X's present in my bed I literally lost my shit. "A FUCKING DYSON!!!!" It felt like I'd won the lottery. I quickly got it out of its box, plugged it in and posed, blowing it against my face and body. It was so strong and light. X thought I was bonkers. I couldn't wait to see how it handled my hair. I shoved my whole head under the bathroom taps to get it completely wet and shouted to Sophie to come into my room.

"Do I need to bring the key?!" she yelled from her bedroom.

Such a joker. Since settling in I'd not felt the need to lock my door at night anymore, but still did when I left for work, which George and Sophie teased me about constantly.

She came in. "A-ha! Happy birthday!"

"Watch this!"

I wanted them both to witness the drying miracle about to unfold. I got my hair in place, turned on the Dyson and started my stopwatch—it took three minutes and 52 seconds!!! And while my hair whizzed dry, I composed the limerick I'd send X in a thank-you card:

On my birthday I awoke to a Dyson

Bigger and stronger than a bison

Kind Guv

Him I love

And I called the hairdryer Tyson

It was the best start to the day. Then X and Sophie treated me to cakes and a birthday brunch and more presents and I felt so, *so* happy.

Fran and Al arrived around 3 p.m. and the five of us drank Prosecco and X got to know them a bit. On his first loo trip they huddled in. Al went first. "I like him."

Fran agreed. "He has a good aura, positive, clean."

I still wasn't interested in any of Fran's crystal shizzle, but this information made me feel very happy and proud.

Dinner was lush. All big chunks of beef and creamy potato dishes and vegetables that tasted like butter. Jay and X sat together, and X joined Jay when he went out to smoke his rollies to keep him company, which I really liked.

At the end of the night, over taking off our make-up in the bathroom, Fran said how calm and different I seemed.

"What do you mean?"

"You seem relaxed, happy."

"What was I like before?"

"The last couple of years when you came down with Three you always seemed quite stressed."

"Oh. That makes me sound a bit shit."

"No, it was just an undercurrent. And now you seem like the you that you were at school!"

That made me feel sad and happy at the exact same time. I was getting back to a self I hadn't realised I had left.

I made a note on my "Don't forget" list.

Don't forget
—You want and like your own time at the weekends.
—To check in with Al and Fran to see if I am seeming like me.

Christmas

As Christmas approached I began feeling a bit sad about things. It was hard to pin-point what exactly, but a TV advert centred around a bunch of woodland animals decorating their tree made me cry for 10 minutes. I think it was linked to having been with X for over a year and him living in a flat that I hadn't visited.

I decided I needed to see it, but would mention this in the new year, as X seemed to be quite worried about Christmas in general, what with it being the girls' first one with him and Almostexwife being split. I worried a lot for him about this too. I had even given up this year's birthday-cake-candle blow-out wish, using it to wish that Almostexwife and the girls would all be okay. Which was *big*, because normally I wished for things like huge success and money for myself.

They had planned it so that X would take the girls to his parents' house from the few days before Christmas Eve until Boxing Day morning, and then she would go there and take over and do from Boxing Day afternoon to New Year's Day. For the last 13 years since they had become a family, X and Almostexwife had spent every Christmas at X's parents' house with X's sister and her partner and their child, and also Almostexwife's parents and sister, who'd drive down on Boxing Day for a few days. X was pleased that for the girls that part would be unchanged. I was pleased too, and the timeshare thing seemed the most sensible and mature plan, but it did also annoy me a bit—the part of Almostexwife being there with his family.

But I guess they were her family also. And then I felt quite sad for her, thinking what her first Christmas Day without her children would be like. So I told myself to stop being a knob, and I genuinely hoped she would have an okay time.

This would be my second Christmas since leaving Three. That first one, only six months after we split, I don't even remember really getting that excited about. I had decided to stay in London and not see my family as I had this weird period of time when I just didn't want to be around normal-looking things. Sophie had offered for me to go to her parents' place with her, but that involved driving to Wales and the full-on-ness of all her sisters, and Al and Fran, who were both doing Bournemouth Xmases with their partners, had both said about going to theirs. But I didn't want to be around all that romantic long-term love. Instead, I had gone to a big "London Friends Dinner" at Mia's with people I knew and liked from work. The idea that it was a fun friends-only day had made me feel far less stressed than the other options.

This Christmas I was more myself and ready to go big. But I still felt a bit weird about where to go, because I very much felt like my old family was over and my new one—X—couldn't be around. Jay had decided to spend it somewhere hot so he was in Thailand, which automatically made the thought of Christmas dinner with just my dad and step-mum a bit shitter. They were okay, but as I got older and started to have feelings about life and politics, I found I could only handle them in about two-hour sessions because their views differed hugely from mine. Plus, Dad only ever wanted to talk to me about how the divorce was progressing, what I was going to do about trying to save to get my own place, how important my pension planning and thinking had to be now, etc., etc. So I decided to spend this Christmas out of the country and go somewhere warmish as well. I had never been on a holiday on my own. I had travelled to a lot of places solo to meet people but had never purposely planned a few days with only myself.

I'm mad about tanning. My skin turns easily and I love being brown. For the last eight years I have practised ever-so-safe-suntanning—gone were the days of factor-six Hawaiian Tropic oil for seven-hour solid shifts, and now I only tanned for a maximum of four hours per day using factor 30 on my body and 50 on my face and neck. Money-wise, I could only realistically afford to go away for four days, and to make the most of my time I needed to fly somewhere under three hours away, so that meant it needed to be a destination in southern Europe.

I created an incredibly detailed spreadsheet charting what the average daylight hours, rain and temperature was for all the places that easyJet flew to within three hours of London, and only recorded the flights that left between 9 a.m. and 11 a.m. and returned between 8 p.m. and 10 p.m., to ensure maximum sun time. I then analysed all the data and settled on Lanzarote, which, judging from the last five years, should have a decent 21–23°C. I can get a tan in anything above 17 degrees.

Flights and accommodation were pretty cheap—I think this was due to Lanzarote picking up a bad rep in the nineties with people nicknaming it "Lanza-grotty," which it had never quite shaken off. That didn't bother me. I gave not one shit what the area was like so long as there was warm, cloud-free sun.

I had made the right choice. Lanzarote was quite windy, but I knew that and had factored it into my choices by picking a hotel that had huge walls surrounding the rooftop tanning area, which meant I'd be sheltered. I had used Google Earth to make sure the walls wouldn't cast too big a shadow on the sun loungers throughout different points in the day. It is this kind of detail that definitely qualifies me as a tanning expert. I would never commit to a holiday where I couldn't get to a decent tanning area within five minutes of my room. Actually, this is how I knew I'd fallen deeply for X, because I had broken all these rules when we had gone on our first trip away. It was a weekend break to Rome, and I didn't look into any of this or give two shits about being in the sun. I had it bad!

In Lanzarote, I spent my days lying by the pool reading and sleeping. There's nothing lovelier than feeling warmth on your skin. I was happy and would smile to myself and didn't get annoyed by any of the other guests, which I always did during all my holidays with Three. Once the sun had set, I'd have a wander and get something to eat, normally involving mussels, prawns or tiny new potatoes that were boiled and then completely covered in a dusty salt, which is a dreamy combination. I sent a potato picture to Sophie.

Me:
You'd love these little pots!!

Sophie:
I'll work out how to make them when you're back!

Over dinner I'd read a magazine or book while I ate my food and drank a local beer, and I felt so grown-up and independent. Happy. Just doing only what you want on a holiday is so amazing. I highly recommend it. It was very empowering. Plus, I loved that I would be brown and therefore hotter looking for Boxing Day night, when X would see me again. I sent him a picture of my bikini-bottom tan marks, which drove him crazy.

Me:
My tan marks are missing you!!!

231

X:
Ahhhh!!!!!!

X:
I am missing you terribly xxxx

X sent me loads of loving and missing-me writings over Christmas—long essay emails and regular texts with songs. On our goodbye, as I left he had said he felt terrible that we couldn't be together over this period, and had handed me five handwritten envelopes which were titled with the time and date I was allowed to open them. Inside were words of love and limericks and generally stuff that made me go a bit gooey.

We spoke loads throughout the days, and on Christmas Eve I asked him how the girls were getting on and he said everyone was doing well. Which pleased me and made me feel better about us being apart. At least they were all doing okay. I had worried that Christmas might make Almostexwife turn, or that it would push her over the edge. Maybe because Christmas seemed to stir something for Three. Last year I had received a bunch of messages from him. But X hadn't received anything negative from Almostexwife so it all felt rather hopeful. I was relieved, and I realised that I had actually been worrying a lot about this all through December in the run-up.

But now, all my excitement was aimed at Boxing Day night. I was due to land at 3 p.m. X would be coming over at 6 p.m. and staying until the 2nd of January. Sophie was back in Wales and George was up north with his family, so I had our house to myself. I COULD NOT WAIT.

X and I had planned what would be our actual Christmas dinner for Boxing Day night, and we'd do presents and other Xmas formalities then. We had already both given each other stockings to open on Christmas Day. His to me had included a Topshop voucher—fuck, I loved him! Before leaving for my holiday, I had bought crackers, condiments and Christmas pudding, and he was getting the meat and veg and other things that would have gone off.

When he arrived, it was electric. That had been our longest time apart since becoming serious and our bodies had missed each other massively. We kissed in the hallway and rolled along the wall kissing and undressing until we hit the sofa. I sat on him and we had the slowest sex ever. Just as he was about to come he picked me up and put me on the kitchen table, pushing the crackers and table settings aside, and then he sat on a chair and licked me, really slowly, until I came. Bloody hell, even with all our explorations I had never been licked out on a kitchen table. It was incredible, and a little puddle of something gathered underneath me, which immediately after made me feel a bit gross as that's where I'd be eating my chicken dinner, but I cleaned it with the antibacterial kitchen spray, twice, and then I felt better. We prepared the food and then took some champagne into the bath where we had more sitting-sex followed by a fingering while I was pressed up against the bathroom door—the heat from the bath making me feel a bit out of it in a good way. After I came, I made a mental note to google if bath water is bad if it gets up your fanny.

We did presents and ate and danced naked to my favourite Christmas song ("Jingle Bell Rock") and had fierce pinned-down-on-the-lounge-carpet sex. It was the best not-quite-Christmas I had ever had. And I couldn't wait to spend the rest of my time properly with him.

As we lay in bed that night, I told X that I wanted to come to see his flat. "I think it's time I started to make the effort to do one night a week at yours. I've come up with an amazing solution to the problem of all my stuff . . ."

I got out of bed and opened my big wicker chest, which

was full of all the essential seconds stuff that I had been buying on eBay over the last few weeks. People in fashion magazines always go on about capsule wardrobes but I had never been into that kind of thing—whatever the opposite was of a capsule was how I liked to shop. However, for the purposes of this I had taken on that theory and replicated my essential fashion items, which involved:

A duplicate of my favourite Topshop leather jacket.

A fake pair of white Converse.

A duplicate of my favourite Topshop high-waisted blue jeans. And then a bunch of T-shirts and tops that I already had doubles of (if you find something you love when shopping, *always* buy two).

(I didn't need to buy a hairdryer after all, as my shite old one could go there now.)

Some shitter-than-GHD hair straighteners, but good enough for one-day-a-week hair.

And a bag of all the toiletry doubles.

X laughed at me. "You are madly practical!"

"Will having all this at yours stress you out? Coz this is in no way at all in the same area as moving in; these are all just slightly shitter clones of my real things in my real room."

"Having your stuff at mine does not worry me one bit."

"Ha, good!"

"And I can't wait to live with you one day."

Ahhhhhh! It felt like a very romantic end to the year, and I couldn't wait for what the next one—our second one together—would bring.

X's Flat

After work on Wednesday the 31st of January, I would be going round to X's. It kind of felt like a big deal, as well as not being one too. I decided that I would print out the Manifesto and create a double-sided option by putting it behind the picture we had bought in Rome, which I had rested at the end of my bed, waiting to be framed.

In Lanzarote I had edited the Manifesto and arranged it into categories. People say your CV should ideally be one page—more and you're annoying, less and you've not got enough experience. So I formatted the Manifesto with that in mind and got it down to one page on A4 (if you took out all the paragraph spaces and used font size eight).

SEX STUFF

- Agree on sexual-fantasy-world ground rules for role-play (no describing of people known).
- No wanking over real people.
- Continue finding new ways to have sex.

Weekly

- Dirty texts should be sent (more frequent during time apart).

At least once a month

- Monitor fanny wetness.
- Fingerings, lickings, blow jobs and sex should occur in multiple rooms in the living residence and outside of the primary living place.
- Have a naked dance.

Couple of times a month

- Lickings and sex should include more than one position.

Once a year

- Create own porn videos.
- Update the sexual aids which make things hot (outfits/sex tools).

When apart

- Phone/FaceTime sex to be engaged in at least once a week.
- Watch the homemade porn.

COMMS

Weekly

- Communicate any change of feeling in regard to sexual stuff. Even the hard stuff (ideally as close as possible to feeling it).
- The only promise you are allowed to make is that you will always communicate honestly.

Once a year

- Set a date for an official MOT to check in and adapt any points where needed.

DOMESTIC STUFF

- Make sure you treat each other like you would have during the first few months (in terms of politely tolerating gross food on mouth, bad breath, lateness, etc.).
- Be wary of feeling urges around all "traditional" relationship stages. Come up with at least four other options before deciding on committing to one.
- Ideally don't live together full-time, or sleep away from the home separately at least once a month.
- Clean your teeth at different times in an evening to prevent a bedtime pattern, which leads into dull bed-only, just-before-sleep sex. (No flossing in front of each other, ever.)
- Domestic bills should be agreed and divided up prior to some kind of serious shared-living arrangement, meaning no dull conversations should be needed concerning them.
- No joint accounts.
- Don't have children.
- When bad patterns occur, clock them, monitor them and set up a reward system over a period of time to help break them (apparently most habits take 21 days to change).

At least once a month

- Prosecco in the bath together.
- Sleep on different sides of the bed.
- Have weekend time to yourself.

I chose a fancy-looking font, turned it into a PDF, shrunk it and then printed it out on special gloss paper. I had found one of those large glass floating frames, which meant I could have the Rome picture on one side and this on the other. We could hang it Rome side facing out, but sometimes turn it round. I was excited to get it to him. It felt important in a way that I imagine saying wedding vows felt to normal people.

At 11 a.m. I asked X to confirm his address—I had it somewhere, after posting him the limerick thanking him for all my amazing birthday treats, but I couldn't find it on my phone. He sent it straight away. I texted back:

Me:
Finally today to your flat I will bring
Lots of good vibes and that kind of thing
Here's to next steps
And your lovely biceps
Listen out for my doorbell ding

Followed by the Honeyz' "Finally Found." It is the best cheesy love song ever. If you don't know it, stop reading and put it on YouTube and listen to it now—sing along. And the second time it gets to the chorus, give it full diva singing.

What a classic.

Under my desk I still had the special bag of move-in supplies plus some extra bits that I had been putting in there over the last few months. I added the framed Manifesto.

At 2 p.m. X rang my phone. "Are you at your desk?"

"Yes!"

"Can you come down?"

"Yes, coming now!"

He was going to do something ridiculously romantic—I could tell!

He was standing by the entrance to the doughnut shop near

my office. He grabbed my hand and took me round the corner. Fuck, what if he was going to ask me to marry him? I knew we were both officially still married and I didn't agree with it as a concept and didn't care about that kind of thing. But if he asked, and even if he didn't have a ring, I would definitely say yes!!!!

He then broke down in tears.

Part Three

FUCK

Everything happened in a flash. My insides went berserk, like they had been told terrifying news. My brain was confused.

X pulled me further into the alley. "I have something awful to tell you."

This was no proposal. My eyes started crying before they knew why.

"I need you to know this hasn't come from a bad place."

"Can you just tell me?"

"There is no flat."

"What?"

"I don't have a flat."

"I've got the address . . ."

"I never went through with it."

"But you got the card I sent you there."

"I went there and asked them for it."

"What??!!"

"I know . . ."

"Where have you been staying?"

"At home."

"I don't . . ."

"I couldn't leave."

"I don't understand."

"I never told her."

"But what does that mean?"

"I didn't tell her I was leaving. She, the girls, they don't know anything."

"I don't understand."

I fell a bit onto the concrete—not like a faint, because I stayed awake, but my body was fainting while my mind kept whizzing. My brain wasn't keeping up. I wasn't asking the right questions to help it sort out this muddle. My nose was tingling and I felt out of breath.

He hadn't left.

He hadn't told her.

He hadn't moved things on.

He had lied to me.

He had tricked me and lied to me ever since our I Love Yous, which were 1, 2, 3, 4, 5, 6, 7, 8, 9, 10—11 months ago.

I didn't understand. I was shaking and cold.

I went into survival mode. I texted my boss, Diana, to say I was ill, rushed back in and grabbed my bag and coat, then booked a nearby hotel and we caught a black cab there. I needed X to talk, a lot, and in private, not on the side of the fucking road.

We didn't speak during the 15-minute drive.

I never got black cabs—they were so expensive and were only for treats.

We got to the hotel. I got out first—he could fucking pay for it.

I had kept my shit together in the taxi, at the hotel reception and in the lift with an annoying old couple who had pressed nearly all the floors by mistake, but as soon as I got inside the room I lay on the floor and I cried. Neither of us spoke. What the fuck? I felt desperate. I was really confused, and shocked. A part of my brain asked me where my anger was—it seemed to have left me to manage this without it.

Eventually I looked at him.

"Tell me everything. But first I need to know what main bits are true. How you feel about me."

He gestured for me to sit next to him on the bed. I ignored him.

"Nothing has changed about how I feel about you. I love you. I want to be with you. I haven't been with her properly for years. I told one awful lie and all the other lies were an extension of that one. That day when I rang you from the Pets At Home carpark, I was too scared to tell you that I couldn't tell her. I had planned to, but I couldn't because I thought it would mean you would end it with me since you made it clear you needed me to move out. So I panicked and said I had told her. The only reason I couldn't do it was the girls. The only reason I lied was my love for you. I had planned to find a time to tell her and sort it all properly. That was always my plan. I know this is not good enough. I did an awful thing, but it wasn't from an awful place."

"Where does she think you've been all the nights you've been with me? What about our phone calls every evening when you were driving back to the flat? I don't understand—what did she think you were doing? What about the first grotty studio flat? And the picture of the keys? And Tammy in the suitcase? And Christmas? And the guest room? You have to tell me everything, in order, with every detail."

"I will."

I got off the floor and grabbed my notebook and a pen.

"And don't stop. I will have questions at the end."

I drew a line down the middle of the page. The left side was for fact bullet points, and the right was for random questions that popped into my head. He began and I listened, taking notes. It was good that I had given my hand this job to do; it reminded my body that life was happening.

X's Version of the Last 11 Months

"I'm so sorry I've treated you this way. I only ever wanted to make you happy and keep you. Almostexwife and I have not had romantic relations[1] since before I met you. We get on pleasantly, we function for the children. When I met you, I still slept in our bedroom together in our bed. We had/have a no-contact relationship. We don't hug or kiss or hold hands. We never had that sort of thing. But we are kind and polite and like each other; we're friends."[2]

I said nothing.

He continued: "When I met you, I didn't expect anything to continue. You had your six-date rule and it was clear you weren't looking for something so soon after your marriage. Then we fell in love and the sex and our conversations were unlike anything I had ever experienced.[3] When you said you loved me and said we could only carry on if I left the house, I felt so strongly that that was what I intended to do. There was no doubt in my mind. Then, on that day when I had planned to tell her, I found it impossible. I didn't doubt us, but I was really terrified for the girls. Not to make this sound like blame in any way, but you asking me not to mention you made it much harder.[4] I didn't feel like in her eyes, my family's eyes, I had enough of a reason to change things so drastically. So

1. When was the last time they had sex?

2. Did they lean on each other when they sat on the sofa watching telly? Did they laugh together a lot?

3. Yeah HONEST!!!!!

4. Why didn't you explain this then?

244

I got scared and said nothing. In that moment that was the first lie to you, and all subsequent lies were only in relation to that one. I told you I had told her, and that she was OK with it all, and that I had moved into the guest room. I didn't move to the guest room. I stayed in the bedroom."

"In the bed with her?"[5]

"Yes, in the bed. But honestly, for me the bed is not the place you are imagining."

My anger had arrived. I wanted to shout at him, I KNOW WHAT PLACE A FUCKING BED IS, YOU CUNT! But I knew I needed to save it until I had all the details. Anger at this stage would not be conducive. I needed him to think it was safe to tell me everything. So I wrote it on the right-hand side instead.[6]

He continued.

"Because she didn't know, I then didn't tell the girls the following month like I said I did. On that day, I had planned to tell her instead. This whole time I had been trying to find a way to tell her. That was never not my plan. I have only ever wanted to leave her and be with you. If we didn't have children I would have done that easily. I need you to believe that."

"I do, but that doesn't make any of this OK."[7]

"I know, I know, I'm sorry. I'm so sorry I've hurt you."

Hurt? Hurt felt fucking easy compared to *this*. I was so full of anger. But I spoke like a robot.

"I want you to continue with the timeline."

"I went and saw all the studio flats that I told you about. In my head I thought this would help me move things on. I intended to do that plan. But a mixture

5. What is their bed size?!!!

6. FUCKING BED!!!!

7. IN OVER A YEAR ONLY 3 MONTHS OF HONESTY VS 11 OF LIES!!!!!!

245

of money[8] and her not knowing meant I didn't sign up for one.[9] There never was a studio flat. So on the day I was supposed to move out, I panicked as nothing existed and you were always so kind and patient, which made me just want to sort it all out and gave me a deeper resolve to do so. I couldn't tell you. I was deeply embarrassed about the situation I had got into. And the lies I had told you. But I had never lied about my feelings towards you, or her. I thought the counselling would help.[10] But the sessions were circular, because he said I couldn't resolve anything until I had told you and her."

"Why did you keep going then?"

"Because I had promised you I would.[11] That's what I'm trying to say—throughout all this I was trying my best to be true to you. In my fucked-up way. I was always honest about where I was when we spoke. I was never not doing what you thought I was doing."[12]

"Apart from having another woman with you the whole time and sleeping in a bed together?!"[13]

"You know that's not accurate."[14]

"I don't know anything. I want to focus on the facts. What about the second flat?"

"I lied about that too."

"How? You showed me the keys."

"I took a picture of my sister's spare house keys."

"I saw the photo of Tammy helping you unpack."

"I got her to stand in the case when I said we were having a clear-out."[15] He started crying. "It's awful, I know."

I wanted to touch him, comfort him, but I didn't move a muscle.

8. Parents lent money, true?

9. What was the first night photo then??!

10. I want to see payment proof.

11. How many sessions did he actually go to?

12. Them— social plans?? Did things with friends??

13. How could he??

14. FUCK YOU YOU FUCKING CUNT.

15. PSYCHO????

"Why did you go to such lies? Why did you leave me saying you were going to pick up keys that didn't exist????"

"I'd already let you down so much and that was the day you had the pregnancy scare. I didn't feel like I could say anything then. I didn't want to worry you further."

Fuck.[16]

16. Swimming day fear!!!

"And the photo of your car full of bags? What was that?"

"That was an old picture from a past holiday with the girls."

"There was no flat, ever."

"No."

"But what about all the evenings you drove there and we spoke at bedtime, the fucking picture of the miserable bed?"

"I would leave my house and drive the route to the flat I said I was in."

"But you were doing that a couple of times a week—what did she say?"

"That's what I'm trying to explain: when I did lie I tried to make it as close to what you thought, to make the lie seem less big. She didn't ever comment —by this stage, since the spring really, we had started living like the other didn't exist. We barely spoke about non–children-related matters."[17]

17. What were they like in front of the children???

"Did she not ask what was going on?"

"No. She withdrew. I found that easier; I figured it gave me more time to sort this properly."[18]

18. FUCKING COWARD.

"What about the Wi-Fi? You said we couldn't FaceTime as you hadn't been able to arrange it. That was all bollocks?"[19]

19. TRICKED ME.

"Yes. I'm sorry."

247

His sorries were getting weaker.

"Fuck! You must think I'm really fucking stupid . . ."

It all got a bit much in that moment. I felt so thick. What a dumb fuck—I'd not realised *any* of this in almost a year!! I put my notebook down and I walked into the bathroom and washed my face. I've never needed to wash my face in the middle of a talk with anyone before, ever. I thought stuff like that only happened in the movies for effect. That thought made me really angry, so I filled the sink and put my whole face in and screamed. I dried my face, left the bathroom and picked up my notebook. The notebook gave me a strength. It made me feel like I was a detective, writing down his statement for me to pick over later.

I had wanted to be a police officer when I was little, back when I thought it would involve solving crimes, having a gun and getting to have a partner who was not only my best friend, but also my dog, Mavis. Mavis and I took on the world busting up bushes and smashing the shit out of mouldy apples in our neighbour's garden. When I realised what being a police officer would actually entail—i.e., wearing awful fashion and not being corrupt—I decided it was not for me.

The detective in me made me continue. "The birthday thank-you card I posted to your fake flat, how did you actually get it?"

"This is how insane I was. Anything you wrote to me meant so much, I couldn't bear it being there, so I went round and asked them for it."

"Seriously?!"

"Yes."[20]

"What did you say?"

20. Where does he keep all the letters etc I've written him and gifts etc??

248

"That my mum had got confused and realised she sent it there."

"Did they think that was odd?"

"A bit—they'd lived there for six years, but I said I lived further down the street and as the envelope was there waiting it seemed to make sense to them."

"Fucking hell!" I actually laughed out loud at this. Even among all this misery, that was really a bit funny. What a loser. He could have just told me it got lost in the post. The thought of him trailing over to some stranger's gaff and asking for some card was just properly silly. And sweet. We shared this lighter moment for about four seconds before the bollocks reality broke our smiles.

"Where did she think you were all the nights you slept at mine?"[21]

"She didn't ask. I would text and say I was staying near work or at a friend's."

"That's so weird . . ."[22]

"She would often decide to stay over in Paris for work or have a last-minute stay at a friend's. It was something we were both used to."

"What about Sunday nights? Surely Sunday nights would be too odd to not be at home for?"

"Yes, they were. I behaved appallingly and in one excuse I told her I had been knocked into by a cyclist and was at the hospital."

"What?"

"It was awful behaviour."

"What about meeting all my friends, and when we bumped into some of your joint friends—weren't you worried then? That Frank guy who was like, 'Oh, I didn't realise'? What if he had told her that he had met

21. Calculate all nights' sleep with me vs her

22. Is she stupid???

249

your new girlfriend?!!! You seemed so normal. It all felt so normal . . ."[23]

23. List who knows

"I know I was acting mad. I was beginning to just believe in our life."

"That is actually mad."

"I wasn't thinking straight. I figured it might just be easier if she did find out that way. I wasn't thinking clearly."

"How could I not have seen this? I thought all your worry and stress was tied into worrying about the girls. I thought your panics were about them, but they were about the fucking lies."

He went to say something, but I wanted a moment. "Wait."

I needed more time to think.

I drew a timeline in my notebook. Looked over our entire 14 months. "OK. What was this Christmas? Where was everyone?"

"It was exactly as I told you, only she was there from the beginning[24] and I told them I had to work over the time in between Christmas and New Year. My sister knew something was wrong. Everyone thought I was ill. My parents were worried about me leaving on Boxing Day. It wasn't a happy, nice time. I was barely there as my head was always with you."

24. Christmas present for her???

At this point I lost it and stopped taking notes.

"THAT IS NOT 'EXACTLY' WHAT IT WAS. I FELT SO WORRIED AND SAD AND GAVE UP SO MUCH OF MY TIME AND FEELINGS TO YOUR FUCKING FAMILY DURING THAT TIME. YOUR FUCKING FAMILY, WHO WERE ALL OK AND HAPPY AND EATING MOTHERFUCKING PIGS IN BLANKETS LIKE A BUNCH OF HAPPY

CUNTS. I WASTED WISHES ON HER BEING OK. MY FUCKING ONCE-A-YEAR BIRTHDAY WISH. HOW FUCKING DARE YOU TRICK ME. MAKE ME TAKE UP MY EMOTIONS WORRYING ABOUT SOMETHING THAT WASN'T EVEN REAL FOR THEM? HOW COULDN'T I SEE THIS? YOU FUCKING LET ME THINK THAT. HOW COULD YOU?!"

I ran into the bathroom and slammed the door harder than any door I'd ever slammed. Locked it. This was too much. This was all too much and all I wanted was for him and me to still be okay. Even knowing *all* these lies, that was the main part of all my feeling. We had to be all right. No one got to do this to me. I couldn't lose him. He didn't get to leave me. I'd rather he was dead than that. I calmed myself down and went back out to continue.

After four hours of talks I had extracted all the information I needed. The new truth. I believed him, I understood all of it, every decision. I completely and utterly understood. But fuck knows what this all meant going forward. I felt fucked.

He had said the thing I needed to hear to know where we stood—that all he wanted was to be with me and he was still working towards achieving that. But what the fuck did that even look like now? And how could that mean anything comforting when the man saying it looked so broken and weak and scared and was sleeping in a bed with another woman?

He said now that I knew the truth he felt such relief and would sort this for good. Within the week, he said.

I didn't let my brain pay that timescale any attention. I realised in that moment that my body had stopped believing in the deadlines he gave me ages ago; they made me feel stressed. And now my brain knew too.

I told him that he could mention me if that made things easier, coz at this stage I didn't want his inaction to be linked to me at all. After all this he *had* to leave. I didn't even care that I couldn't see what our future would actually look like or if I could trust him. I just needed this huge wrong to be righted. No one gets to do this to me. I needed to stay calm and supportive so he couldn't use me flipping out as a way out of this. I would not give him an easy way out.

I opened my phone notes.

Lies to admit to X
—Lying about being pregnant
—That I'm pretending to be ok with any of this

Rice Cake

Over the next few days my hardcoreness came and went. When I felt hard I felt mafia-hard, and when I wasn't feeling hard I was feeling desperate—life-over, hard-to-breathe kind of desperate. They were shit states to be stuck between.

Since being told The Truth I hadn't been able to eat.

That was over a day of no food. I had *never* gone for longer than two hours without eating during awake times. Even through all the Three ending, I ate. But this thing had ripped my stomach out. People say you should try to eat even a little food for fuel, to give you energy, but my energy was coming from an alternative source. My upset.

By the afternoon on day two of still not eating I had got smaller. My jeans were actually loose and I felt really light. Just from not eating for two days. I couldn't believe stopping food for this little amount of time made my body look so different and a part of my brain felt a tiny bit happy about this because although I loved my body, everyone wants to be a little bit slimmer, don't they?! It was the one upside to this pile of pain. Sophie asked what was wrong and I said a stomach bug. That's all I was able to come out with.

I hadn't been able to go to work. My brain was like a nervous bird flittering around the place. Plus, I had a new project. I gathered every song and limerick we had ever sent each other, hundreds of them. Every love letter and poem. I collated them into one document and printed them out. I was seeing X at the end of that day, just for a brief meet-up after his work, and I wanted to present them to him to read through in the hope that it would help him do the right thing.

I'm sure "the right thing" would have been considered different by other people from the outcome I wanted. But for me, anyone who can have a proper relationship with someone else behind their partner's back either had to own up or admit they're a psycho. Not being brave enough and continuing on at this stage was the wrong thing. Regardless of whether children were involved.

My brain alternated between deep hate for the pathetic person Notalmostexwife obviously was for putting up with that non-relationship, to deep sadness that she was a woman being treated in such a bad way by a man. I tried to stay in the latter thought, as I knew she hadn't actually done anything wrong. But that meant I had to hate X a bit more.

I met him in a Starbucks to present him with the documents. It was one in Southwark that had a really discreet downstairs part that no one ever went in. He had fingered me in it sometime near our beginning, before going to watch something at the theatre. I sat in the same seat I had then, feeling teary about that better time. As well as not wanting food, my fanny had also packed up. I hadn't felt horny since the big reveal.

When X arrived he looked awful, and thinner too. The tiny bit of hate in me commented, "And ugly?" but no—he still looked like everything to me. When we are treated badly by people, why can't something automatic happen in our brains that switches the feelings off? Protects us? Like when you overeat something and then can't ever have it again. I had done this with crabsticks a few years ago—I'd had an amazing three weeks snacking on them, then one day I ate 20 in one sitting and ODed. Since then I have never, ever craved or wanted them again. Why couldn't I have that response now? What he had done to me felt much more sickening than the crabsticks aftermath.

He got his wallet out as he approached. "Would you like something to drink?"

"No, thanks."

"Anything to eat?"

"No."

"That's not like you. You should eat, you look . . ."

He looked pained. He knew his hurt was the cause of how I looked.

In my head I shouted I'LL EAT SOMETHING WHEN YOU FUCKING LEAVE HER, but my mouth said in a kind and reassuring way, "I'll eat something as soon as I'm hungry, promise."

I wanted him to feel bad. I was pleased my change in shape caused him more worry. I actually had felt a bit hungry earlier that day but I didn't allow myself to eat anything as I wanted to continue in this way, like a silent protest that made him feel worse. But I was pretty sure I'd eat a chocolate-covered rice cake once he left.

I made him read the bits of paper—pages and pages of our love written down.

He got teary and I said, "Our love is amazing, isn't it?"

"Yes."

At the end I had put something new in, a verse from a song I had heard:

When people are scared and not living their true.
They're wasting their life, there's nothing more blue.
Pretending to be happy playing the game,
But you can step out at any time, there's no shame.

Things are changing.
It's OK just to be.
Blink and you're 80.
Memories with me.
Come out of the dark.
Come to me.

Life is short.

It was the "life is short," and "blink and you're 80 . . . come out of the dark" bits that I'd highlighted and underlined.

I didn't tell him that the song was from someone who had spent their life struggling to keep their addiction to heroin hidden, because that actually felt like a much bigger problem than the situation X had got himself into, and I didn't want to distract from that.

Two nights after that, on day four of this hell, X finally told Notalmostexwife. He said that those final words of the song had really stuck with him and I silently thanked someone I don't believe in.

This was actually three days before he had aimed to, which was a massive relief, and helped with my new trust issues as it made things actually feel real. In darker moments I had been struggling a lot with that. What was real, what wasn't. It's so hard believing someone when they've done this kind of lie to you, and it was made even worse by the fact that I hadn't picked up on any of the signs. I always thought I had good gut instincts, but now it felt like there was nowhere to anchor myself to; I couldn't tell shit.

He said that now I knew everything he didn't need to wait, and he'd spoken to her that evening when the girls were in bed. He'd told her everything—the people before, the lies he had told me. He rang me after, when he was in the Uber on the way to mine.

"Did she shout or scream?"

"No. She was very quiet."

I went into Sophie's room. I'd been avoiding her for the last few days.

"Hey."

"You feeling better?"

"Yes, thanks."

I told her the truth of what had been going on and apologised for not saying sooner, but that I just needed to see how this first bit went. I told her everything apart from the bit about him sharing their bed still. I lied and said he had been in the guest room as that was just too much information to be honest about. She was kind and supportive of me, but pretty angry with him about it; she told him so with a finger pointed at his face when she answered the door to him. I listened from the top of the stairs. She said there'd better not be any more messing me around now or he'd have her to deal with, and then she softened and went back to normal and asked if he was okay.

Sophie had agreed that X could stay until he sorted himself out. I promised it would be very short-term and thanked her.

We went to the shitty pub opposite our place. After a year and a half of living in Walthamstow, I had never been in there. Sophie had once, to buy us some Prosecco when ours had run out, coz the Tesco Metro was closed and the shitty pub stayed open really late.

X had a pint of pale ale and I had a Baileys, as I never considered it alcohol and was not currently interested in proper drinks, what with feeling not over the moon about life in general.

X didn't really know the plan. He had told her and left, and that felt massive. That night we had sex for the first time since

257

the news. It was so intense and close and felt very urgent, and he made me come twice. I felt such relief. It had only been a few days but, bloody hell, it felt like months. I intended to eat a steak tomorrow!

He was so very positive and hopeful over that drink that I assumed that meant everything would be okay. I guess he was probably in shock, because it wasn't okay.

Three days later when he arrived at mine after an early evening with the girls he said he had to end it with me. Explained that Notalmostexwife had told him he had to—for the children. She wanted to continue to be with him, make it work. What the fuck was wrong with her?! He had told her he was in love and had been putting his dick in someone else for over a year, and she still wanted him. Their thing was obviously wrong. I didn't get why she would want to cling on. She had even rung his parents to help. They had told him the same message, and his sister, who had turned up at his work, tried to convince him too. They all told him he had to end it. I hated them all. And I hated him for being a fucking wimp after already doing the hard thing.

This was way too much drama for me. My body felt exhausted and when the words came out of his mouth, I fell to the floor in a sort of elegant knees-led body bend. Kind of like the child's pose stretch they do in yoga but without my arms out. I stayed there, on my bedroom floor, like a folded-up sun lounger, with my forehead pressed right against my knees and my shins pressed tight against the carpet and I wanted the ground to take me away. I had not seen this coming. He had completely bent me to the floor. I wished that I wasn't alive, and then that thought worried me and the always-reliable strong part of my brain caught it and threw it out. I was not the kind of girl who had thoughts about being dead. This shouldn't be happening to me. How dare he? I wanted him dead. I wished he would die, then no one could have him. I didn't mind suffering my pain if they all did too. I wished I had never met him, never had this kind of love, never seen what being with a really caring and reasonable person was like. Away from the lie, he really was the best person I had ever spent time with.

When I eventually came out of my fold-up position, I asked him if he loved me and wanted to spend his future with me. He said yes and yes, but that he had to end it with me.

I was so tired. I hadn't realised how draining the last few months had been. Even throughout the time when I didn't know anything was wrong, all the specifically timed phone calls and limits on when we could talk or see each other had taken things out of me. And it had also made me hard. He was expected to break up with me, now, and go back home there tonight? No fucking way.

I pleaded with him to take more time with all this. Speak to some people who weren't me or them. Friends. People who could help him see that leaving was not the end of the world like they were making out. That pretending was. Pretending to live a life you didn't want when we aren't even around for that long anyway is madness.

"Please can you stay over?"

"I said I'd go back."

"I deserve a longer conversation. Don't I?"

"Of course."

"Then text and say that. We don't have to do anything sexual. It's not fair to me otherwise. I deserve a longer conversation, surely?"

"Yes, I'll text her."

"Can I see it?"

I hated having to ask and apologised but explained that my brain felt like it was under attack and needed the confirmation. He had no problem showing me, and I felt huge relief and also satisfaction. He was staying here. A tiny victory, but it felt very important.

I had every plan of making him have sex with me. That felt like the answer, like us shagging would break this spell they had him under. It was our language, not to be broken. We never lay naked with each other for longer than 20 minutes without it turning into something hot. Sex with him felt like *the* most crucial thing to achieve tonight.

He wasn't having any of it. He said it was unfair to me and her until things were clearer.

What? Since when did we stop being us? And now he wanted to remain faithful to her? This sounded crazy and it hurt me so, *so* much. But the time for arguing this wasn't now. I was just so relieved he was there. We fell asleep with me crying in his arms. I hated him.

I woke really early and started pressing myself against him, and he let out a little groan. I knew that sound; it meant he couldn't stop what would happen next. We had sex and kisses, and afterwards I felt pleased that I had got my way and also *really* shit. It was the worst sex he and I had ever had. I cried as he got ready to leave. He hugged me and it made me feel worse. This was mine; how could it all be so out of my hands? I asked him again, "Do you still want your future to be with me?"

"Yes."

"Do you love me?"

"Yes."

"Well, that's it then. We have to come up with a better plan."

There were actually loads of options; he just wasn't thinking straight. I told him that due to not wanting the normal relation-ship stages I was willing to consider something unconventional—maybe where he still lived at home for the girls but our relationship was known, for example. We just needed to think outside of the norm, come up with some alternatives.

He said he couldn't see how staying there and being with me would work, but agreed to take some time away from her and me and to speak to some of his friends, think of some options. It was so important to me that he did this, to give himself time to think and get advice from someone who was outside of this. He had only been talking to himself for so long. I really felt hope that other, normal people's perspectives would help him.

X planned to go and stay at his mate Neil's in Oxford for five nights. I had wanted it to be a whole week, but this was better than nothing. He sent me screengrabs of the text and train ticket—they flooded me with relief. I could almost handle all of this if he wasn't around her and his family. He wasn't leaving for Neil's for two days, so he would be staying at his home till then, which I hated, but he showed me a text he had sent explaining to Notalmostexwife that he needed time and his Neil plan, and that he'd be sleeping in the guest room. She had responded, "OK." Even though he didn't make me feel bad about asking, I felt awful making him show me his text again, but I was so paranoid about everything now, it was the only way for my insides to operate well at this point. We had agreed not to see each other until he was back, but we would still text/call.

I was very worried about him having two evenings at his house. I imagined Notalmostexwife manipulating him into staying. He told me that, when telling him he had to end it with me, she had brought up the wedding vows he had said to her and had listed the names of their friends and family he had said them in front of. She told him he was breaking that promise to all of them, which is fucking ridiculous. We can't be held to account for promises we made years ago; this is why marriage vows are bullshit. People change. Promises break. Clever people should not offer long-term promises to anyone about anything ever. Clever people should understand that long-term promises may not work out. I just wanted him away from her.

We kissed goodbye and he left to take the girls to school. It felt awful and hopeless having him go. Leaving all of this down to him. I had no say, no control. My head was fucked; I've never felt lower. I knocked on Sophie's door lightly to see if she was awake. It was 6:55 a.m.; she wasn't. I waited an hour and tried again, and then she was (sort of), so I went in. I sat on her bed, desperate, and updated her on the latest turn of events. I was the weakest, most broken I had ever been. Shaking, I told her I didn't think I could carry on. I had never said words like that out loud to anyone, ever. She was always so kind and loving to me, I just wanted to get in her bed and be hugged.

But Sophie was pissed off. She was really angry. It felt like she was angry at me.

"This is enough now!" She had her eye mask across half her face and she ripped it off and threw it on the floor. "Just ENOUGH NOW. I don't want more drama in this house. I don't want him coming back here."

I was really shocked. I'd never heard Sophie raise her voice before. I backed out of the room, saying, "Sorry, sorry, you're right," and shut her door.

What the fuck?

I waited in my room for a bit, half expecting her to come in. She didn't. I looked at myself in my mirror and wished my reflection could hug me. I wanted someone exactly like me on a good day to help me through all this. I got my phone and opened an email to my mum. Then closed it. I heard Sophie wash and then go downstairs to start her day—she had a little office space in the back of our kitchen. She wasn't planning to check on me.

I didn't feel like I could stay at home after that, so I got myself together and cycled to work.

Fuck knows how. It was raining and I cried for the whole 55-minute cycle, the tears and the weather feeling the same on my face. I remember going through a red light thinking, "Who gives a fuck anyway?" I thought Sophie would probably text me or something during the day. I'd told her I wanted to die; there was no way her anger would ignore that. I watched my phone, waiting for a text from her; looked at the last ones she had sent me before I had turned into whatever it was I now was for her:

Sophie:
Shall I do mash for dinner?

Me:
With butter so will be extra creamy???!!!

Sophie:
Yes

But she didn't get in touch. I spent the day not doing any actual work and instead found research on Google about how fine children could be if a break-up was handled well, and how there was no actual proof that parents separating would cause them to have problems. I gathered case studies and edited them into a master document with links and quotes pulled out. I emailed it to X near the end of the day. I wanted him to consider the facts. During some of my research I saw a stat that said 90 per cent of married men with children never actually leave their family after saying they would. This was not the kind of equation I expected to have to be dealing with in my life. I hadn't planned for this. I hated the website for telling me that, and I immediately found ways of discrediting it—and if it was true, X could be the 10 per cent; that wasn't the lowest chance. But it still made me feel more worried.

Home

At the end of work at 6 p.m., because of the Sophie situation, I felt I couldn't go home as normal. I'd fucked that up now too. The only place, out of all the homes I'd ever lived in, where I had actually been truly happy. I saw that now. Having grown up across different houses, with stuff split between them and feeling in each one that the space wasn't properly mine, or that I wasn't actually wanted there all of the time, was one of the side effects of the parents I had and the partners they had picked to live with. Even though growing up I thought this constant-adjustment feeling was all normal and I bombed about in my happy self, I've realised now that neither of my parents' places were the open, free homes I saw that my friends had.

Mum's place in San Francisco was like visiting a foster home for animals; it smelt hamstery and there was always some animal in crisis that they were nursing in the lounge. There were shoeboxes filled with straw where there should be rugs and a coffee table. It felt like an extension of their workplace and it didn't hold any kind of real home feeling. I hadn't felt that with Mum since the last flat she'd lived in, in Salisbury. At my dad and step-mum's it was ridiculously strict. I wasn't allowed in their room or bathroom, I wasn't to put posters on the walls of my bedroom, I had to ask before making food outside of normal food times, and I wasn't given my own set of front door keys until I was 16, but with the caveat that I was never permitted to stay there overnight if they weren't there. Even when I was in my twenties! It was the same for Jay, although he didn't care as much as he had his mum's place round the corner.

All I've actually wanted was to have a place where I didn't have to constantly adjust. The home Sophie had created for us. Why do these great insightful understandings always have to arrive in the moments when something might be lost?

Sophie was right, I had brought a lot of extra stress into her life, into our home. I hadn't regularly downloaded on her too much about X and me, but when I did it was big, complicated things, and why should she have to take that on?

I booked a hotel for the night. It was grubby, and I had never felt lower.

I wrote a list of people who usually helped me feel better about things.

People
Defos
X
Al
Fran
Sophie
Three

Maybes
Jay

Wildcard
Mum???

I crossed off Three and Sophie from the list of defos. And then also Al and Fran as they were too far away and it would involve so much explaining. But I made a note that if I was still not feeling better in a week, I would ring one of them.

X was not an option—he was the whole problem.

Jay wouldn't be of use and I didn't know why I'd put him down.

Mum. I'd still not really had a full conversation about all the Three stuff with her. She had kept emailing to ask about it but I'd been ignoring them.

I had loads of phone cards in my wallet as she had gone a bit mad and sent me a whole bunch when I gave her my Walthamstow address. I hardly had enough energy to hold the phone, fuck finding a phone box. I rang her number from my mobile.

"Hello, Bay Sanctuary for abused, neglected and unwanted animals, how can I help y'all?"

I almost hung up. I can't stomach the insanely slow and long-winded, super-cheery way Bobby answered the home phone.

"Hi, Bobby, is Mum there?"

He got her straight away—he knows not to try any small talk with me.

"Darling! Such a lovely surprise! Are the new cards quicker?"

"I don't know, I'm on my mobile."

"Oh. Is everything all right?"

"No, I've had a falling-out with Sophie."

"What happened?"

"I don't want to go into it."

"OK. Well, that must feel especially hard now you're not with Three."

"Three has nothing to do with this."

"Darling, why did you ring if you're not wanting to talk properly?"

"Can you just say something useful, please?"

There was a pause as she shooed away one of their latest guests.

"It's hard to feel OK when things feel out of control. When your father left me and you were so little I had to just be OK, but I wasn't. And I didn't have any friends nearby, so when you'd gone to bed I'd put on the Contours' mashed potato

266

song and dance to it, at least three or four times in a row, in the lounge. Even if I was crying I'd make myself do it. It always helped."

After we hung up I put the song on and stood up. "Like a mash potato I can do the twist . . ." I was moving in half-dance mode and not at all in the mood, but hearing it out loud reminded me of all the times I had danced to it: end-of-school party, cheesy uni disco nights, with Three any time a friend put it on, our wedding with everyone dancing it with us. Those thoughts got me through the song and eventually sent me off to sleep.

I'm a morning person. I love waking up and always have loads of energy, and 99 per cent of the time within minutes of waking I experience happy thoughts around what I might eat and wear that day.

I woke with a black anger. X had done this. His actions had jeopardised one of the most important friendships of my life. How fucking dare he?

On my way to work I texted him to tell him that because of all this I'd had to stay in a grotty hotel. He felt awful. Good.

I went home that night. Normal me would have argued it out, said where I felt Sophie was being unfair, but I was in desperate survival mode. I gave Sophie a card I had written saying I would be careful and more considerate going forward and please let's just be okay.

She agreed and we hugged. She asked if I was okay and I lied and said I was/would be. Then I went up to my room and cried. Inside me, in a separate place away from the X grief, I felt like I had lost something big, because I knew I couldn't just be how I had been before with her. That I had to keep things from her.

I felt really alone.

X kept ringing, trying to support me, but it didn't make me

feel better. Later that night we had phone sex and it only took me one minute and 45 seconds to orgasm. I think weirdly all the pain and fear of him leaving made me come more quickly.

The next day X was due to go to Neil's, so we met in my lunch break for a coffee as I had a few terms I wanted to be clear about. He had previously implied that if he chose to leave me and stay with Notalmostexwife that this would *only* be because of the children and not because of her. In which case I wanted him to agree to certain things:

1. Tell me to my face it was over and also have it in writing too, as my brain wasn't the best at remembering and processing things, therefore I wanted to be able to read over it as well.

2. Pay me £15,000—I had looked into it, and this would cover me for three years of weekly therapy as well as six months for a sabbatical from work. I knew I would have serious issues coming out of this and I had done some research and apparently therapy takes a very long time to have an effect. I couldn't afford that on my salary and he should fucking cover it. Plus, I now didn't have my best friend to help me so this was only fair. The sabbatical was linked to point three . . .

3. He had to quit his job and not work in the same industry as me. I would take my sabbatical during his notice period. He could either get work in another sector or she could increase her job and he could become a stay-at-home dad (if staying was about the children). I couldn't handle him being around my life if this was done, and why should I have to be reminded of him when I was working? He was the one who fucking tricked me.

4. Tell her EVERYTHING!

5. Never cheat on her again.

He didn't take well to the contract. He wasn't angry, but very firmly he told me it was like blackmail. I disagreed. Actions have consequences. I wasn't asking for anything unreasonable. I knew he could borrow the therapy money from his parents. This was the outcome of him choosing to lie. Atonement for it. If I continued to park my car without a permit in the wrong place, I would get automatic fines. This should be treated like that. Plus, he'd be spending that money on rent if he left anyway, so I really didn't see why he was acting like this. The agreement would help ensure my wellbeing—something he claimed was most important to him. Was he lying about that too?

"But it is a version of blackmail."

"I'm sorry you see it that way; it was not what I intended. And I need to put myself first. Can't you just agree to it?"

"No. I want you to be OK, of course, but I can't sign this."

He passed the make-shift contract I had printed out back to me, so I left it, because we weren't going to agree and I was still trying to be the calmer, supportive me in front of him even though inside I was livid.

He was wrong about this. For me, blackmail would be threatening to write to Notalmostexwife with a detailed account of everything as I understood it, from the day we met, to the sex we had the other day, during the time that he wasn't supposed to be seeing me. And then sending that same account to his work colleagues and his company's board. *That* was blackmail.

I had written that letter to Notalmostexwife the night before at 4 a.m. while I was lying awake worrying. It took me an hour and it made me feel calm knowing it was there in my saved items. A timeline of his awfulness to her pre and post me. It wasn't a nasty letter; it was purely factual. If he left me I felt very strongly that she should definitely know *all* the information, including the first time he had cheated on her and all his other one-offs.

When he initially confided this info to me I had been impressed that the first time had been after quite a few years of them being together. Now, in my current confused state, I felt sickened by the kind of man who could choose to continually cheat on a woman who was stuck at home looking after the children he wanted. What a cunt.

I had no idea if I'd actually go through with sending this letter to Notalmostexwife, but having it ready made me feel a kind of control that I didn't have in any other part of this.

I never told X about that letter, precisely because I am *not* into blackmail. I wanted him to make his decision because he loved me and thought I was great, not make a decision out of fear. That was the whole point of him going away to take time.

I told him I'd support whatever decision he made. Which was a massive contradiction of what every part inside me wanted—to ruin his life if he stayed with her.

I had these two opposing sides to me constantly during this time. Deep love and care; deep hate and revenge. It made me a bit schizo and I couldn't be entirely sure which version was actually me now.

Lies to admit to X
—Lying about being pregnant
—That I'm pretending to be ok with any of this
—That I will support his decision and not take revenge

We kissed passionately as we said goodbye outside the café, both our bodies desperate to have the other. Even though he had booked onto a specific train and needed to head off soon, that kiss was the start of something that needed a finish. I knew the swimming pool at the end of the street—it used to have unisex changing rooms. We both paid for a swim and met in a cubicle. My knickers were soaked from the walk there. He held my face tight while we snogged. I unbuttoned my trousers and he his.

We muted all our noise. He picked me up so I was standing on the bench bit; he then crouched down and licked me until I came, which did not take long at all. It was much warmer up the top of the changing cubicle and I almost passed out during the orgasm. I then manoeuvred him to a sitting position on the bench and slowly fucked the very end of his dick while holding my hand across his mouth. I liked the power.

Back at work I had my weekly meeting with my boss, Diana; she was no-nonsense but kind and very observant. We spent the 30-minute session discussing my situation because she had asked with kindness at the start of my meeting if I was okay, and I broke down and spewed it all out. All of it!

She was 20 years older than me and pretty wise. She often had quite big ethical decisions to make at work and she would discuss these with the team, listening, taking advice, but her instincts were always a few steps ahead of ours, and I realised over the last six years of working with her that I trusted her judgement more than anyone else's.

Maybe this was the kind of thing normal people felt with their mums, but Mum had been so far away for so long that when she did try to give advice it wasn't always relevant. And she had such bad judgement over other things that once she moved away I just kind of retired her from that role. I had never asked Diana for her advice on personal things before, but with this, very nonjudgementally, she gave me some and it felt like I had something to anchor onto.

She said I had two options. One, to keep communicating with him while he made this decision and thereby become "the other woman"; or, option two, leave him to it. Cut all comms and give him space to do what he needed to do. And if that was not choosing me then he was not the thing I thought he was and I'd be better off without him.

I didn't want to be the other woman; that version would

not work for me. My step-mum was "the other woman" and growing up I disliked her immensely for that. I didn't want his girls to feel that, ever. Plus, I fucking wasn't. Well, not of my choosing. So I decided to do option two. Cut all comms. I never would have done this if one of my friends had suggested it, but there was something about it coming from Diana, like a work order, that changed my mindset, and I knew I would achieve it. I never failed at my job.

I decided to email X something kind and thoughtful and strong. I told him that I thought it best we stop communicating until he had worked it out, and that me being in touch was obviously what I'd rather, but how helpful was that continued presence when what he really needed was time and space?

I told him I loved him and was there for him, and obviously I wanted to be his choice, but until he knew I needed to leave him to it. I told him I would of course talk to him if he had news about his decision, but if not I'm afraid we couldn't be in touch. I said he could respond to the email.

When I gave up smoking, on the day I decided I would, I did it, there and then. Never had another puff. I can't explain why then, as I had flipping loved smoking—it was one of my favourite enjoyments, but for some reason I'd had enough, and so I set up the tools to prevent me from relapse, i.e., to have two fully charged vapes on me at all times so that when I was pissed I wouldn't slip if one ran out of battery. On nights when I wanted it really badly I allowed myself to get another smoker to blow their smoke in my face at the same time as I inhaled my vape, giving me an extra hit. Six months into vaping I planned to slowly reduce the amount I used them until finally, 10 months after stopping real smoking, I had stopped the electronic cigarettes too. That was over four years ago and I haven't slipped once, even though in my heart I will always love smoking. Plus, Three had said I could have a Topshop spending spree on my six-month anniversary of being smoke-free. Which helped.

If I succeeded in the X-no-comms I told myself I could buy a pair of boots from Russell and Bromley that I really wanted as a reward. I had never been in that shop as it is *soooo* expensive, but I walked past it most days on my way to find lunch and I knew the black cowboy ankle boots in the window display were The Boots I had been searching for my whole life (or at least for the last few years). They were the right style to go with everything from cute short dresses to jeans or shorts, and they were the right heel height for looking dressed-up, but also for fighting or running in (a must for any shoe I buy, as you always want to be able to run away from trouble in whatever footwear you happen to be wearing). If I could go a week without communicating with X, I decided I would put them on my credit card. I didn't actually feel in a shopping kind of mood, but I was relieved that even throughout this harsh time, my brain's muscle memory still responded to incentive buying. It knew I'd be pleased with them in the future.

No Contact

Day one of No Comms, and Day 12 of "The Truth."

Don't contact him don't contact him.

Don't contact him don't contact him don't contact him don't contact him don't contact him don't contact him don't contact him don't contact him don't contact him don't contact him don't contact him don't contact him don't contact him don't contact him don't contact him don't contact him don't contact him don't contact him don't contact him don't dontcontacthimdontcontacthimdontcontacthimdontcontacthim-dontcontacthimdontcontacthimdontcontacthimdontcontacthim-dontcontacthimdontcontacthim.

It was only 9:30 a.m. and it had already been the *biggest* struggle to not contact X. I typed the longest text to him and then edited it right down to just the shocked ghost-face emoji—our sign for "missing you." I had the text ready—my phone waiting in my hand. This was rubbish, and so hard. I deleted the text and went into my inbox. Yesterday X had replied to my email, saying how wonderfully generous I was and that he felt such privilege to be loved by someone like me and that he would use this time wisely and he loved me and hoped he found the calm inside him for us to be together. I wanted that so much. I read it over and over—"for us to be together, for us to be together, for us to be together." It's so weird how we do that as humans: pore over the same few words, get feelings in our chests from them, give our own tone and meaning to them, kiss the shitting screen . . .

At the end of his email, X had asked if we could have a quick phone call before the No Comms officially started. I agreed, of course, and kind of knew this would be his response to my email. I had planned a few key messages I wanted to slip in to our final chat; little seeds that would resurface for him over the next few days. My last hope.

On the phone we said we loved each other, and I said I hoped he'd find the courage he needed. I played it very relaxed, kept all the feelings of desperation I had out of it. It was Valentine's Day in four days and we had a reservation in a restaurant that I'd wanted to go to for ages—I had booked it back in December as a surprise. I told him and was pleased he sounded disappointed. I said I was mentioning it not to make him feel bad, but to be honest, as I planned to still use the booking—I'd be taking Paul from work as a thank you for helping me with a big project I was stuck on. I knew full well that X had shown tiny bits of jealousy around mentions of Paul before. I asked if that would be okay, that I didn't want to miss out on eating there and that this killed two birds with one stone. I could tell he was trying hard to not show that he hated the idea, which made me feel powerful.

I had no plans whatsoever to go to this dinner or hang out with Paul. I just wanted it to be in his head. Figured it would be a good nudge. He said he understood and thanked me for being honest. It surprised me that giving him the wrong impression and making him feel shit felt very pleasing!

We ended the phone call at 4:08 p.m., and that was that. No more chances of subtle manipulation to ensure he didn't forget how much he wanted me. It was now all down to him and his brain. I wouldn't be talking to him again until he had made a final decision and chosen either them or me. In a true gesture of pure supportive love, I hadn't specified a deadline. What a dick—always specify a deadline!!!!

I shut my eyes and I pleaded with a higher power I don't believe in that he would choose me. Desperate times make non-believers want to believe in something. After my plead-prayer, I felt ANGRY. I hated that I'd made some bullshit dinner scenario up, and that I was waiting to be picked. By a fucking man. It made me feel so pathetic. The week before we had discussed how neither of us would ever regret the love we had experienced together, and the things we had reached as a couple that neither of us had come close to before. But I realised now I didn't mean that. I'd rather be unaware. If he ended up staying with her I wouldn't want to be left with all this love that I only want to give to him and if I was offered a way to remove all memories of our time together, I would take it.

Someone's patronising voice who I didn't know came into my head and said, "It is better to have loved and lost than never to have loved at all." They are wrong. To love this greatly and then have it taken away is bullshit. If I had to get over this I didn't want the sadness of how great it could be to stay with me. I didn't want any kind of reminder.

I made my eyes stop looking at his email response and they settled on a picture across the room—an arty photo of X's silhouette walking down some steps. Maybe I should prepare for the worst. I got out of bed and took all the pictures off my wall of art that involved things we had done together, as well as removing all bits of him from my room. His eye mask for sleeping, books, toothbrush, the treble-clef bracelet he had given me, and all of the letters and notes he had written to me, which I kept in an almost-bursting A4 envelope in my jumper drawer. I put it all in a cardboard box and left it in the garage so that it couldn't make this harder for me during this awful limbo stage.

I spent the rest of the day watching *The Vampire Diaries*, which wasn't my usual kind of telly choice, but there was something comforting in all the death and biting.

Day Two

Waking on Day Two, the first thing I did was check if X had messaged. He hadn't. I typed some of the things I wanted to say to him on my phone's "X Thoughts" note diary. By now it took forever to scroll to the bottom of it. Hundreds of words, recording my feelings from desperate to fair to sad to hatred to regret to threatening to missing him . . .

In a continuation of my preparing-for-the-worst by getting rid of visual reminders of him, I caught the train into town and went to my favourite jewellery shop. X had bought me a gold-and-silver skull from there for Christmas, to represent the ghost-face "missing you" emoji. I loved it, not only coz of what it symbolised for us, but because I still loved wearing gold and silver mixed together. On their own they felt like too much of a commitment, but together they were perfect. My love for this jewellery shop had existed way before I had met X. He knew about it because one day we were passing and I went in to stare at the giant silver shark's-tooth pendant that I so desperately wanted to own one day. It was £250, so not something I was going to buy myself since in general my necklace cravings were ever-changing and never-ending, although it had been over four years since I first saw and fell for it, so obviously a stayer. I had worn the skull necklace X had got me every day since our Boxing Day-Christmas, right up until the night when he had tried to end it. I'd taken it off that morning and put it

278

back in its box. I still had the original bag it had come with, and I handed it to the lady in the shop. I asked her if I could exchange it, lied and said I had never worn it, and explained that my boyfriend had got it for me but then broken up with me and I couldn't ever bring myself to put it on.

She said yes without any hesitation and told me I could swap it for something else. I pointed to the shark's-tooth pendant. She said it would mean I'd have to pay an extra £105 to cover it, but I didn't mind and put it on my credit card. It felt empowering to get something that I had wanted long before I knew of him.

The lady in the shop had obviously been through this before and asked, "Are you sure you won't regret this, my love?"

I never once considered getting rid of any of my jewellery gifts from Three, even the ones I wasn't really into, because they all had memories that I didn't want to forget from our time together. I hadn't been able to wear the bracelet he gave me on our actual break-up day, but I was hoping I would be able to one day. It's why I was still keeping his special cufflinks safe, because I know at some future point, when he has someone great and probably a baby or two, he will be able to wear them again and I can give them back to him. But maybe my feelings around wanting to keep Three's gifts were because ending it had been my choice. Whereas if X and I didn't end up together, I knew I wouldn't want to ever see anything he had given me again because they would remind me of the lies and upset.

"I won't," I replied. If we did work out, I would just come and buy it again. So definitely no regrets.

Outside the shop, I took a close-up necklace selfie and posted it on my Instagram. X didn't do any social media himself, but I was pretty certain he would take a look at my page, as he had mentioned that at times of missing me he found himself on there—he wouldn't know what this photo meant, but I did.

I left Soho feeling stronger, the silver point of my new tooth slightly stabbing into my upper chest when I walked. The pain made me feel good.

It was Sunday and Sophie and George were both away for the weekend, which was a relief and awful at the same time. Once home I went to the kitchen to find a light bulb for my bedside lamp, saw my "All You Need Is Love" cushion on the armchair, grabbed the kitchen scissors and stabbed into it, tearing it apart. Stupid fucking saying. Life would be easier if we could ban all forms of love. It's the last thing you need. It lets you down, it goes away, it doesn't even necessarily exist in the places it is supposed to.

After I had worn myself out slicing the cushion to shreds, I lay on the floor feeling panicked and cried for quite a while. What if this never ends? I rang Fran. I told her everything. She didn't say anything for ages. It took quite a while to explain it all. She listened and understood and had nothing mean to say, but encouraged me that I was doing the right thing.

"If he really wants you in his life, he'll find a way to sort it out."

"Do you think?"

"Yes, definitely. And if he can't, it means he's not fit for you."

"I hate people not being 'fit' for me. I've had enough of them."

"I know."

"Any chance you could come up for a visit this week? I'm happy to cover your train ticket."

Fran was a bit broke at the moment as she had gone down to part-time so she could study for a master's in theology.

"Yes, of course. I can come on Tuesday?"

Tuesday was only two days away and was Valentine's Day, so it would be especially nice to be with her then.

"Do you not mind being away from Jules? It's Valentine's Day."

"No, we never celebrate it, it won't be a problem."

"Thank you so much. I'll book us into a nice spa hotel so we can have massages and it can feel like a bit of a treat at least, and not just a heartache chore for you!"

Fran said not to, that there was no need, but I was so relieved I wanted to do something nice for her. It gave me something to focus on.

That night X cracked first—of course he did. He sent a picture of a sunset from Neil's back garden, and I was flooded with relief that he was actually where he said he was. He said he knew he shouldn't be in touch, but its beauty made him think of me, that I was all he was thinking about constantly, and then he signed off with the ghost-face emoji. Normally this kind of wank wouldn't actually be my kind of thing and would repel me a bit, especially as the picture was actually quite shit and not even that beautiful. But given the current situation it made my heart beat super-fast and go gushy. And, weirdly, it also made my fanny wake up too—I had a super-quick wank while I looked at the actually-shite sunset picture—a landscape porn first.

After coming, I looked at the cowboy boots online for motivation before considering if I should reply. I didn't want to ignore him—I wanted to encourage him—but I also didn't want to break my No Comms rule. I figured a swift, to-the-point response wouldn't jeopardise the boots.

Me:
Hello, obviously it's very nice to hear from you but I think we need to try and stick to the no comms. I'm going to bed now. Goodnight 👻

No romantic gush—I was being so strong!

X being in contact helped me to fall asleep more peacefully than the night before.

Day Three

Monday was the third day, and by bedtime I had received no response to my text. I felt the least amount of hope. I didn't even have to persuade myself not to contact him; it was like I had no energy or feelings for anything. I'd gone to work, barely eaten, got teary in the staff meeting and came home again without taking in any part of the day. As I lay in bed in the stage just before sleep, I wished over and over that I could wake to a message saying, "It's you. It's *always* been you." But this wasn't a cheesy American romance film.

It was 11:59 p.m. and if we had been in normal comms I would have sent him "You're the One that I Want" from *Grease* as his song to wake up to, because it was almost officially Valentine's Day. I fell asleep to dreams of X and me on a sandy beach both wearing leather trousers and dancing together as we belted out the chorus, but it was too hot and the sun was melting the leather and we were getting burnt and stuck to each other while a chorus of angry children in pink bomber jackets and multiple Notalmostexwives shouted at us.

Valentine's Day

Even when times were good I thought Valentine's Day was proper bollocks. It had no meaning to me. Until today.

If things were where I thought they had been with X, we would have woken up together and had some intense and flipping exciting sex. I'd bought a giant red-ribbon-bow underwear thing, and had planned to put that on for him to "unwrap." I know it sounds shite, but the picture of it looked much hotter than my explanation!

Last year X had written a card with a double limerick for the occasion. I went to the box in the garage and dug it out to look at.

You're the only sun that shines for me
I want you all the time you see
To hold and caress
Don't want nothing less
Than to be with you for eternity

Have a lovely Valentine's Day
Hurry home the quickest way
For bed and lurve
Like heaven above
Then homemade pizza on a tray

This year's limerick would have probably referenced our exciting restaurant plans. I hated him for doing this to us.

There were two things that made me feel slightly better: 1) that X would wake thinking I was going out for dinner with

Paul, and 2) I had posted a picture on Instagram of me wearing a new pair of jeans and a top and I looked particularly happy and hot. It pleased me that if X looked on it today he would be greeted with it. The picture was actually from a few weeks ago but he wouldn't know that.

I had planned to leave work at 4 p.m. to meet Fran off her train. I'd ended up booking us into a couple's massage. I couldn't quite imagine what that entailed, but it meant we'd be done at the same time. Some roses turned up at work, and I felt a bit sick—they must be from Three. X was not the kind of man to do flowers, especially not roses, and Three was still sometimes sending things like that on special occasions. For Easter he had sent my favourite flavour of cake (carrot) and for my birthday he had sent the massive yellow roses we had got married with, which weren't my favourite flowers anymore as I could now only associate them with our five-year-anniversary break-up and them lying knocked over on the floor during that dreadful talk. It's weird that he thought sending them would make me think good things, and I had told him this tactfully afterwards. Hence the small red roses this time. As a flower, I hated these small ones. I found them dull, and the red ones especially tacky. I've never been impressed by them.

I put them in the communal kitchen and ignored them. My approach with Three was to never respond on the day but bring it up a few days later, explaining in a nice way why that wasn't appropriate anymore, etc. It made me feel uncomfortable, getting nice things from him, because the follow-up was always stressful and full of sad questions from him. I just wanted him to move on.

I took a cup of tea back to my desk and went to make a start on logging the IP for someone's latest discovery.

From: X
To: Me
Subject:

Did you get my flowers? xx

They were from him! I legged it to the kitchen and grabbed them back. Suddenly they were the most beautiful flowers I had ever seen. And then I felt angry. How dare he send me flowers! How dare he keep breaking the No Comms plan that had been really hard for me to suggest and implement! He was taking the fucking piss now.

I wrote him a firm email back.

From: Me
To: X
Subject: RE:

Hi, yes I got the flowers. In a different scenario I would have loved them, but actually they made me feel shitter as none of this means anything until you know what you want to do.

Please don't get in touch again until you know.

I didn't sign off with any ghost faces or kisses.

This love-sadness was getting boring. I needed a new conversation in my head. Something pro-active. When I was in primary school, before my mum left, I had taken our new dog, Jim, to dog training every Saturday morning. Even though he was a Labrador, he was a naughty little fucker. Nothing like Mavis. Mum had got Jim from a rescue place and he'd obviously picked up some bad habits. He used to run away and go and eat the ageing and less mobile sheep in the surrounding fields. Farmers hate that and Mum had received quite a few threatening phone calls saying we either sorted him out or they would. In the dog training they explained that it is much easier to teach them from puppies, and since Jim was already two it meant I'd have a harder time undoing his naughty ways. They said he needed constant actual reminders to help him recondition his behaviours. In the dog-training world this meant a water squirter in the face and a Coke can full of pebbles shaken in front of his ears. In eight weeks I had trained Jim to be very obedient and to stop eating people's sheep.

I went to one of our meeting rooms and worked out my retraining plan for myself. I started with making a list of all the things I wouldn't miss about X if he ended things. I would then study this list and reprogram my brain to care a bit less, see him through a shitter lens.

X Won't Miss List

1. Toe Fungus

The very worst thing about X, the if-I-concentrate-on-it-properly-it-makes-me-feel-a-bit-queasy-and-sick-pops-into-my-throat thing—is that he has toe fungus. I don't mean one gammy nail, but a severe overtaking of all his toenails by what appears to be at least 10 years of fungus growth.

Google image search "severe toe fungus." It's sick. I first discovered it when I had been in the reverse cowboy position on his dick. I was trying a new version of it and stretched my hands and body down towards his ankles, clasping them near his heels in a kind of pinned-down move. It was hot. Until my eye refocused and it was looking right at a completely yellow and fungus-thickened toenail. I quickly looked up and down the rest of his toes and on the other foot too, and they were all as bad. He was a big guy; he had big feet and huge toes—the size of his little one was much bigger than my actual thumb. It

286

was fucking gross. I tried to put it out of my head but that ick feeling wouldn't go away.

Knowing that his toes were roaming around free on my bedroom carpet, in my bed, my bathroom floor, little fungus-crumbles flaking off around me, meant I had to bring it up with him.

"What's going on with your toes?"

"What do you mean?"

"*That* stuff!"

"They've always been like that."

"Are you sure?"

"Yes. It's an ageing thing."

"I don't think it is. In fact, I printed off these for you"— I handed over some pieces of paper—"about toe fungus. That's what you've got. It's very common and very treatable."

"Oh. I thought it was something to do with getting older."

"No. And it only gets worse. Will you do something about it?"

He did; he went on some strong-arse fungus pills that damage your liver if taken for too long, and nine months later one foot was completely clear and the other was on its way too. Except for his stubborn big toe on his right foot. That fucker wasn't improving at all. I took a close-up memory screenshot of it in my head to have as top of the list of things I wouldn't miss about him.

2. Baked Beans BO

Very occasionally X got stinky armpits. It wasn't often, but he had some weird thing about not using deodorant; said he didn't really sweat and if he did, it hardly ever smelt. Which was kind of true apart from on an incredibly hot day, after hours of shagging, or a really long cycle. After those occasions his sweat smelt weirdly like baked beans. I really dislike that smell on human skin. I would remind myself of this constantly—his smelly, beany sweat.

3. Yellow Teeth

His teeth were more yellow than white, with brown stains forming around some of the gaps. I took great relief in what they'd look like in five years' time if he continued to not have regular dentist visits. I go to the hygienist every six months and had also whitened my teeth before I got married, so next to my beauties, his were really lacking. He rarely flossed, which overall was not a good sign and could lead to bad breath—which I hadn't encountered with him yet. But I had hopes this would develop if we ended.

4. Stupid Saying

He said the phrase "reaching out" in emails like he was an American businessperson. "I'm just reaching out to see . . ." It was just such a ridiculous thing to say and always turned me off. I will repeat it over and over.

5. Frown Fluff

Sometimes his deep frown lines gathered fluff and stuff. Ninety-six per cent of the time I was besotted by his looks and actually found his lines part of his handsomeness. However, 4 per cent of the time they were so deep that things would gather in them. I never checked but always feared they might sometimes smell too, as normally things that hung around in places like that were prone to. For the purposes of this list, his frown-lines fluff did smell, and I visualised how much more stuff would be gathered in them when they got 10 years deeper.

6. Completely Unphotogenic

This didn't really bother me, and was more of an inconvenience in the early days when looking for images of him on the internet to wank over, but X always looked really minging in any photograph. He'd always have this expression where it looked like he was just really struggling to understand anything. I had noticed similar characteristics in pictures of his dad and sister.

7. Hair, Part One
Ironically, even though he had minimal hair on his arms and legs, fucking hell the rest of him was hairy and it moulted worse than a moulting dog. Once his hair had come off his body it looked pube-like, which grossed me out, and piles of it gathered any time he spent more than five minutes in a room.

8. Hair, Part Two
When we met he was a tiny bit embarrassed about a patch on his left shoulder blade that was even more massively hairy than the rest of him. It was not a normal place to have a lot of hair, but I had always told him I loved it. I didn't, I had lied—mainly because I was in the still-getting-to-know-him stage. I hated those clumps of freak hair; they choked and tickled my nose when I hugged him from behind in bed. And they were fucking ugly.

9. Thrush
He was a massive thrush instigator. All the hours of sex without cleaning ourselves in between meant we were getting thrush quite regularly. It always lasted worse for me, so I will remind myself of the uncomfortableness of it whenever I drift off to think about his dick.

10. Piles
He gets piles quite regularly. When he had them it meant all bum-hole licking/fingering was off. He was normally quite good at knowing when they came and would warn me, but my fear was that one day he'd be between not having and

having them and my tongue would accidentally discover them, which would be awful because in my head piles were tiny little poo-smelling grapes that dangled out of the bum-hole.

11. Disgusting Eater (when eating meat on the bone)
The way he picked at meaty bones with his fingers, with gravy dripping all over them and it going under his finger nails, was disgusting. This was how I had first encountered him, on our first date, and it was important to remember how much I didn't at all fancy him then.

12. Bill Splitter
Making me pay half on that first date—defo not cool or hot.

13. We'd never had bum sex
Even though this was strictly down to me having such a tight bum-hole, I like to think if he was "the one" that somehow this would all be compatible too.

14. His penis alone had never made me come
At this stage I think it is pretty clear that biologically my bits were made to only orgasm through stimulation of the clit, which according to scientific studies is the same for 80 per cent of all women, but still there could be a penis out there that might be able to make me come, and it defo wasn't his.

15. He had lied to me for a year

16. He was a coward
And wimps are not hot.

I had my list. I went over and over it, learning it, wishing it to change me.

When I felt specific needs, like my body longing for him, wanting to look at a picture of him or read an old text, or trying to remember a lovely time, I would assign one of the above to that urge and focus on that instead.

I repeated in my head: "HE IS NOTHING, HE IS NOTHING, HE IS NOTHING. YOU ARE STRONG, YOU ARE STRONG, YOU ARE STRONG. YOU DON'T NEED HIM, YOU DON'T NEED HIM, HE IS NOTHING, HE IS NOTHING . . ." muttering this to myself any time I was walking somewhere or alone. My mantra.

Normally I would have been walking around in my life listening to music or podcasts, but since this had happened I couldn't concentrate on other people's words, spoken or sung. I found anything and everything too upsetting. Music was completely banned, even instrumental stuff—all sounds reminded me too strongly of something lovely about me and X.

I met Fran from Paddington and we did the hour walk to where the spa was. We had a long conversation about why I needed this to work out so much. Why couldn't I just tell him to do one?

"He is the best person I have ever met. Having him near me makes me feel lovely. And I haven't enjoyed being me so much as I have since meeting him. I've known me for over 30 years, so that feels big!"

"There could be other people that you feel those things with."

"Maybe, but also maybe not. All I know is I've never operated in such an honest and exciting way with anyone. And also calm and kind and no crazy arguments. Even with all this, it feels totally different to all the bad ways that Three and I had. For ages I thought that was down to me, and that the screaming and the yelling meant passion and true love, but I've been in something for over a year that has shown me otherwise. That's why I'm holding on so tightly."

"That does all sound much healthier, but then the maybe not being able to leave his kids is—"

I interrupted her. "Him finding it hard to leave the girls makes me have *more* faith in him."

"Why?"

"I think if parents who leave their children find it easier than this then they shouldn't be trusted."

"OK, but I worry you are only seeing the two extremes—your parents' way and then this."

"Of course I compare, but I think that's something positive, to have a scale for me to see how I want the people in my life to be."

"Yes, but I wonder if there are some other things that are at play here too."

It pissed me off that Fran had brought my parents into this.

"Look, it's simple, my dad left Mum super-easily and it's clear he's not the best human. And then my mum left me super-easily and likewise she isn't the best human example. She said she loved me, but essentially she did the leaving thing really quickly and without a lot of thinking. I love that X is doing all the thinking. It makes me feel secure in him for that."

But there was something in what Fran was nudging at that wouldn't leave me alone. That maybe the reason I wanted it so much was so I could be the one who is chosen, and then that would allow me to choose. I didn't really know how it would be long term—X, me, his children and Notalmostex-wife always in the background. It might be awful. I might stop fancying him once all that reality hit. Stop wanting it. But I wanted the chance to know and decide myself. We had gone too far; I needed the option.

And then one of my nastier thoughts surfaced—a kind of fantasy I'd been having that if he chose me, then six months later I would change my mind and dump him out of the blue.

I'd tell him that while he'd gone through the agonising decision process, I had already known I didn't want to be with him and purposefully not told him—lied, pretended I wanted him so it would cause as much damage to him as possible.

The nastiness of that pleased me. And then I felt teary at having such a thought. I confused myself constantly.

I had no clear sense of what I was actually feeling. I wished there could have been a person who could see through all my anger and fear and just tell me what the fuck I actually wanted. Fran said that person could only be me. But I wanted a God-like leader who I had complete faith in telling me the answers. When I was younger, from about nine until into my twenties, for any hard decisions I would ask the Magic 8 Ball. I'd had to chuck it out when it broke. Three had thrown it against the wall in a rage. It hadn't burst open or anything, but the magic-answer bit got stuck on one of its triangle sides so no answers would ever come through. It was okay though, because I could use a virtual one on the internet now.

While Fran went to get some chewing gum I went on to www.ask8ball.net and typed in:

"Will X leave his family for me?"

I pressed the shaker button and it responded:

Ha, of course. That is the absolute accurate fucking answer. Then I asked: "Do I actually want to be with X forever?"

OUTLOOK
NOT SO
GOOD

Seeing that answer didn't make me feel good, and I quickly edited my question to remove the forever, as of course that wasn't an accurate measure because in terms of human life there is no such thing as forever. So:

"Do I actually want to be with X?"

CONCENTRATE
AND ASK
AGAIN

Yeah, no shit. Concentrating was my biggest issue at the moment. But the Magic 8 Ball was good, right?!

Day Five

By Day Five of No Comms, X had worked it all out.

The night before, he had sent some cryptic message that I didn't see until the next morning because Fran had told me to turn my phone off over dinner and keep it off until the morning. With her there this was easier to do. His email had said:

From: X
To: Me
Subject:

Not long I promise my love, I will be in touch with good news soon. Sorry about the flowers, they were supposed to make you feel hopeful, sorry if that wasn't their effect.
xxxxx

That did seem hopeful, but again, what the fuck? I had told him to only send me something solid. Over breakfast I was working out a way to respond to it with Fran when a new one came in from him:

From: X
To: Me
Subject:

I love you and I am so sorry to have put you through all of this. This time has given me the clarity I needed. I need you to be part of my life.
The girls will be ok.

I will continue to be there for them as much as I can.
When I'm back in London I will tell them all.
Yours xxxxx

He was leaving, he was leaving, he was *leaving*!!!!!!!!!!!!!!!
I believed him.
I felt it.
I had won.

I didn't know what this meant for me and the cowboy boots, since the No Comms didn't need to carry on now, but it felt like I shouldn't get them. Instead, I asked the waitress to add a sausage to my avocado on toast.

X asked if he could see me after his train got in late that afternoon, before going to tell them all.

Fran and I discussed the pros and cons of this, and I responded saying that although it was great news that he was clear on his decision, until the actions had been carried out I didn't feel secure meeting up with him.

Fran headed back to Bournemouth, and as soon as she went into the tube I rang X, because there had been five missed calls from him in the last hour.

"Hey."

"Hey."

"I've missed you."

"I've missed you too."

"Please can I come over? I just need to see you before I do all this."

"OK."

Of course I was going to say okay.

I checked Sophie wasn't at home. If she was I'd have booked a room at the weird James Bond–themed hotel up the road in Tottenham. She wasn't, so it was all good for a home visit.

I was supposed to be in work for a half-day from lunchtime,

but I called in sick and rushed home to wash, shave and find the most incredible not-trying-at-all outfit to be wearing, finished off with the shark-tooth necklace. It was really important to me that I wore that.

X knocked on the front door at 3:47 p.m.

I had never felt such excitement, although calling it just that isn't accurate. It was all the feelings, jumping around in my chest together. He came in and he looked like a stranger and family at the same time.

I took him into my room. We hugged tight. Pulled away to look at each other and then came back in for another hug. We kissed, sniffed, stroked, just generally held onto each other. He noticed that I had removed all of the framed pictures and the other reminders of him. He said that made him feel so sad and apologised to me again for all this. Seeing him there saying these things, I didn't mind one bit. My brain retraining and regular mantras hadn't changed anything. I loved him so much.

We fucked. THE MOST INCREDIBLE SEX I HAVE EVER HAD. Which, bearing in mind that all the other sex had always been amazing, meant my mind was literally blown. It just kept getting better. Slow and careful and smooth and long kisses with intense eye-locking and tight face-grabbing. Two orgasms for him and two for me.

After the sex we lay and talked. He told me a few remaining things that had been on his mind about before, when he had been living in the lie—stuff like friends' dinners that he and Notalmostexwife had been to together as it had been easier to go along than not, and also a holiday their friends had booked for them all this summer, which he still wanted her and the children to go on. He said obviously he wouldn't go but would have to deal with all that after this. I told him about exchanging the skull necklace and also about there never being any Valentine's dinner with Paul. He said that had been his worst night, seeing my outfit on Instagram (ha!) and imagining us out together—it had been one of the things that had really spurred on his action. My instincts had been correct!

It was great to be able to talk, but the main reason I was glad X had come over was because, seeing him, I could tell that he was in a calmer, more grounded place. He said he would go back and tell Notalmostexwife, said he had already rung his mum and dad and asked them to support her through this but not to get involved in trying to change his decision, as it was final.

He said that he had found a flat in Brixton, a poky studio through a friend who was away for the next three months so needed minimal rent. It wasn't ideal being that far from the girls, but it would do until he had found something closer. I was relieved that he wouldn't need to stay at mine as I couldn't see a way to have *that* conversation with Sophie. He said that he had sent Sophie an email that morning, apologising to her for bringing this all into her house, and letting her know that he was serious about sorting this all out, looking after me and giving me the love I deserved. I was quite surprised he had contacted her. She hadn't responded, which made me feel all kinds of anger towards her, but that was probably linked to our other thing. X said he had picked up the keys to the new flat on his way to me. Took them out of his bag from an envelope with instructions written on it. Showed me a picture of the flat. It was all actually happening. It felt so odd really living through the things I had already thought I had lived through. Made me feel a bit faraway, not really there. And the opposite of grateful/excited. I made supportive sounds and face movements while my insides talked to me. Morse code was going mad.

X said that he would never delay or mess me around again; that wasn't the real him, that was the panicked, not-able-to-be-truthful version. That he wasn't that person, that he was actually good at getting things sorted and that's what he'd continue doing, to prove to me that everything would be so much easier now.

I told myself to just wait and see. Don't get overly hopeful. I wouldn't be packing overnight bags or getting his move-in flat-survival bag out from under my desk where my framed Manifesto lay on top, Rome side getting dusty. He still had to do this final big thing of telling Notalmostexwife.

But it felt real, all really real.

The following night I visited him in the Brixton flat.

Almostexwife had thrown a vase and smashed it against the wall when he told her. And that was the end of them.

Crap

I had got what I wanted.

The right thing had been done. Truth spoken to all parties. Now we were at the start of something else. X expressed such happiness and hope that now, really, truly, everything would be great as it would all be so honest—but I had felt that happiness and joy last year, when I had believed that's what we were in then. I had thought together we were the most committed either of us had ever been.

I had.

He hadn't.

And even though my brain absolutely understood why he had done what he had done, and it wanted only to forgive and move forwards, I couldn't. My inner bits had been so monumentally changed by everything that had happened that they were now fearful, untrusting, insecure, sad and *very* angry.

I kept having pull-back moments. We'd be doing something and then suddenly I'd remember having the same conversation the first-time round, during the fake bit. Like last year when he'd said he was waiting for the Wi-Fi to arrive, but I knew now that he wasn't coz he hadn't ordered any coz there was no flat then. Living through these now-repeated but actually real moments made my cheeks go red and my chest area feel tight with embarrassment, quickly followed by rage when I remembered their fake predecessors. X having taken the truth away from me over such a long time had totally fucked with my bearings and I was now continually disoriented. It meant that my body and its paranoid thoughts were slow to allow the forgiveness I so wanted to have.

Whereas before I hadn't been at all bothered about when X saw Almostexwife at their home, now I was filled with dread any time he was there. Which was pretty much every day due to taking the girls to school and trying to show them that he was still very much around. I could picture him in the kitchen chatting to her as she heated something on the hob. I hated their kind of hob; they always seemed to take three times as long for anything to be ready. X agreed. We'd spoken about it when I had visited his house for a long weekend when Almostexwife and the girls were away visiting her parents. I had felt a bit weird being there for about five minutes, until we'd had sex in the guest room and balance was restored. He had a bunch of his stuff in there, so I'd had no reason to think it wasn't the room where he slept.

When he went out to get dinner supplies from the shop I'd quickly gone on a tour of the whole place. I wanted to go into every room and see every photo. It hadn't been on my mind before being in her home, but I wanted to see what she looked like.

I'd found a bunch of recent photos on the fridge. Ones of the girls and a recentish one of them all together in a field; it felt weird seeing them all together. She was the complete opposite of me—tied-back grey hair, and she looked old, much older than him, even though she was only five years older. She dressed very averagely, which surprised me as I had pictured her as very chic what with all her work trips to Paris. Maybe she was when she was younger, so I went looking for more pictures of her, ones closer to when she was my age. I found a wedding album in their lounge cupboard, and to my relief she did have something about her when she was younger. She had long reddish hair, in a natural way, not like a bad colour job. She looked much hotter than X, who, of course, looked terrible in the wedding photos, what with him looking completely confused and lost. There were some other pictures of her in another album. Her dress sense looked cooler in those too, kind of like how stylish people make Cos clothing look good. Defo not for me, but she had good taste. I couldn't imagine them together. I didn't feel anything like jealousy, just some kind of familiar feeling because she now really reminded me of my favourite primary school teacher.

Now, any time X would text me to say he was heading to the house it made my head feel awful and my chest too, and I wanted to stake out his road and observe his comings and goings with binoculars. Which I had a go at but it wasn't very successful because where they lived was one long line of terraced houses with no trees or side roads to hide around. God knows how people successfully stalked—the few hours I had tried it I had found it to be very stressful, even with wearing my Elvis wig and baseball cap as a disguise.

I told myself that my brain would find this much easier after a week or so. That I was the one he had chosen.

He picked *me*!!

But annoyingly that huge fact didn't make a difference to my new insecurities. It actually made me feel really distressed, since I never realised I was going to be in something whereby I had to be picked. It's a really shitty feeling when you already thought you were on your way to amazing relationship bliss. To have it all burst with doubt coz there was a bit where the person you loved was trying to decide who he'd rather have. He said it was only tied into the children, that her being their mother was the only way he had love for her, but I'm not thick—the staying-thinking must have definitely involved her too, because at one point it had really felt like there was a big chance of him picking her over me. This now made me feel like there could be, at any moment, a situation in which he unpicked me. Maybe that doesn't make sense, but the picking shizzle was taking over all my thoughts and it was doing my head in.

I spoke to Fran about it—at this stage I would actually have taken one of her weird healing crystals in the hope of it helping me to find calm.

"You do know this is the basis of all relationships?"

"What do you mean?"

"Well, at some point any of us could choose not to be with the other."

I got it. I had unpicked Three. But it didn't soothe the batshit-crazy dialogue my thoughts were having with me. I had never felt this kind of under-confidence with any boyfriend before. Never doubted that any of them wanted to be with me. Semi-consciously I always played the who's-hotter-than-who game in my head with the guys I was with. Before this mess I was definitely hotter than X (younger, fitter, got my original hair colour, white teeth, no toe fungus, great at tanning). But now it felt like he had been propelled to a 10-plus and me relegated to a two. It was so shit. I don't know why but I felt like I was not at all important, and I decided that somewhere in his mind he linked me to the misery he was going through in being separated from the girls. That in his head, getting back with Almostexwife would give him a sanctuary from that grief. It scared the shit out of me constantly, even though he never once said any of that.

Fran said maybe it was guilt, what I was feeling. But it wasn't.

When he was over at theirs doing homework or bedtime, I'd get physical chest-stressed reactions. Close to what I imagine anxiety attacks are like.

I was not the kind of girl whose body did this to them.

This was serious. Overwhelming.

And my overpowering fear now was that he wasn't communicating the truth. I worried about it all the time. Not in terms of cheating, just everything else—was he where he said he was? Was he being honest with telling me his feelings?

I wanted some kind of relief from this, so I went to start an "X Head and Chest Pain" diary in my phone notes, but as I did I remembered my fanny pain diary and I stopped, because although this was bad, it was not at all in the same category as that. This was just about my head catching up with what had happened and feeling clear again. I needed something practical to help speed things up, so I worked out the passcode to X's phone by looking over his shoulder when he put it in and then, whenever he was in the shower, I kept close surveillance on the tone of his texts with Almostexwife. Checking that she wasn't begging him to come back and that he wasn't considering it. And that things were how he described them to be. They were, and that was so relieving, but only for that moment. I always felt I needed to look again.

I had agreed with myself that I could look on his phone for information on their communications for the next few months, and that I wasn't allowed to go snooping in other places in the phone, as that felt unfair. But this was still not cool. And so not what I wanted to be doing. During my five-year relationship with Three I'd never looked on his phone, and now I was the kind of person who did this. I didn't like it, so I spoke to a professional about it. My work offered a free counselling phone service. I'd seen the poster at the sign-in point at reception every day since I'd worked there but not been interested in it before. I rang the number and spoke to someone whose name I didn't remember. She told me, "Forgiveness from a betrayal takes a long time. Things will get easier."

I took it in.

"Out of interest, would my situation be quicker to move on from than someone who was trying to get over a proper sexual-cheating betrayal?"

I wanted some kind of indication or scale for this.

"It doesn't really work like that. The feelings you are having around this current betrayal will not just be about this, but will also be pulling on times from your past where you have been let down before, by past boyfriends, family members, etc."

Great.

I thought about the big betrayals in my past and realised that even though they had been carried out by people I loved, after the thing had been done to me I no longer liked them very much, which made it simpler in the long term to disengage with them, move on, and have my version of "forgiveness." Which was basically to tolerate them but keep them at a distance. I had been doing this very well since my teenage years, and as I had expert practice of it with my mum, I had assumed I was an excellent person at my kind of forgiving and moving on. But the problem was the "like" bit. I both loved and liked X. I didn't want to keep him at a distance, but having him close was shit too. Nobody had taught me how to forgive with those given factors.

X had said to me, the afternoon before telling Almostexwife for real, that he knew the next bit would be hard and that he'd need my support more than ever, which he acknowledged was bad timing and an unfair thing to ask of me given how he had treated me. But thinking it would be okay as I wanted him so badly, I had said I would be there—100 per cent support.

He had asked me if I'd move in with him once he had left the temporary Brixton flat—he'd been looking at two-beds back in West London. I said I would, but I knew I had no plans to. No way. I'd be a fucking idiot to do that in this state of things. It pleased me to give him the wrong impression—

something I would have taken no pleasure in before all this. I noted it in my lies list.

Lies to admit to X
—Lying about being pregnant
—That I'm pretending to be ok with any of this
—That I will support his decision and not take revenge
—~~That there was a valo dins with Paul~~
—That I like his extra-hairy shoulder patch
—That I've been looking in his phone
—That I will move in with him

I told myself I'd give it a year. Get through all the actual firsts for this first/second time. See if lapping the lies would make a difference to my feelings. I still found him to be the best man I'd ever met. My fanny still only wanted him. I wanted to still believe in us and my Manifesto. I just needed to be less angry, less untrusting.

I gave myself a pass for it being hard, told myself to ignore the mean feelings I'd started to have, and that so long as my fanny continued to want him I'd give it my best shot. The hardness and meanness would pass, once I'd processed it all, healed.

I made him do weekly couples' therapy. It was one of the conditions I asked him to agree to that afternoon in my room after the "support" conversation. We couldn't risk where not communicating properly might lead us. We'd both done that route before, plus fuck knows what his emotional state would be like a few months into not living with the girls.

I was right.

It had been bad enough the first few weeks, him moping around missing them so much even though he was seeing them every day when he took them to school or the sports centre. But as time went on it got worse. It was like being with

306

someone who had depression. I didn't look forward to the future when it came to their birthdays and X not waking in the same house as them, or spending Christmas apart. *Christmas*!! That thought fucked me off and hurt me somewhere deep, as I already thought they had done a version of Christmas apart. It made me want to shout nasty things at him like, "Snap out of your blues, you pathetic, weak man, you shouldn't have cheated on Almostexwife in the first place if you were that bothered about your children." But I kept that one to myself.

Don't forget
—You want and like your own time at the weekends
—To check in with Al and Fran to see if I am seeming like me
—To be less angry

Susan

I liked going to Susan's house.

I got the impression most couples went to couples' counselling when one of them wanted out, like with me and Three, but as X and I were pretty much near the beginning and both very much wanting "in," it felt like an interesting experiment rather than needing crisis almost-breaking-up help.

It was very expensive and I had already agreed with X that he should cover the first eight sessions over the initial two months. I had prepared a spreadsheet ready for stating my case but he didn't need me to go into it. He thought it was right he covered the first few months. I said all sessions after those ones I'd then split with him, as we were in it together. But then I immediately regretted offering that as it was £60 a week, each. Which I couldn't really afford. But then I reminded myself how easily I used to spend more than that regularly on coke, without even stressing. Funny how something that was potentially lethal I was cool with blowing money on, but something that was known to be lifesaving I was more hesitant about—so I told myself to shut up and pay it. I could work out a repayment scheme to my credit card.

In the early sessions, I'd save up my weeks' worth of noted-down feelings and emotions and fire them off along with some of my older thoughts and questions that I'd had since The Truth came out. Susan, our therapist, called it my quick-fire round.

"When did you last have sex with her?"

"The July before we met."

"On the sofa did you sometimes lean on each other?"

"No, I always sat on the armchair."

"Did your parents actually lend you both money?"

"Yes, we asked for it to fix the roof."

"What happened to it?"

"I made sure we didn't do the work as I was planning to use it for rent once I told her I was leaving."

"Where did you keep all the letters and gifts I gave you?"

"At work."

"Where?"

"Locked in my filing cabinet."

"What Christmas present did you give her?"

"A bottle of bath oil."

"What birthday present did you give her?"

"A bottle of port."

"Do you think you are a psycho?"

Susan cut it off there, which annoyed me as it was a simple yes or no answer.

We had bigger conversations about why he had cheated on Almostexwife on that very first occasion (years of lack of comms around sex changing), what his biggest fear now was (the girls not missing or needing him), and general parent-background stuff for us both, as well as some of my dark fantasy-land thoughts.

"Susan, why do I have such strong dreams about him being dead and why am I so happy in them?!"

I left out the awake times when I'd had really horrible and violent thoughts towards him.

"Why don't you describe what happens and we can see what feelings that brings up?"

It felt powerful being able to have a hypothetical discussion about X not existing in front of him.

Susan had logical explanations for everything, which we discussed calmly and kindly, and we always left her sessions feeling tired but good. Apart from week four's session, when I just screamed at neither of them in particular for ages and out of nowhere, shouting, "HE'S SO SELFISH SO SELFISH SUCH A SELFISH SELFISH SELFISH MAN YOU'RE SELFISH HE'S SO SELFISH."

I was actually quite impressed that I hadn't used the word cunt. Susan had a bit of a mother-like quality to her, which I think made me accidentally be more polite. I mean like an ideal mother, how I imagined nice, normal ones were, where you liked and respected them and therefore didn't say the c-word in their company.

After I had stopped shouting the room went quiet and calm again and eventually X said, "I know I'm selfish, and that's the hardest conversation I have with myself."

And then he cried a bit. Which made me immediately feel a lot of love for him again. Those tears. We had really, *really* good sex after that one.

It took me until our eighth session to admit to breaking into his phone regularly. I brought it up as the whole thing had become unhelpful. I'd find out from reading his texts that he might be planning to have a drink with a pal or making a future family plan and then I'd time how long it would take him to tell me about it, and if it was more than a couple of days I would read negative things into his lack of communication and think more sinister things were happening. Which they weren't. So basically it wasn't a great mix for my current state of mind. I had been darting around checking it at not-quite-safe times—loo trips, when he was changing the bins, once when he was struggling to get something out of the freezer. Plus, I had also broken my rules and was now reading all incoming and outgoing texts, all received and sent emails, his phone notes and his call lists, and had also wasted at least an hour studying all of the photos he had taken prior to meeting me. Which drove me nutty. It had become a bit too addictive and dangerous. And not very rewarding. It felt such a relief to be honest about it, although I didn't tell him the whole extent of it; I just said I had been reading his texts to Almostexwife and it was becoming a bad habit so could he change his passcode?

"You're very welcome to know it and look whenever you like."

"Thank you, but I'd rather stop."

It took me a few weeks to get the urge of wanting to look fully out of me.

I crossed it off my "Lies to admit to X" list and popped it on my "Don't forget" one:

Don't forget
—You want and like your own time at the weekends
—To check in with Al and Fran to see if I am seeming like me
—To be less angry
—To never look in partner's phone

X was very kind about it and appreciated my honesty, and although he agreed it was not a healthy or ideal thing to have been doing, he said he understood why I had, which helped me not feel too awful about it all.

Mia

After three months of being in the shitty Brixton place, X found a nice one-bed flat to rent within 10 minutes of the girls. I had helped him choose it as I would be spending lots of time there—and he thought I'd be moving in at some point in the not-too-far-away future, as that's what my mouth had told him.

It was on the same street as the fake address he had given me when I'd sent my birthday thank-you limerick card. Walking down the road made me feel massive hate at being tricked, but then confusingly straight away also feeling huge satisfaction that the flat he eventually got was actually near the fake one.

Urgh!!!

It was all so confusing.

We set a date for September for me to leave Sophie's, which would be seven months after him (for real) moving out of the family home. July the first was when I would have to give my landlord notice for my move-out. And as it neared, I let all the days around the end of June go by without mentioning anything to Sophie or George or my landlord. And then all the days in early July too.

X asked me if the conversation telling Sophie and George had been okay and I said it had.

Lies to admit to X
—Lying about being pregnant
—That I'm pretending to be ok with any of this

—That I will support his decision and not take revenge
—~~That there was a valo dins with Paul~~
—That I like his extra-hairy shoulder patch
—~~That I've been looking in his phone~~
—That I will move in with him
—That I spoke to S&G about moving out

I *really* liked the feeling of him thinking I was moving out but me knowing there was no plan to. Except I did really want to be with him and I really liked being there at his flat. I enjoyed him cooking me dinner and us having a private space, and now that I had deposited all my eBay essential-seconds wardrobe items at his flat the toing and froing from Walthamstow to Ladbroke Grove was less annoying. But something was stopping me from fully committing.

I eventually brought it up in couples' therapy, asking Susan why she thought I hadn't been able to give my notice in on time to move out. I could tell X wanted to say something but this was directed at Susan, so he had to wait.

"What do *you* think it means?"

"Can't you just tell me?"

"No. Try to say what feelings you have around doing it."

It was a complicated mix of things—change, trust issues, punishment, loss of independence, telling my friends, the girls' sleeping arrangements. How would that even work? They'd not even met me yet.

"I'm annoyed at his general lack of thinking around this."

"Tell him."

Urgh, I hated when Susan did this; he'd already heard me. It felt so cringe. I turned to look at him.

"We'd previously agreed that this should be a slow process, led by when the girls felt comfortable. But ahead of me supposedly moving in, you haven't even acknowledged any of this. I want you to be the one to bring something up for once."

The girls knew I existed; Almostexwife had told X he had to be honest with them when he moved out. But it was a big step from knowing about me to actually meeting and being around me properly. I wanted the girls to have decent time with their dad on the one night they actually got to sleep over with him every other weekend. I shouldn't be there as well. Why hadn't he been thinking of all this?

He, as always, listened and agreed, saying he should have done that thinking, but then didn't offer up any kind of tangible solution.

After the therapy session we went for a beer to discuss it further, and I came up with a plan whereby I would pay 70 per cent of my rent budget to X and 30 per cent to Mia, who had an almost-room in her attic, which she was doing nothing with and where I could dump a load of my not-so-important everyday-living stuff and also have a bed for the nights the girls were over. I'd then move my eBay seconds over to Mia's, meaning the nights I stayed there I could just turn up and not have to lug stuff around with me, preventing this feeling like a big ball-ache.

Obviously I'd prefer to have just one home, but this seemed like a suitable solution for now, plus—and I didn't say this to X, but—I still didn't really see what the version of the future looked like where I was around all the time living somewhere where two children slept over regularly. That life felt weird, not mine.

Mia had been great during my move-related worries. We had spoken most mornings on my way to work as I built up the words to talk to X about it. As well as offering her spare room, she gave me very fair thinking around the full X and me situ, said how I had every right to freak out in the way I did about the things that upset me, mainly Almostexwife. She made me feel like I was normal and not a hopelessly shit person at for-giveness. She never judged X or made me feel bad for wanting to stay with this. She got it. And it was really nice having one person that I could be completely myself with. I'd still been keeping Sophie out of most of the me and X up-and-down feelings as I wanted to give her space from it all, in the hope of repairing our friendship and not making it worse.

On the 1st August I finally told Sophie and George that I'd be moving out, and that was it. I would be semi-living with X from October. I told them separately. George first in the morning before he went to rehearsals, and then Sophie after work. I was really nervous about telling her so I prepared a speech.

"I love you, and this has been the best home I've ever lived in, and I'm probably going to regret moving out, but I think I need to do this next step and please be OK with it?!"

She told me she understood and could see that we both loved each other very much.

It hadn't been as bad as I'd been dreading. Which made me feel sadder to be leaving her. My original hero.

From: Three
To: Me
Subject:

I hope whoever you meet next is actually a nice guy.

From: Three
To: Me
Subject:

Sorry I shouldn't have sent that. I just worry about you.
x

Three had really cut back on his late-night emotional emails, but the odd ones that did still come had started to have a weirdly prophetic quality to them.

It had been a while since we had sold the flat, and the divorce application had felt simple in comparison to that.

Probably helped by Three having started something new with someone. Which made me feel relieved, as all I wanted was for him to meet a partner who was nice. We had the date for when the divorce would be read out in a court room somewhere up north, and we'd even spoken about maybe having lunch or dinner on the actual day. Steps towards the friendship I knew we both wanted. But this last email made me feel really stressed and gave me a deep dread of bringing up the "I've met someone" convo—Three would definitely not think what X had done was okay. I had easily avoided telling him so far, as the mechanics of our lives were so very separate now. And the 70/30 living plan meant I could just tell Three I was moving in with Mia.

X and I took a trip to Madrid in early September, before the big move-in. Summer had passed in a mass of complicated feelings with my overall goal being to balance out my intense love and bubbling hate towards X. The time together away from everything felt good, like original us. X fingered me on *both* plane journeys, and we had incredible sex hanging over our hotel balcony as protesters marched down the middle of a main road throwing paint bombs at the bank. I had fewer questions and worries whizzing around my head during this time and things seemed close and hopeful. More so than they had done since he had left home. It really felt clear the two people we could be together.

On the day I finally moved out I told myself to be extra-cheery about it, but as we drove off in the van X had hired I felt really upset and doomy, which is totally nuts considering how poo Walthamstow is to live in. I tried to cover up my feelings of dread by doing silent looking-out-of-the-window crying, which lasted all the way to Tottenham. But even with these feelings, I did think it was the right thing to be doing. And like Three always said, I was just shit at moving homes.

I moved the majority of my clothes into X's flat—we had to

buy two extra clothes rails from Argos to fit them all in, along with a big laundry bin for the bathroom for my okay-to-be-folded dresses, and a big wicker chest for the lounge for my jumpers, as well as a smaller chest by the kitchen for my bags. My shoe boxes lined all the walls in the hall, and my books were squeezed by the one spare wall bordering the kitchen/lounge area.

The place looked a bit shit now that I had used up every single bit of space.

All of my other furniture I had either sold, crammed into Mia's or got my brother to store in his shed.

X made a comment on whether I really needed all the things I was bringing to the flat, and I told him in a stern don't-fuck-with-me voice that I'd already got rid of more than I'd planned to.

Bags full of clothes, binned.

The best table ever sold.

Amazing kitchenware left for Sophie.

All my garden furniture left there too.

He didn't push it further.

It was a good job his girls were already aware of me as it would have been hard not to see parts of me crammed into every corner of that flat. But I wanted to be mindful of them, so I kept my jewellery, photos and perfume out of sight. I thought it would be weird for them to see or smell me before actually meeting me.

I'd always loved hanging my jewellery in creative ways on top of my chest of drawers for easy access and fashion inspiration. I'd been doing it like that since I was a teenager. Dangling necklaces off teacup stands and stacking bracelets on the wooden kitchen-roll holder. But now, for the first time ever, I created a new storage situation for them. Before the move, I had been in Homebase looking for extra-big plastic boxes for stuff to go into Jay's shed and found myself down the toolbox aisle. Holy shit there were some incredible creations down there. Turns out storing tools and jewellery is not that different.

I bought an amazing toolbox which had seven compartments and big pull-out bits—this would house my head crowns, bangles and chunkier necklaces (I had gone mad the year Zara brought out the statement necklace and had about 20). For rings, smaller necklaces, dainty bracelets and earrings I bought five smaller flat plastic tool containers, which they'd advertised for storing nails and wall plugs. They had removable mini internal walls in the different-sized sections and it was very satisfying organising all my bits into them. I proudly called Sophie in to show her the results laid out on the bed.

"That is impressive."

"And I went with the see-through ones for these, so when they are stacked in a drawer I only need to scan the top to see what's inside."

"You're making a lot of big changes—you sure you're feeling all right about it all?"

"Oh, this I don't mind, feels nice to have a shake-up, plus it means my jewellery won't get dusty!"

When I had finally finished unpacking, X stood in the middle of the bedroom and commented unhelpfully, "Blimey, there is no sign of the flat it was before! My minimalist days are over . . ."

And then he said he was going for a walk around the block.

As soon as he left I cried.

On our Boxing Day–Christmas last year, after the kitchen-table licking, we had excitedly talked about our eventual move-in plans—and they had not looked like this.

When he came back, X apologised for deserting me and explained that he'd found it hard as all his belongings apart from his clothes were still in the family home, so he had momentarily found it a bit overwhelming. I felt sorry for him, but also it felt shit and unwelcoming, and I was upset at him not making it the exciting thing a move-in night should be. He reminded me, not in an unkind way, that I had spent the first three miles of that morning's drive crying out of the window and not talking to him, and even though he didn't say it at the time, he had found that a bit upsetting. Which made things feel equal and we apologised to each other, and he suggested having some Prosecco in the bath—something I had hoped would be part of our move-in night.

His bath was wider at the top than the bottom so I always took the tap end so he could be more comfortable.

He topped up my glass. "Cheers to clutter, love and you!"

I twisted round to turn the tap off. "You do know that you are actually quite lucky?"

"How so?"

"Because 40 per cent of my things are distributed around other postcodes in London. You'd have spiralled into a proper meltdown if this had been a 100 per cent occupation!"

He splashed some water at me and things felt as they should.

Shift

After a few weeks, even without my frames and photos, it did start to feel like a home of sorts. I stayed at "ours" most of the time, with visits to my room at Mia's every other weekend and more stays planned during half-term and the school holidays. In theory I didn't mind sleeping at my room there, especially as it meant I got to see Mia, but when it came to leaving to go to hers I always had quite difficult feelings. Not so much because I wanted to spend all my time with X—I didn't—but because knowing I wasn't "allowed" at our flat during those times felt sad and depressing. Even though I knew logically it was right, and something I had suggested.

I would have quite low and mean thoughts on the nights I was sleeping away. It wouldn't cloud my whole day, it would just hit me as I lay in bed in the dark waiting to fall asleep. It reminded me of the feelings I had when I was younger, that first night I'd be staying with whichever parent I'd not seen for a while. A different bed in a different house. Re-feeling that made me hate it more. The thing that helped me to balance it all out was that I was glad the girls weren't having their dad's girlfriend pushed on them. I thought how little me would've really appreciated some of that consideration. Plus, as I was a proper grown-up adult now, I was also very happy to have the night to watch back-to-back episodes of *Big Little Lies* and finish the evening with a wank.

~

Sex with X was still very good but had definitely calmed down a lot. We did it most days, but now it was more like one orgasm each plus less romantic talking afterwards. Gone were the times of lying around for hours continually rediscovering hotness for the other's parts or discussing places we wanted to go to with each other. I was still open to this but he'd be gone, normally to the bathroom to wipe his willy. He had always left it to air-dry before.

With our new commitment to always communicating, I brought it up. "Do you think there is anything in you always rushing off after sex now?"

"Do I?"

"You do. I have been keeping notes!"

"I hadn't noticed; maybe it's because I'm getting older and need to pee more. But I still give you a run for your money!"

He did seem to wee more than he used to, especially during the night. And I agreed that our sex life was still incredible; however, that didn't take away from it not being what it had been.

"We almost only ever do hot stuff on the bed now."

"Do we?"

"Mostly."

I thought of the Manifesto, which was now in my knicker drawer, Rome side facing up. I still hoped to present it to him at some point, I'd just not found the right time. I had made sure I was cleaning my teeth at unexpected times and making him do things with me in other places—a fingering in the hallway between the bathroom and the bedroom, sex bent over the pile of books in between the kitchen and lounge area. But it all just felt a bit different, and I didn't have the ability to know whether this was a) because of normal (not-quite-full-time) moving-in-together shizzle, b) part of the leftover betrayal stress I still felt or c) due to him being in absolute missing-the-girls-pain hell.

Don't forget
—You want and like your own time at the weekends
—To check in with Al and Fran to see if I am seeming like me
—To be less angry
—To never look in partner's phone
—To go through the Manifesto

It had been over nine months since The Truth had been known, but I still wasn't like the self I'd been before and was still waiting for that proper forgiveness feeling to settle in. And to just feel secure.

On my worst days I hated X a little bit all the time. Not so much his behaviour now or anything. He was kind and thoughtful and clear at communicating, like he had promised he would be. But I just hated that thing he'd done, and how it had shifted everything for me.

My wanking fantasies had changed.

When I was on my way to coming I had started picturing him cheating or, more accurately, licking or knobbing other women I knew he knew, and I would be there also, but it was like I was him or something. It would be the hot thing that would make me climax. But then immediately after, in non-fantasy land, it made me stressed because it was the exact opposite of what I would ever want and it wasn't a helpful addition to my already-long list of insecurities to worry about with him.

I didn't feel like unpacking that one in our therapy sessions as we had so much other shit to pick through. X was still sad a lot of the time. He wasn't worried about it, said it was to be expected, and he would always be quite positive and not very moany. He said he knew that things would get better. But having him give off an often low vibe was a real drag. A downer. It felt like being with someone who had a force field of non-emotion around their body. On good days it could be penetrated in small areas so you could reach skin or heart or lips, but once that moment was over it would seal up again and those things would be harder to get to. And if a bad day was happening there was no chance for getting through, as the layer became foggy and bumpy, like trying to move through really awful turbulence. There was no pattern for when it would get really thick. It could be at the end of a nice weekend with the girls, or at the start before leaving to pick them up, over a breakfast when they weren't there or while watching TV or a film. He was raw and lovesick over his children and in those moments there was no room for me and my insecurities or my fanny, and I felt completely pushed out and on my own.

We spoke about his sadness in therapy, and Susan confirmed that everything X did or felt was all to be expected and therefore I just had to keep on being okay with it all, holding out for a time when it would lessen, with fuck no idea of when that would actually be.

But this wasn't what I had signed up for.

They kept forgetting that.

Back when we were starting out, if he had demonstrated these things then I might not have been as attracted to him. Our thing wouldn't have necessarily become what it did. I wouldn't have fallen so mad in lust with a man who had children-related depression fog. This might sound harsh, but I think it's the truth.

Jay has had depression since his early twenties following a car accident he was in where he lost the movement in his right eye. After that he always saw himself differently (that isn't an eye joke). His depression comes for a few weeks, then leaves for a few months, then comes back again. When it's with him, it is completely impenetrable. I know how to support and be around him during those times, know to lower my expectations, me talk more, him talk less. And coz he's my brother, me doing that goes without saying. But in a new guy I wasn't even looking for? No way. And if X had just been honest with me from the start or just left when he'd said three months in, I'd have seen all this sooner and not have been tricked into thinking life after leaving the girls would be easy.

These should have been the best years of my life; I was in my thirties and officially in my sexual prime. But they weren't. I was with a man who was grieving for his children and it was like I was grieving too, for the amazing thing X had been before, and the love and sex I now missed. I wanted to believe it would come back once he felt more settled with his new parenting ways and had arranged the new financial stuff with Almostexwife, but a) that seemed like a long and far-away journey for them and b) after such a time of things now being this way, I couldn't be sure it would ever return to its previous glory.

And that made me feel the saddest.

I created a fold-out calendar chart in the back of my notebook to monitor how often I felt happy or low because of X and his situation. Through initials and tallies I recorded how many times we had sex, how often my insecurities came, how often I felt lethal hate, and the times I felt like he wasn't really present. I colour-coded each category. My plan was to track all of this so that at the end of this year of trying, approximately three months away, I would have the evidence to help me work out if things had got better or not. And then I'd make a non-fanny-related decision about what to do, as I couldn't rely on my bits going off him any time soon—I still wanted him all the time. I hadn't fancied another male person since we met; he was still my only type. I'd even searched out "men with deep frown lines licking fannies" porn, which had soothed me during our apart time. I was doomed. My only hope was the chart.

Susan had encouraged us to talk more about the hard feelings we were both encountering, so I brought up that I was keeping a lot back.

324

"I have all these worries constantly about what he is thinking and what he is feeling when he's at the girls' house, and I don't know what I should or shouldn't be saying, especially as I can see that he isn't in the best place with all that."

X responded before Susan. "You can tell me when you're worried. I'm always happy to reassure or have a conversation. I know it's me that has put those thoughts in your head."

I nodded.

Urgh, I was now the kind of girl who needs their boyfriend's reassurance—how pathetic.

Susan gently said to me, "You are looking a little uncomfortable—what is this making you feel and where?"

I hated it when she tried to make me say where in my body I was feeling things.

"In my chest. And it's making me feel that he says that now, but if I say all the things I want to and be the real me of now, with all my sad and angry and paranoid thoughts, it'll be too much and he'll leave."

Good, I got that out without crying and sounded quite objective. Susan slightly turned her body to focus on me.

"Do you mind if we talk about your mother and father?"

"OK."

"Can you remember how you were after your father left?"

"No. I was too young; all my memories don't start properly until I was near the end of primary school."

"You've mentioned before that your mother used to say you were very difficult at the age after your father left her."

"Yes, in like a badass cool-child way."

"Do you think that after your father left your mother and you, with all your difficult feelings and reactions, that was part of why your mother then left?"

What the fuck? No, I fucking didn't.

I went to say this to Susan, but by the time I had finished

thinking it in my head my nose had gone tingly and my eyes were welling up and I couldn't actually speak.

Fucking cunt.

X moved closer along the sofa to go to put his arm around me. I shrugged him away. "I'm fine."

I looked at Susan angrily. She looked back at me. We held eyes for what felt like a very long time. She knew. And now I did too. We continued talking through our eyes until my anger left.

I was so thick. How had I not known??!!!! I thought my feelings towards Mum leaving were that I found it annoying, rude, weak. I didn't realise it was actually *this*. That I thought it was to do with me.

I drank some water. One of the best things I've learnt after being given shocking news is to drink shitloads of water.

Susan continued: "I think you struggle with being your true self with people when things aren't feeling good for you, in fear of them finding you too much and then them leaving. You need to separate the you from back then, the confused, scared child, from the you now, an adult who is in a secure, loving relationship, and start trying to communicate honestly and without fear."

So I added how often I voiced my insecurities on the chart too and started to do exactly that.

"When did you last kiss on the lips?"

"When was the last time you had sex with her?"

"Did you accidentally touch skin when you shared the same bed?"

"Did you wake up with boners?"

"When did you start wearing your boxer shorts in bed?"

"When did you last communicate that you loved her?"

"When was the last time that you actually meant it as a romantic thing?"

"What was she like when you took the girls to school this morning?"

"Has she asked you to come back?"

"Is part of you wishing you'd not left?"

"Does she look more beautiful to you now you've left?"

"Do you want to comfort her?"

"Have you comforted her?"

"When the girls make you laugh do you share a nice look with each other?"

"Where will you sit during the school play?"

"Will you walk with her back from parents' evening?"

"Did you talk at dance handover?"

These thoughts were never quiet in my head, and if I could have got away with it, I would have constantly repeated the same questions over and over to X at every breakfast, lunchtime phone call, dinner or middle-of-the-night wee.

He had answered all these questions, quite a few times, but I learnt during this period that I didn't have a hear-it-once kind of brain.

I had been right about being cautious at voicing them too often, because it did lead to arguments and stress, which then sometimes turned into hateful words from me. I worried constantly that it would push him away. I'd hated it when Three had been needy with me like this and especially never felt hot exciting things about him in those moments. I didn't want to risk that with X, so I tried to be more careful with what I voiced and cut down on some of the new jealousies I had developed.

I also added a fight log to the chart.

Me:
Where are you? xx

X:
Headed to see the girls xx

Me:
How long do you plan to be there? xx

X:
Picking Tammy up from friends
then will do bath and bed xx

X:
Will also eat with them xx

On his way home he called me and the first thing I asked was who was sitting next to who at dinner?

I couldn't stop myself.

X breathed out a deep sigh. "I'll be back in five. Talk then."

I got stressed at myself for being this kind of desperate girl but reminded myself strongly that for that whole first year I had been with X I had not once been at all jealous of Almostexwife, or had any of these kinds of questions, even though I knew he saw her every day. This was his doing, not mine.

By the time he walked in I was pretty angry and I engaged immediately in a fight.

Fight Diary
—Beer with Tom
—Parents' evening
—Tammy's bday
—Convo with his parents
—Eating dinner

I logged our fights because in his pressured state when we had one, X would claim that's all we did, when actually that wasn't the case. There would be days, weeks, between our fights. It annoyed me that he wasn't seeing this, that he was walking around with an incorrect version of what we were.

Don't get me wrong, we did have a few big blow-out ones, generally linked to nights when I had drunk wine and always led by me saying something really mean about past-him. Particularly about the guy he was before he met me, as it seemed

I now had more and more trouble accepting the past-him who had cheated on Almostexwife. The meaningless one-night stands he'd had when he was with her before he met me angered me. Surely he knew each one of those shags was risking the family he claimed to care so deeply for? It made me feel insulted on behalf of her, and fucked off that he worried so much about the girls now but not then.

My hate grew with pints of cider and glasses of Pinot Grigio. The therapy was helping, but it wasn't a miracle cure. After one vicious yelling-at-him fight in which I informed him he'd never find someone who would put up with all this shit in the way I had, and that he was a cunt, I decided not to drink for the next two weeks as it was clear he didn't have the emotional resources to navigate those kinds of fights where my tongue went off on an alcohol-fuelled rant. He had just sat in the corner, shrinking.

I hated that my behaviour reminded me of the kind of toxic fights Three and I would have. Hated that I'd thought that version of me had gone away, but it hadn't.

X's eventual response would be to walk away, leave the flat, saying he needed some space. On returning, he would say my hate was making him too unhappy and then, in a really solemn and serious tone, say maybe we should leave it—and that would always *really* fucking scare me. Because it was clear that in those moments he didn't mean just the conversation we'd been having. He meant us. This would immediately bring me back to normal-and-kind mode, and also make my insecurity go crazy and make me feel really unsafe in there being an ongoing us.

Don't forget
—You want and like your own time at the weekends
—To check in with Al and Fran to see if I am seeming like me
—To be less angry
—To never look in partner's phone

—To go through the Manifesto
—To not make fights happen when drinking
—No booze when feeling shit
—No swearing in fights

X had been through so much with leaving his family that he didn't now have the room to argue without everything feeling too much. Surely, I deserved at least a year of going ape-shit at him whenever I fancied? But because I didn't want to give him any reason to walk away during this extra-emotional time, I modified my fighting style (i.e., stopped shouting swear words at him). It wasn't easy, but I told myself if I didn't call him a cunt in the next ten arguments, I was allowed to reward myself with some a-bit-too-expensive earrings I had been desperate to have.

This earring incentive really helped me; I managed to give up the expletives and quickly learnt to call him much calmer and more considerate mean names during disagreements.

X's speed of giving up in the face of an argument wasn't the only thing that now made my insides feel under threat from him. For months after The Truth, if X paused in a certain way and said something like, "I need to tell you something," my heart would actually stop, or my breathing would, until he spoke again, because my body always felt certain in those moments that he was going to drop a horrendous bomb. It made me feel like I'd been transported back to that day outside my work. When actually he was only wondering if I'd like his special steak and mushrooms for dinner.

I'd not experienced this kind of fear before, and now it was in overdrive. It made me feel like I had no control over anything. It was exhausting, and it was 100 times worse than the quicksand feeling.

The Strangler

A couple of weeks after setting myself the earring challenge X and I had a *really* bad fight. One I would never have expected us to have.

It was extra-disappointing that it had happened, as I was (annoyingly) only one disagreement away from achieving 10 arguments without any name-calling, but then I fucked up big time.

It was over an escort. Previously, we had sometimes done this hot thing during sex where we'd say we wanted to get an escort and then we'd find one off a real website. We'd talk through what she would do to both of us as we scrolled through the photos. I found it really sexy, and was always the initiator. On this day during our scrolling, which I had encouraged, I flipped out when X described something about what "she'd" be doing to us. I had been enjoying it up to a certain point but then just suddenly switched, pushed at him to get off and out of me, threw the iPad across the room, jumped out of bed and screamed at him for being a cunt.

"How dare you fantasise about another woman after treating me so badly? You fucking disgusting CUNT."

That once-safe, anything-possible sexual place now felt compromised too.

I slammed the door and he followed me, confused. I turned on him and pushed him into the wall and he said firmly, without physically reacting, that I couldn't treat him like that. Which

I knew in my head, but I was so angry I couldn't admit that I agreed with him and instead I grabbed at his neck with both my hands, in full mafia strangling mode, shouting in his face, "I CAN DO WHAT I FUCKING LIKE."

But actually, if I wanted him to remain being my boyfriend, I couldn't.

After batting my hands away from the neck shake/strangling, he said I had gone too far and told me to leave him on his own in the kitchen.

I'd lost my reward earrings, and maybe X too.

It didn't take me long to calm down, as realising you have actually gone too far is a horribly sobering moment.

I slowly went back into the kitchen and apologised. Deeply, sincerely. He had a red mark on his neck from my rough grabbing, and that made me sick with regret. How dare I hurt his skin? I told him this. Said I would never hurt him again, meant it. Knelt on the floor at his feet, asked him for forgiveness and then pictured the situation with me being a man and him being a woman, which made me feel even more sick.

I pleaded with him to believe me. "Do you? Do you believe I don't want to ever do that again? I won't hurt you out of anger again? Do you believe me? I mean it. I really mean it . . ."

Eventually he spoke. "I believe you believe you mean that."

I cried with relief at his feet, although it still didn't feel like very safe ground.

"I do mean it, I'm sorry, I'm so sorry, I'm not trying to excuse any of my behaviour at all, but I think I've still got a bit of a way to go before I'm over everything."

I had *never* brought up his year of lies to get out of trouble before, but I did that night as I knew I needed something epic to counter my massive aggression.

It worked.

Reluctantly he came back to bed and said we'd talk about it properly in therapy that week.

We hugged as we fell asleep.

The next morning I committed to drinking nothing around him for the next three months, and even though I still had a lot of anger, I found that by always being sober I was able to control it better. I started the earring challenge again. And created a new chart to log it all in my notebook.

A few days after Shake/Strangle-gate I sent X another sincere apology with "Something Better Change" by the Stranglers at the end, which made him laugh. But I knew it wasn't funny. It's easy to do something horrific to someone and then, when forgiveness is given, to wipe it from your mind. I didn't want to forget. I wanted the fear and regret I felt from my out-of-control aggression to stay with me, so that I never acted like that again.

I wrote myself 10 Post-it notes—

Don't forget you strangled him
Don't forget you strangled him
Don't forget you strangled him
Don't forget you strangled him
Don't forget you strangled him
Don't forget you strangled him
Don't forget you strangled him
Don't forget you strangled him
Don't forget you strangled him
Don't forget you strangled him

—and put them in private-to-me places at home and at work. When I had started to try to floss my teeth in the evening instead of the morning (apparently this is best practice) I stuck a Post-it on the mirror saying "Don't forget to evening floss," but after the third day of it being there it became invisible. I didn't want this to be the case with these notes, so I stuck them to the top of my necklace toolbox, on the tongue of my dry-weather-only Nikes, on the lid of the shoebox of my third-favourite boots, on top of my blusher (which I only used at weekends), and some in random pairs of socks. Spots I didn't see every day, so that the words and warning would really hit me when I came across them.

I really mustn't strangle him again.

~

We kept on going to therapy every week, and we kept on wanting to try to be the thing we'd believed in before, to get through this hard time together, as we still wanted to be in each other's futures. And we had a calmer and easier time for a little bit following that.

But five months after 70 per cent living together, among many happy and loving times, I realised that I did really, truly wish I had never met X.

His lies had forced me to face a whole bunch of constant, unsettling feelings that wouldn't have surfaced had he treated me right.

Susan had said that it probably would have been pushed out at another time in my future, but I wasn't so sure. I'd been alive 32 years and had amazingly easy and positive internal conversations with myself throughout the time before his lies. Even through the majority of my not-so-great Three sexual handling, I was still largely at peace with my brain. I didn't really get it, but all the times I had horribly fought and shouted and sworn at Three, it had never made me feel as brain-stressed and anxious as this. Back then, I never once felt guilt or gave myself huge internal tellings-off when our fights had exploded.

But now, if I slipped and spoke too harshly to X, I was

racked with guilt at not being able to change my old ways more quickly. Control my hate better. Forgive faster. It was so frustrating being with someone who only ever disagreed like a gentleman. He had never said a mean word to me during fights and didn't really do full shouting. He was such a fucking adult and it felt unfair that I continually looked like the shit one when he was the one who'd done the really shit thing.

I was trying so hard. I had charts and notes coming out my arse!

I asked Susan if she thought the X throat-grabbing moment was linked to my X-dead dream thoughts.

She took a pause before replying. "It's your feelings around what X has done to you that you want gone."

X looked drained and worried.

It wasn't. My ideal situation would have been: 1) he had never lied to me when we initially met; 2) he had actually been properly single when we met; or 3) he didn't exist and was already dead at least a month before we first met, meaning I could never have met him.

I was tired of trying to be this fair and forgiving person I so desperately wanted to be.

Maybe some other girl with some other upbringing/different life experiences would have been able to hold all her shit together and just be fucking ace throughout this time, but I was uneducated in those areas and angry. And I didn't know how not to fight about the things that made me feel sad.

Fish Pie

"Bay Sanctuary, how may I help you?"

"Hi, Mum."

"Darling, how lovely to hear from you!"

"Do you remember how you felt when I used to have my fish-pie paddies?"

"Oh, um, annoyed probably, as I would take a lot of time cooking them. Why?"

"Why did you leave?"

"Can I call you back in 10 minutes?"

I waited until my phone rang back.

"Hello."

"Hello."

"What's brought this on?"

"It's really important to me that I know."

"OK. I had to move because of your father. I found it incredibly hard and stressful, them living so close, and I'd never wanted the marriage to end, and my feelings didn't seem to be improving. A couple of years after he left I was still feeling horribly sad, and it was very tiring always having to pretend I was doing OK, in front of you, them. Most of our friends had ended up becoming their friends; I had no one. I was in a very dark place. He'd done wrong, but I was labelled the unreasonable one. So when the job came up in Salisbury, I decided to move there. I couldn't have managed the new job *and* looking after you. Things were different back then; employers weren't

336

as flexible to women as they are now. Your father made it very clear he wanted to be close by you, and Jay was near him so they couldn't move, and so we came to the arrangement we did. I missed you terribly, it was horrible. But being somewhere new did help me get to a better state of mind."

"Why didn't you ever say?"

"I never wanted it to affect your relationship with him."

"But it affected my relationship with you."

"I would have done things differently if I could have."

Neither of us said anything for a bit. Then Mum said, "I'm not as strong as you."

"I'm not strong. I stayed with Three for so much longer than I should have."

"No. You left to look after yourself. I'm very proud of you."

Normally I'd interrupt or quickly move the conversation on when Mum said things like this, but I stayed quiet for a bit. Closed my eyes and really pictured her, back then, my age, dancing for everything in the lounge.

"I wish I could be the age I am now and know you back then. I think we would have been great friends and I would have come and danced the mashed potato with you."

"I would have liked that!"

South Korea

X had to go away for work for two months to South Korea. A big software firm wanted to take on his company's latest algorithm and he said this was *big* news and could lead to something serious.

I wasn't positive about his trip. At all.

As an adult, even when things were okay, my feelings always got confused when people I loved went far away for chunks of time. It made me slow to open up and very quick to shut off to them. Susan had suggested I do an individual session with her after the Mum Big News, and she had helped me see that this was due to childhood stuff and trying to get love from a parent who was geographically far away. It was kind of annoying knowing all this about me now, as I preferred the me when I thought I was just super-hard and didn't need anyone. But it turns out I wasn't, and that I'd created a version of tough for the moments I felt most vulnerable. I wanted love and family and calm and stable commitment. Apparently awareness is the first big step to changing, and once you accept that, you can be in a more authentic state, which will eventually bring joyful calm. I was aware now but did not feel at all close to joyful calm. I think I had been getting there naturally, with X during our first year together. I had graduated from having emotionally open conversations with him where I could only say soppy things with my back turned to him or in the dark or while I held my hands over my face, to being able to look him straight

338

in his eyes while speaking such things. It was a big step, and by month six I had even moved on from not allowing him to comfort or hug me when I cried, to embracing his love and care and arms. Because of the trust and hope I felt in us I had stopped being my previously mafia-like self around him. But now I had reverted back to turning my head away from him when I communicated hard things, and I noticed I had stopped letting him hug me when I got upset. My new awareness of these returning old traits meant I was doubly screwed, as it upset me twice over.

Susan made us discuss this so we could be prepared for his time away.

X wouldn't be able to come home during that whole period so he had negotiated into his contract for them to pay for me to visit for three weeks during the middle of his trip.

We'd had a huge disagreement when he had told me the news. I say disagreement, as all the training I'd been doing around not swearing and shouting in arguments so he wouldn't give up and end things had really worked, and we'd recently been able to talk through tricky issues without me calling him the c-word, which felt encouraging. I'd had to do a lot of underwater screaming during this time and was now visiting the swimming pool at least twice a week to do so. It seemed to work.

When X raised going to South Korea, I said that after the year we'd had it was too much. That it was the worst possible timing for it. He agreed, but it was work, he had no actual choice, plus they were paying him £5000 just for going, so what with his new financial worries and escalating debt while he and Almostexwife continued to not work out how to split their assets, this was a no-brainer.

I understood of course and agreed, but I was pissed off and felt all the work we had done would be put back due to my imminent mafia shut-off default.

He said we'd cope, that me going out there would be fun, something to look forward to, and that he'd be able to take three days off for us to visit somewhere else away from Seoul.

I had zero interest in visiting South Korea, as apparently it was a cold place at that time of year. If I can't tan, forget it.

But on a Sunday night watching telly on the sofa, I told him I was looking forward to going as he'd got himself upset about what the trip meant for him not seeing the girls for all that time and I wanted him to feel better, so I lied. I hated my involuntary reaction to always want to make him feel better whenever he got properly upset. I didn't even bother to write that one down in my lies list.

In the weeks before he left, when he prioritised seeing the girls over me, I covered up my sadness with smiles and encouraging words.

On the day he left I hugged him goodbye and gave him an envelope with four pieces of A4 paper inside that I had written on.

I told him to open it on the plane.

He said he would look forward to it and kissed me again on my cheek. He said he couldn't wait for me to visit, that he would have sussed all the best places for us to eat. They did some kind of incredible chicken dumpling thing, which I'd apparently love the taste of.

I smiled and waved from the door as he carried his suitcase down the stairs. Fuck, I loved him.

He sent me the ghost-face emoji from the Uber and I replied back with one.

And then I started packing up all my stuff from the flat.

I had been a pretend version of myself with him for the last too long. Holding back upset and real feelings. I felt tiny and not the size of the person I used to be. My chart was off the scale with how much sadness being with him caused me and

I couldn't help but think that maybe the sad I'd feel without him would be less than the sad I felt with him.

I needed to know for sure.

I had found a flat to rent near Sophie in Walthamstow. I had used the South Korea plane-ticket money for the deposit. Mia and Sophie were coming in the morning with a hired van and their hands.

Mine and Three's divorce papers had come through, and with them the split of our flat money into our individual accounts. I had decided to use a bit of this money to subsidise renting a one-bed flat that was too expensive for me on my current wage. I hadn't planned to touch that money, but Three had persuaded me to. We'd gone for lunch the week before X left and it was the first time we had met up where it felt like his pain had moved into something better. I told him about my current X situation; I didn't go into big details, but explained how it had revealed the Mum stuff and how I was finding it hard not having a proper stable home place.

"I think you should do it."

"But you were always the one who said we had to save, save, save."

"I know. But maybe this is more important. Savings can come later!"

We squeezed each other's hands and I felt something reassuring.

I placed a box on the table.

"I brought you these . . . I understand why you needed not to have them back then, but they were bought with proper love and so, could you take them and then maybe one day, you might want to wear them again?"

Three put the special wedding cufflinks in his work bag.

"I will wear them."

~

341

It had been over a year of trying with X. A year of feeling less than me. Of having madness in my thoughts. Of biting hate down on my tongue. Of not being my true self with him.

I needed things to change.

To give my thoughts a new story.

It was time to leave.

We packed up the van and, as Mia and Sophie waited outside, I struggled to walk out of the flat door. Fuck. This felt like the hardest door yet.

I wanted the version we had both been so excited about before his big lie came out.

I wanted to stay. Wait for X to come home. Try some more.

My hope in our love was making it so hard for my legs to move.

I got my phone out and found the limerick I had written the night he went to Neil's to "decide." I had wanted so badly to send it to him then, but I wasn't ready.

Go and fuck yourself, you stupid, selfish man
Guess what? I'm no longer your greatest fan
You're boring, old and a liar
Fucking baby bullshit crier
And I'm sick of trying to get over this scam

You had me, yours truly, forever
To lose this great thing you're not so clever
Fucking thick
There's other dick
But love like this you'll feel again never

All you'll have is a life of missionary fucks
Your tongue in this fanny no longer you'll tuck
You're so average
With your lack of courage
You pathetic, weak and undeserving schmuck

And all those fucks your dick never made me come
I'm going to let some other guy do me up the bum
I'm going to have great sex
Forgetting about you, my ex
While your life it slowly turns to numb

I'm fabulous, I'm great
I was your best mate
But you've ruined this
Our previous romance bliss
And in you I will forevermore hate.

It was a very angry and very past me. I thought a lot about if my story with him had ended back there. How much simpler it all might have been. But at that time I so desperately needed him to choose me—I just didn't realise that him doing so wasn't the answer I thought it would be.

I don't think there are ever any proper resolutions from really sad things in life. Important people hurt us, we try to move on, but really, we take that hurt to our death. And that's okay, as long as we've lived and been happy in between.

I wasn't being happy enough.

The raw anger in that limerick, translated into the feelings I now understood them to be, still lived in me.

I wrote him an updated version and put it on his bedside table:

I love you a huge amount and find you hard to resist
But the pain you've caused I can't dismiss
I'm being someone I don't want to be
I need to work on a couple of things for me
I haven't the ability to carry on in this

I want you to be a good dad and be happy
I want to be part of you but it can't be

343

You need to heal
I need to heal
This is my goodbye. I'm sorry it's a bit crappy
xx

I walked out of the flat door. Sophie was on her way back up to get me. But I was already heading down the stairs.

She went to hug me, and I let her.

...

I didn't intentionally plan to end things a year after trying, or trick X into thinking I was going to join him in South Korea. At every step I had hoped we could return to the thing we'd been. That I'd reach the forgiveness and it would open up to some other, more joyful level. But it didn't. And I hadn't. And I just couldn't quite press "buy" on the plane ticket.

I would never know if ending things back when X's big lie came out would have worked out better or stopped me feeling mad things in my brain. But this way, now, with it being on my terms, after trying my best, felt some kind of empowering.

I had given up painful sex with Three to end up in a different kind of painful love. And even though the sex was still amazing, and I genuinely thought he was brilliant, the pain I carried with all his other stuff wasn't enough to balance it out with X.

I know I said I would let fanny lead, and my fanny still very much wanted him, but my brain needed to be taken care of too, so on this occasion I was thinking of it.

I have no idea what'll happen after he reads the letter I gave him. The still-insecure part of me wonders if he will actually be relieved, maybe eventually consider having another try with Almostexwife.

Once he lands in South Korea he'll probably try to call me. I've blocked his number and plan not to go on emails. I'm not a complete cunt—I've explained this kindly in the letter I gave him. I know I can go full No Comms on him again. I

345

was the strong one at that. Plus, as back-up, I found the Russell and Bromley black cowboy boots new on eBay and made an executive decision to buy them but not wear them until I had succeeded in the two months of No Comms. Fuck, I can't wait to wear them.

Realistically, we will talk again. But the point is, I have two months to get back to me. Get back to being strong and not always worried, and give my brain the chance to not have to think constantly about Almostexwife and his children. Have a break from feeling sad about the situation X got us into. Get rid of my insecurities. Think I'm fabulous again.

Coz I am. I'm fucking amazing.

Plus, I'm an ever-hopeful optimist, so, if we're the greatest sexual match that ever was, if we're *really* meant to be together, well, it'll find a way to work out. Won't it?

Acknowledgements

Thanks to Rose Lewenstein for being my first reader and for making me feel like a proper writer of books. Closely followed by Arifa Akbar and Jessie Thompson, whose early thoughts gave me an added level of confidence, particularly around all the sex stuff!!

And a big thanks to all the team at Doubleday. Especially Lee Boudreaux—who only ever made me feel in very safe and flexible hands. (The best kind!)

And finally, LAURA BONNER!!!!, my US agent who has made it possible for me to have my book in ANOTHER COUNTRY!!!

P.S. A final thanks to Margo Shickmanter for opening and reading it!!

About the Author

ANOUSHKA WARDEN is a British writer for stage and screen. Her second play won the 2020 Platform Presents Playwright's Prize. She is an associate artist at Pentabus Theatre Company and is the producer of two podcasts—*The Playwright's Podcast* and *The Lockdown Plays*. This is her debut novel.